playing doctor

KATE ALLURE

sourcebooks
casablanca

Published by Sourcebooks Casablanca, an imprint of Sourcebooks, Inc.
P.O. Box 4410, Naperville, Illinois 60567-4410
(630) 961-3900
Fax: (630) 961-2168
www.sourcebooks.com

Library of Congress Cataloging-in-Publication Data is on file with the publisher.

Printed and bound in the United States of America.
VP 10 9 8 7 6 5 4 3 2 1

CONTENTS

The Intern 1

My Doctor, My Husband, and Me 101

Seize the Doctor.. 165

The Intern

～ 1 ～
PHYSICIAN, HEAL THYSELF

DR. LAUREN MARKS LOCKED the door to her small medical practice and sighed. All day she had felt an unshakable, bone-deep ennui, a quiet weariness that permeated her very soul. Brooding over it as she pulled out of the parking lot, Lauren decided it was time to take stock of her life and figure out what was missing. *Well, who am I kidding? I know exactly what's missing in my life. I just don't know how to get it, that's all!*

Three simple letters…S-E-X! That was the big hole in her life. Oh, that and a husband, best friend, and partner in her medical practice, she added to her mental list.

As Lauren drove the short distance home, she ruminated about the good and the bad in her life. At thirty-six, she was the proud owner of the only medical practice in her tiny, rural hometown of Plum Banks, Illinois. It was a small general practice she had started with her new husband almost ten years ago. They had seemed so profoundly connected in those early years, so much in love, that subtle issues she should have paid more attention to—like the fact that Ted was really a big-city kind of guy, born and raised—had seemed immaterial.

He had lasted nine years in Plum Banks before moving out and moving on to follow his original dream of a career in medical research at a prominent hospital. One night when she was out with friends, Ted had secretly packed his bags and left a note. *A note!* Lauren still couldn't believe he'd taken off that way. But he had left the entire practice to her in the divorce, a sign of how deeply he regretted abandoning her. Almost overnight, she had become the sole owner of the small clinic, debts and all.

With a sigh, Lauren acknowledged that she had been lucky, in a way. The initial shock of his betrayal had almost destroyed her, but somehow she had managed to pull herself together in the months following and had continued on with her life. At one point, she nearly had to close the practice due to finances, so she had looked for a second doctor to help grow the patient list and make ends meet.

She considered herself fortunate to have found Dr. Kelly Walsh, who had the funds to buy into the practice, thus helping to relieve some of Lauren's debt. If all went well, Dr. Walsh would become her full partner. Kelly was about Lauren's age and very capable—she had quickly become a close confidant and ally. Along with some childhood pals still living in her hometown, Kelly's friendship had helped relieve Lauren's loneliness. Yes, she mused tiredly, she had friends...just not a boyfriend.

The rest of Lauren's small practice consisted of Brenda Roberts, a mostly retired nurse working part-time at the clinic, and young Jessica Smith, who was receptionist, bookkeeper, and office manager all rolled into one. Oh! She'd almost forgotten that another young woman would arrive on Monday, a summer intern named Courtney Sinclair. Lauren still couldn't believe she had hired someone sight unseen, but this had been an emergency of sorts, and she owed her old college friend Sara—now Dr. Rhodes—big time. During her final year of med school, Lauren had been flat broke, and Sara had let her sleep on her sofa for nearly six months until she finished school. With her parents retired to Florida on a fixed income, Lauren had no one else to turn to for help.

So when Sara had sent out the urgent email yesterday to all of her contacts asking if anyone could take on an intern from Chicago, Lauren had read the attached résumé and realized this was a way to finally pay back the debt she owed her friend. Dr. Rhodes had unexpectedly received a once-in-a-lifetime job offer at Stanford University Hospital, halfway across the country, but had already hired Ms. Sinclair as a favor to a friend. Sara felt terrible about leaving the girl in the lurch without her planned summer job. The recent college graduate was already accepted to med school starting next fall but could not decide if this was really her calling. That's why she wanted to spend the summer working in a general practice.

So, without even a telephone interview, Lauren had agreed to take the intern. It was only for three months, after all. With staff vacations coming up, the extra help would come in handy. She was a little concerned the young woman would prove useless in her clinic, but Lauren trusted her friend's judgment. One way or another, she'd meet Courtney on Monday and find out.

Putting thoughts of the intern out of her mind, Lauren returned to taking stock of her life and contemplating why she was mildly depressed. She had a career she loved, a cozy home, and good friends, and while she had no family in the area, Lauren kept in close contact with her parents. Not wanting to face it, she ultimately had to conclude that the only thing missing in her life was a significant other, a romantic companion—and the much-needed sex that would come with such a relationship. But as a thirtysomething adult living in the same tiny town where she grew up, she had to admit that there were no single men her age left, truly no romantic prospects anywhere in sight. None…at…all!

Opening the door to her small bungalow, Lauren smiled slightly as she thought of a solution for at least one of her issues. She could get a dog that could at least provide a welcome home each night, a friendly, loyal companion without the other entanglements of a romance. And, being totally honest with herself, Lauren acknowledged that she was not ready to jump back into a long-term commitment. Even though the marriage had died long before Ted left, she was still mourning the loss of what she once had with him. She still needed more time for her heart to heal. After pouring herself a glass of cold chardonnay, Lauren sat on her porch swing and continued pondering where her life had gone wrong.

2

REVIEWING THE CASE HISTORY

LAUREN HAD MET TED during her residency, and they had quickly become best friends and lovers. They had moved in together almost immediately, allowing her to finally vacate Sara's couch. They had definitely needed a place of their own because they had enjoyed boisterous sex, often and loudly. The two were married in a small ceremony exactly one year after meeting, and from then on, their lives had become intertwined. She had taken his name, and they became known by their friends in St. Louis as the Doctors Marks.

By then, Lauren had spent more than ten years in a big city, but she had always known she wanted to move back to her hometown. The small, close-knit community needed a doctor, and Lauren wanted to fill that role. Ted had followed both Lauren and her dream back to Plum Banks, a quaint town that bordered the Shawnee National Forest and had a population of less than a thousand. It was the kind of charming, warm place where she wanted to settle in and raise a family.

Everything had seemed perfect at first—at least for Lauren. But the stressful, hard work of starting a practice from nothing, the mounting debts, and Ted's dissatisfaction at being in such a rural place had quickly begun to take a toll on their marriage. He had tried to hide his unhappiness, but it seemed to permeate their relationship anyway. They didn't have huge fights, so it was easy for Lauren to pretend nothing had changed, especially because the amazing sex that had been so much a part of their union did not erode as quickly as their bond of friendship.

As she rocked slowly back and forth on the porch swing, Lauren chided herself yet again, acknowledging that she should have paid more attention. She had refused to see the truth until the night she came home and found Ted gone, along with his clothes and personal things. His brief note had said that he felt responsible for the decay of their marriage, and clearly he considered it over. There had been no point in her chasing after him.

She had been truly devastated at first. But slowly Lauren realized that she, too, was no longer in love and had just been going through the motions. The shock she had felt when he left so abruptly was more about having her life suddenly and unexpectedly ripped apart. It had thrown her into a panicked depression made worse by the loneliness she faced each time she came home.

Even now, she could hardly believe Ted had managed to secure a job with a renowned hospital behind her back. It must have happened when he went to that medical conference in Chicago, she mused. A part of her also wondered if there was more to it than that. Had Ted found someone else in the city, someone who shared his goals? Lauren hadn't pursued that question. What was the point? Ted was gone and she was alone.

Now, six months later, she was slowly emerging from the fog. Lauren realized that she had needed time to let go of the dream of her marriage, to grieve its loss, and then to heal. She knew it was way too soon to jump into another deep relationship, but what truly depressed her was that when she *was* ready to try love again, there wouldn't be any prospects here. Lauren didn't know what she would do then, but for now she would try to put the thought out of her mind while she made a life for herself as the now single Dr. Marks.

So that evening, while reheating some leftovers, Lauren made the decision to go to the nearest town on Saturday and check out the rescue dogs at the shelter. That, she figured, would help with at least one of her problems. A friendly companion would ease some of the loneliness.

However, she didn't have a clue what to do about the lack of sex. Carrying on a torrid affair in Plum Banks was out of the question. Actually, any kind of casual sexual relationship with a local would become the biggest gossip of the year—and, as she reminded herself for probably the hundredth time, there weren't *any* available guys here anyway. The nearest town, Marion, Kentucky, was thirty miles away, and she wasn't sure how to go about meeting someone there either, never having been a barhopping kind of gal. Besides, with a population of three thousand, Marion wasn't that much bigger than Plum Banks.

As Lauren sat at her small kitchen table eating dinner, she finally acknowledged that there wasn't any easy solution to her problem. Her physical state was made worse by the memories of the terrific sex she and Ted had shared here in their cozy home. It seemed like every time Lauren went to bed, she remembered their sensual nights, stirring vibrations within her that were best left dormant. Even time alone with her Doc Johnson wasn't cutting it anymore. Lauren wanted a living, breathing, warm body in her bed to bring her the release she craved. She wanted a man.

Thankfully, Lauren was so busy over the weekend with her new dog project that it provided a measure of distraction from her physical needs. On Saturday morning, she made the trip to Marion, which although tiny, did have an animal shelter. There she fell in love with Rufus, a charmingly cute beagle-setter-whatever mix. Before driving home, Lauren visited the pet store to buy things she would need to make her small bungalow "dog friendly" and even managed to get Rufus in to see the veterinarian. She was reassured that the dog was healthy, but bemoaned the fact that her community didn't have its own vet. On the plus side, she was pleased to discover that her adult rescue dog was already house-trained.

Lauren happily took Rufus on a long walk late Saturday afternoon and several more on Sunday, all of which helped to keep her attention off the one area of her life that seemed starkly lacking in hope.

3

THE DOCTOR WILL
SEE YOU NOW

BY MONDAY, LAUREN HAD successfully put her nonexistent sex life out of her mind. She gave Rufus a hug good-bye before leaving for work, then, deciding better safe than sorry, she tied him up in the kitchen, promising to come home at lunch to take him on a short walk. Rufus seemed to smile at her as he wagged his tail and looked back with his big, brown doggy eyes.

Yes, I made a good decision getting you, and now when I come home I'll at least be greeted by a friendly face and your wagging tail.

Upon entering her clinic, Lauren wished her receptionist good morning and then remembered the intern.

"Jessica, I almost forgot. I've hired a summer intern to help out around here, a young college grad named Courtney Sinclair. I'm not sure exactly what she'll be doing, but we will figure it out as we go. She should arrive sometime this morning, so please show her into my office when she gets here."

"Will do," said the always-pleasant receptionist. Although just twenty, Jessica had proven to be very efficient by learning basic book-keeping on her own and adeptly running the small office. Lauren thought perhaps it was time for a small promotion, maybe to office manager, along with a small increase in salary. Unfortunately "small" was all that the practice could afford at the moment.

Jessica called after her, "I just made a fresh pot of coffee. I'll bring you a cup. Your first patient is due any minute. He's new and his file is waiting on your desk."

"Thanks, Jessica," Lauren called back through the open door of her private office. Yes, it was definitely time to let the young woman know how much she was appreciated.

After donning her lab coat, Lauren settled into her desk chair and logged onto her computer before opening the manila file folder to scan the patient record. When Jessica brought her the coffee, she mentioned that the small local pharmacy had called. Their online prescription system was down again. As Lauren sipped her bracing hot, black coffee, she mused that at times Plum Banks was a definite pain in the ass. This had never happened even once during her residency, but stuff like this seemed to be a regular part of small-town life—power outages, Internet disruptions, and more. But she did love living in a place where people knew each other by name and were friendly rather than frantic.

Taking another sip, Lauren remembered she had a pad of old-fashioned paper prescription forms buried in her large, antique wooden desk. Bending over, she opened the big bottom drawer and dug around until she found the pad. Sitting up, she was disconcerted to find someone standing just inside her door waiting for her. But *someone* was surely not the correct word to describe *this* person.

As she stared openmouthed at the dazzling young man before her, all Lauren could think was *You...are...gor...geous!*

He was tall, broad shouldered, and smiling—the polite smile a person offers when they first meet someone. As her eyes skimmed over him, she noticed how his healthy tan set off his flowing, corn-silk hair and beautiful turquoise eyes.

How would it feel to run my hands through that hair?

Lauren was startled by her inappropriate thought, but the next thing to meander through her scattered, giddy mind was: *I wonder how old you are?*

Followed quickly by: *Are you married?*

Lauren's eyes darted to his left hand. *Nope.* She didn't see a ring there, but glancing back at his face, she realized he was young, very young, maybe still in his teens. But even his youth couldn't change the fact that Lauren was unmistakably drawn to him, and the reason slowly registered in her addled brain—he was hot...super hot. Lauren could see him plastered on billboards in sexy Calvin Klein underwear. Something about him just screamed SEX! Despite his young age, Lauren knew without a doubt that he would be good in bed, very good.

She stifled a gasp as all this hit her like a physical blow, leaving her dazed and wary.

As the handsome youth walked toward her, he reached out to shake her hand—his smile fading slightly at the doctor's mute response—and Lauren suddenly realized that she was ogling him openmouthed like a complete idiot. Even worse, she became aware of a rush of shocking desire coursing straight down through her body like a lightning bolt to settle between her legs. Jumping to her feet, Lauren could feel the spread of an embarrassing blush rise up from her neck.

Get a hold of yourself, she silently ordered. *He's probably the son of one of your neighbors, home from college for the summer.*

Ignoring his outstretched hand, Lauren adopted her most professional demeanor as best she could under the circumstances, those circumstances being that she knew with certainty that her nipples were tight and she was starting to feel damp between her legs.

Introducing herself brightly, she said, "Hi, I'm Doctor Lauren Marks. I'm sorry about this. I can't imagine why our receptionist showed you in here. Let me take you to an exam room Mr....ah... Simpson," she added after glancing at the file on her desk.

The young man's hand dropped as he muttered, "Umm, actually—"

Cutting him off abruptly, Lauren repeated herself, "Really, I do apologize. Follow me," and she started to walk out of her office.

Reaching out, he touched Lauren's arm gently to stop her. "Wait! I am not a patient. I'm sorry about the confusion, but I'm Courtney Sinclair." Looking a little worried now, he asked, "I believe Dr. Rhodes arranged for me to intern here this summer?"

Lauren stopped dead in her tracks, feeling her arm tingling where his hand had touched her. Spinning around, she proclaimed, "But you can't be the intern. Courtney is a girl... I'm sure of it."

"Ah, well, I'm sorry but I am Courtney Sinclair, and the last time I checked, I was a man." Smirking slightly, he added, "I believe I'm still a man. Did Dr. Rhodes *say* that I was a woman?" Incredulity dripped in his tone.

"I'm sure she did!" Lauren responded sharply. "Well, I don't know," she added more uncertainly. "As I think about it, maybe Sara didn't say at all. The arrangements were all done via email, very quickly last week."

Feeling deeply embarrassed, Lauren walked slowly back to her chair, wondering just how red her face was now—cherry flaming scarlet, if she had to guess. In her mortification, she felt hot, sweaty even, as she turned back to look at him. She stared mutely as Courtney—*the young man!*—restarted the conversation.

"I appreciate so much that you are taking me on. I know it was sudden and that you hired me sight unseen, without even a telephone interview."

Feeling like a total moron, Lauren finally said, "Please sit down, Courtney, and we can discuss it."

As the young man took a seat, he said, "Actually, I mostly go by the name Court, if that's okay with you?"

"Of course." Lauren nodded, still gripped by almost paralyzing humiliation.

Court hastily added, "I promise I'll work very hard to do whatever you need done. I'm a fast learner, and really, I'm so grateful I'll get the chance to work at a real medical practice all summer. I'm sure this will help with any remaining doubts I have about becoming a doctor."

Watching him, Lauren thought Courtney—no, Court, she re-minded herself—seemed anxious now, as if concerned, perhaps, that he might have lost the internship based solely on the fact that he was a man and not a young woman. However, the real reason she wanted to send him on his way was that he was too damn gorgeous for her peace of mind...and raging libido!

"I'm sure you'll be fine," Lauren reassured him, going against her better instincts. "Your résumé shows that you've successfully held jobs before, and I'm pleased to see you have a certificate in first-aid training along with your science degree. I have the highest respect for my col-league Dr. Rhodes, who recommends you highly, so I'm sure you will be an asset to our clinic."

"Thank you," Court said as he relaxed back into his chair. "I'm ready to start now and will do anything you need done. I really mean that! Answer the phones...even clean the place, if that's what you need."

"Well, I have a couple projects in mind for the summer—reorganizing our patient files and the supply closet, for instance—but for today, I'll ask Jessica to train you on the phones and computer system. She'll be gone for a couple weeks in July, and it will be helpful if you can take over her duties then."

"Great, I'll go out and get started," Court said with all the confidence of youth.

"Ask Jessica to introduce you to the rest of the staff, and then you can fill out some new-hire paperwork. Oh, do you have a place to live in Plum Banks yet?"

"Yes, I was here over the weekend. I'm renting a furnished studio apartment over a garage just a couple streets away. So I'm all set to start working." Once again, he unleashed his killer smile on Lauren.

After he left, she got up to microwave her now-cold coffee. Upon returning to her office, Lauren shut the door with a sigh. She needed a few moments to catch her breath and gather her scattered thoughts. How had she not realized that the intern was a man? She had tried so hard over the weekend to get her mind off sex. Until now, Lauren had believed she'd succeeded in turning that part of herself off, at least temporarily, but now one idea kept popping unbidden into her mind. *He's so hot!* Beyond a doubt, Court was eye candy of the finest quality, which had flipped her libido switch back to "on." With a sense of panic, Lauren realized this was going to test her deeply.

Well, at least he wasn't a teenager. Lauren figured Court was twenty-two or twenty-three. Like that mattered, she noted with some regret. *Not only is he more than ten years younger than me, he's also my employee.* Sighing and resting her head in her hand, she tried to forcibly will her libido to go away. This was going to be one tantalizing, squirming summer! *How am I going to get through it?*

As the day went on, Lauren managed to maintain her professionalism, but it was wearing thin to say the least. By five o'clock, she was in no mood for the enthusiastic reports from her staff about the new intern, grinningly shared behind her closed office door. Nurse Brenda reported that even though she was an older lady, her still-working eyes appreciated having such a "fine, decorative addition to the clinic." She gave Lauren a wink as she departed. Her colleague Dr. Walsh jokingly asked if she could "send Dr. Rhodes a thank-you note for the gift of this hunky intern for us ladies to ogle all summer." Further, Kelly suggested, only half jokingly, that he might help bring in some business as well, perhaps going door to door handing out clinic flyers.

"Humph," was Lauren's response to that idea.

The worst was Jessica. She was absolutely glowing with excitement at having Court working with them for the next three months. Before leaving the office, she drilled Lauren with questions: "Is Court single?" "Is he dating anyone?"

To those and others, Lauren replied that she really didn't know.

The worst question was the last. Jessica asked Lauren, "Would you mind if I go after him?" Jessica didn't wait for a reply, prattling on that of course Lauren wouldn't mind, since she was "so much older" and wouldn't be interested in Court. And that she and Court were "the same age after all," not leaving an opportunity for Lauren to say anything. Just before Jessica raced out of the office, she promised conspiratorially that nothing she and Court did together—wink-wink—would interfere with their work in the office. Then Lauren overheard Jessica offering in honey-sweet tones to show Court around Plum Banks.

Lauren gritted her teeth and "humphed" a second time. What *was* she going to do?

Nothing was the answer, of course!

And her receptionist was right—Jessica was the same age as Court. Yes, the two of them were now coworkers, but there wasn't any official policy against interoffice romance. Knowing that Jessica was going after him, even though there were other guys her age in Plum Banks, made it somehow worse when there was no one here Lauren's age. If Jessica and Court did hook up, Lauren realized she would be haunted by images of them together having sex—the wild, sheet-twisting kind that she herself had needed for months now!

Just that thought had her tingling. Lauren squeezed her thighs together tightly in response. No, that was the wrong answer—the clench-ing just made the erotic itch more pronounced as blood poured down to fuel the ache. Breathing deeply, she tried to calm herself and relax the tight fists that her hands had become.

"Well, I guess I'll head out."

What? Lauren woke dazed from her lusting daydream.

"What?" she said aloud, giving her head a little shake as she looked up from her desk at the Adonis standing in the doorway, now officially her employee.

"I'm going to leave now, if that's okay with you," Court said again with a friendly but platonic grin that showed off his handsome tanned face to its best advantage.

Glancing up at him, Lauren attempted to plaster an equally pleasant but professional smile on her face. However, given where her thoughts had just been, she could feel another blush blossoming up from her chest. Grasping at any option to keep him from noticing, Lauren jumped to her feet to look out the window.

"Looks like a nice evening tonight," she said—her feeble excuse for turning her back on him. "A nice night for your first night in Plum Banks or…whatever," she finished lamely. Without turning around, she called brightly, "Thanks for your help today. I'll see you tomorrow."

"Ah, ohhh…kay," he responded, sounding taken aback. She felt his eyes staring at her from behind. "I'll be here early, and again, thank you for this opportunity."

Lauren was still trying to regulate her pulse, so she just fluttered a hand at him in good-bye without turning around.

TAKE A DEEP BREATH, PLEASE

As COURT WALKED THE three country blocks to his garage apartment just outside the village, he could not stop thinking about pretty Dr. Lauren Marks. She was not at all what he had expected, what he'd been prepared to meet. She was older for sure, but somehow he'd expected the friend of his mom's friend to seem older, look older.

When she had raised her head from digging in a desk drawer, his first glimpse of her had hit like a sucker punch to the gut that had left him slightly stunned. As the day wore on, Court found he could hardly take his eyes off her. He wondered if she had thought him vastly immature and tongue-tied. He certainly felt that way around Lauren—Dr. Marks to you, he reminded himself sternly.

But Dr. Marks appealed to him immensely. She had the clean and sexy girl-next-door looks that really turned him on. He may be a city boy, born and bred, but that kind of friendly Midwestern beauty always made him think of sex—of taking the sweetling's clothes off and teaching her some naughty, big-city bedroom tricks.

Trying to get a hold of his thoughts and his libido, Court focused on the fact that she was going to be his boss all summer. He really needed to stop seeing her as a hot, fuckable woman—but to him she was the epitome of that. Shaking his head, Court told himself once again that this was no way to think about his new boss. Not only that, she isn't some young, naive girl, but a mature, experienced woman—way out of his league!

He just wished that she hadn't done that, had not stood there in front of the window with the setting sunlight flowing in through the glass around her—and through her clothes! It had provided him with an

X-ray-vision outline of her voluptuous body. Having battled his growing attraction all day, he would have been better off not seeing the side and back views of her body that Dr. Marks had unknowingly provided.

She had full, round breasts that his hands were now itching to caress and an ass that he wanted to snuggle right up behind and feel pressed against his pelvis. His penis had started twitching the second he saw her sexy outline. It had been hidden from him all day by her puffy cotton dress and white lab coat, but now her hot body was emblazoned in his memory. Taking several deep breaths, Court tried again to calm his lust. This just wouldn't do, he told himself as he walked slowly up the stairs to his apartment.

Maybe he should have tried to get some wheels for the summer, he thought. He'd never had a car while in school, and it had seemed like a good idea at the time to save money over the summer, especially since his friends had promised to visit and drive him around. But Court now felt trapped in this small town, knowing that she was here somewhere very close by and so ripe for the picking. It didn't help that he was currently unattached, had been for months now, with no outlet in sight for his growing lust. As he unlocked the door to his furnished studio, Court decided maybe he should go for a long run. Only exhausting exercise would help get his mind off sex with his new boss.

BLOOD PRESSURE RISING

As THE WEEK WORE on, Lauren became increasingly irritated with Jessica—and with herself for caring. Lauren had never thought of efficient Jessica as a flirt, but suddenly she saw a new side to the receptionist. There was more jiggle in her hips and a sparkling, beckoning smile directed at Court, and Lauren knew she wasn't imagining that Jessica's skirts were shorter and her tops tighter.

It was none of her business, *really*, but Lauren was making such an effort to be professional and keep her distance from the young hunk that watching Jessica vamp it up was like pouring salt in a wound. More accurately, it was like a bothersome itch, and there was nothing she could do about it in public—or in private, for that matter. Only one thing would fully satisfy her, and *that* wasn't going to happen, Lauren reminded herself again and again.

To work off the sexual tension, she'd begun running nightly with Rufus. It was such a relief to just run as fast as she could, working to exhaust herself so that she could sleep at night rather than lie there hot and bothered with thoughts of her much younger intern. Rufus was turning out to be quite useful, both as a friendly companion welcoming her home and as an exercise buddy. At night they would sit together on the sofa while Lauren watched TV or on the veranda's swing. Later, Rufus would snuggle beside her on the bed and she felt less alone.

After a long, exhilarating run on Friday night, Lauren gave Rufus an extra yummy dinner and a big hug, very pleased with her new four-legged companion. Feeling better than she had all week, she turned out the light and had her first really good night of sleep since Court's arrival on Monday.

It's Contagious

ON THE OTHER SIDE of town, Court was having no luck whatsoever falling asleep and had given up even trying. Finally, he got out of bed to have a cold beer on the couch while he pondered the problem of his undeniable attraction to his boss. Lust hit him every time he looked at Lauren. He had never before lacked female companionship in his adult life—Court guessed he could thank his good looks for that—so he'd never gone long without a release. Having to fight arousal all the time was a novel condition, and going home with a raging hard-on every night made Court wonder how he would get through the next couple of months.

While Lauren was the type of woman he hoped to settle down with someday, at twenty-three that was a long way off. Court knew he needed to stop thinking about her all the time, or he would go absolutely nuts. He should set his sights on something more appropriate. The receptionist's seductive overtures provided a mild distraction, and she was pretty. While she didn't immediately raise his blood pressure, lust wasn't everything, he told himself.

Court guessed that Jessica was someone he could enjoy spending some time with over the summer. At the very least, he thought, chugging down the remainder of his beer, if he was fucking someone, anyone, he might just be able to stop lusting after his boss. He was in a quandary—torn between right and wrong—since it didn't seem right to ask Jessica out when he kept hungering for someone else, even someone so far out of his reach.

He rose from the couch and chucked the empty bottle into the garbage, then walked over to the window to stare down from his small second-floor apartment to the dark street below. Court suddenly wondered if Lauren might consider dating someone much younger. It was a ridiculous idea—but now it was lodged in his brain. Still no closer to finding a solution, Court just stood there staring at nothing, fighting the desire that even now stirred in his groin.

⌒ 7 ⌒

APPEARING ASYMPTOMATIC

LAUREN FELT LESS STRESSED during the week that followed. Her exercise routine was helping her to get a good night's sleep, putting her in a much better mood. Court was fitting in nicely and learning to help in all areas, everything from answering phones to taking blood pressures to billing. The staff enjoyed teaching him, and his presence added excitement to the clinic.

Even the patients were more lively and engaging—the female clientele, that is. Plum Banks was a small town, after all, and there wasn't much else going on, so news of a hunkalicious newbie traveled fast. Women, old and young, came into the practice in droves, sometimes just to say hello and get a look at Court. Lauren was grateful for the additional patients and only slightly scornful about the cause. With her improved finances in mind, she began to plan for the clinic's first-ever employee picnic to celebrate the ten-year anniversary of her practice.

Being around Court was getting easier. The daily shock of seeing his astonishingly good looks was growing less powerful as she got used to him. Now that she was less twitchy around him, she began training Court to assist with exams so he could fill in when Nurse Brenda went on vacation. Realizing she could be near Court and not act like a lovesick teen or sex-craved nympho restored Lauren's confidence, and she was able to relax and join in the playful banter that the other ladies engaged in with the summer intern. Court was always very friendly, seeming pleased to be in her company, which delighted Lauren even when she knew it shouldn't.

A mild outbreak of stomach flu in the area had kept the practice very busy at the end of the week. By Friday evening, the entire staff was tired, especially Lauren, who had stayed late and arrived early to see the extra patients—but on the bright side, she'd managed to keep her libido in check while overseeing her sexy intern's training. A date had been picked for the summer picnic, and everyone was looking forward to it. So, her fatigue was the good kind, not the bone-weary ennui she had suffered just a couple weeks ago.

After her staff departed, Lauren locked the clinic doors and headed to the grocery store to restock her empty fridge. Finally driving home, she was ready for a glass of wine and a hot, soothing bath. She parked her old car in the driveway that ran alongside her tiny bungalow and walked around to the front carrying two heavy bags of groceries. Lauren could already hear Rufus's welcoming bark and looked forward to seeing him, but maybe for tonight she would put off their nightly run. She was just too tired. All she wanted was that bath and then bed.

Approaching the short stairs leading to the veranda, Lauren abruptly stopped dead, her grocery bags slipping from her hands. There relaxing on the porch swing was her ex-husband, Ted. She had not seen him, not once, since he'd abandoned her. Even the divorce had been done long distance via phone calls and lawyers. As soon as he saw her, Ted quickly jumped to his feet and offered an apologetic smile.

"Ted! What are you doing here?" Lauren demanded.

Inside she felt dreadfully unsettled, almost sick with anxious surprise and confusion. But a small part of her was pleased to see his deeply familiar face as long-ago memories of their once happy times flooded back unbidden.

"Hi, Laure," he responded, his smile warming. "I just had to see you. I miss you, and…I decided to come see you this weekend. I was…"

"What?" Lauren interrupted hotly. "You just show up here without calling after all that happened?" Looking around confused, she asked, "And where is your car?"

If his car had been parked there, Lauren realized, she would have had a little warning instead of experiencing the heart-stopping shock coursing through her now. Or, she could have just pulled back out of the driveway and driven away.

"Oh, the engine warning light came on as I drove down from

Chicago, so I left it at Harry's Garage and walked over," he answered. Stepping closer, he reached out to take her now-empty hands in his as he looked deeply, pleadingly into her eyes, searching their depths with his own.

"I miss you so much. I should never have left the way I did, and I want to talk with you about getting back together," he said quietly.

Lauren would have pulled her hands free, but Ted's hold was strong and firm.

"Please just hear me out. I can stay the whole weekend. I think we had such a good marriage for so long that it's worth a try, don't you?"

"I...I don't know...? This is so sudden. Why didn't you call me first before coming down?"

"I was afraid you would say no," he admitted truthfully. "Please, just hear me out."

Not sure what to do or say in response to his astonishing announcement, Lauren avoided answering, asking instead, "Where are you planning to stay?"

"I was hoping...that maybe I could stay with you? We'll have more time to talk that way."

"Look! It's totally inappropriate for you to just show up and think you can move back in—even for just a weekend," she said, growing more upset by the minute.

But Lauren also felt torn. She wanted to hear what Ted had to say. "You can stay just one night...on the couch. That's all I'll agree to for now."

Cheerfully, as if he had just won the first round, Ted reached out and hugged Lauren warmly as she tried to pull away. "Thank you, really! I just want you to hear me out. Let me help you," he added, bending down to begin gathering up the spilled groceries.

"Fine," Lauren said, wondering why she had agreed to let him stay with her. "I need to take a bath, so I want you to take Rufus for a much-needed walk...for at least thirty minutes."

Ted readily agreed. After helping put away the groceries and being introduced to a happily wagging Rufus, he left the bungalow.

Lauren was confused, not sure what he could possibly say or

whether she even wanted to try reigniting their love. She actually felt settled now. Was he proposing to move back? Stewing about it while she undressed and the tub filled with hot water, Lauren wasn't sure what to think. She added some sweet-smelling, perfumed bubbles to the water before sinking in, deciding just to luxuriate. After the hectic week, she deserved a few minutes to herself before seriously thinking about *anything*.

She was so comfortably relaxed that the time went by quickly as she allowed herself to daydream about old times with Ted. Too soon, she heard him returning and a friendly bark from Rufus as they entered the small cottage. She took her time getting out of the tub and drying off. As she put on her robe, she heard a knock on the front door. Ted called that he would answer it, so Lauren went ahead with brushing the tangles from her wet hair.

Hearing the door open as Ted said "Hello," Lauren wondered who had stopped by. She was not expecting any company. Lauren heard Ted answer a question she couldn't hear: "Laure is in the tub, but let me see how long she'll be."

After a few seconds, Ted called through the door, "Laure, there's someone here to see you, a young guy…Court Sinclair?"

Oh *my*, she thought. *What is he doing here?*

Hurriedly Lauren secured the tie on her robe and went out to the small living room. The two guys were still at the door—sizing each other up, if she had to put a name to the look on their faces.

Thanking Ted, she paused awkwardly before suggesting, "Ah… how about you start a salad for dinner?" He nodded and turned toward the kitchen.

Lauren stepped out onto the veranda and completely shut the door behind her. Maybe Ted wouldn't be able to eavesdrop if he was in the kitchen.

"Hi, Court," she said, smiling brightly. "What can I do for you?"

Court looked very uncomfortable as he shifted his weight from foot to foot.

"Umm, I thought, umm…maybe you might want to catch a movie tonight if you weren't doing anything. I really don't know many people here so… Well, never mind. You obviously have company or something," he muttered.

Lauren was so surprised that she couldn't think what to say, especially since the shock of Ted's unexpected arrival had already frazzled her brain. Standing there with wet hair and naked under her robe, Lauren felt self-conscious as she realized what Court must think was going on. He might even think they'd just had sex! This possibility embarrassed her so much that she felt the warm spread of a blush on her face.

Court started to turn away as he said, "Have a nice weekend. Sorry to bother you."

Finally finding her voice, Lauren called brightly after him, "It was not a bother, really! Maybe another time… Have a nice weekend… Ah, bye!"

Turning to go back into the house, she felt stupid for having called after him like a teenage girl with a crush. Surely he hadn't meant anything but friendship, but now she would never know. Lauren realized she was more upset about the lost opportunity to spend time with Court out of the clinic than she was excited that Ted wanted her back. She figured that meant something, but she wasn't ready to go there…yet.

As Lauren walked in, she saw Ted leaning against the door frame to the kitchen and looking at her skeptically. Not meeting his eyes, she marched into the bedroom to get dressed and grabbed some of her oldest sweats. She would be comfortable, rather than looking like she cared to impress him.

After dressing, Lauren glanced in the mirror, saw how dowdy she looked in the stained, ragged gym clothes, and changed her mind completely. Forget that, she decided. If she was about to go out and face her ex, she was going to look her best! What was the point of all that jogging and exercise if she didn't show off her now tighter ass and slimmer waist? She pulled out a newish pair of skintight jeans and her skimpiest low-cut tank top. After dressing, Lauren added just a hint of color to her cheeks and took a look at herself in the floor-length mirror. *There! That's better. Might as well make him realize what he threw away.*

Once again, Lauren bemoaned the bad luck that Court had chosen the same weekend as Ted to come by her home. Now she would never know if he wanted friendship or something more, and Lauren couldn't think of any simple way to let him know who Ted was or why he was here. She was again struck by the realization that she was more excited about the mere possibility, however remote, that Court might be interested in her than she was that her ex-husband wanted her back. That, it seemed, was her answer, not that she would tell Ted that exactly. However, unless he could rouse some excitement or longing in her, there was really nothing to discuss, was there?

Lauren took one last look in the mirror as she got ready to face Ted. Feeling considerably more confident than she had just a few minutes ago, she strode out of the bedroom to meet head-on whatever he had to propose. Her gut told her that whatever it was, it would not call to her, not set her pulse racing like the mere idea of a date with Court! She wondered absentmindedly where Court was and what he was doing at that moment.

MISDIAGNOSIS

.

AS HE HEADED BACK to his apartment, Court was stomping mad, so angry that he would have kicked himself if it were possible. He kept wondering, what had he been thinking…going over uninvited to his boss's home at night to ask her out on a date! Shit, she really must be laughing it up now—a young, naive kid thinking he had a chance with an experienced woman like her.

Bumping a small rock with his foot, Court then grabbed the rock and hurled it at a tree. That felt good. He heaved another one into the woods, and yet another. If the trees could talk, they would be telling him he was a fool, he thought dejectedly.

Well, that was that. Lauren had a boyfriend, someone more her age and who clearly knew her very well. The guy had called her the sweet nickname "Laure" and seemed to be staying at her place. *Oh well*, Court thought again, better to know for sure she was unavailable. Maybe now he could free himself from this inappropriate desire and look elsewhere. Maybe he should start making an effort with Jessica, he decided. She was clearly available and undeniably interested.

At least there was one good thing about his internship, Court realized. He was learning a great deal and enjoying every minute of it, so much so that he wondered why he had ever doubted that he should go to med school in the fall. That helped settle his feelings, knowing his future was set. Not only that, but the work would look great on his résumé. Now, if he could just get his sexy boss out of his mind once and for all, he would really enjoy this summer of hands-on medical training. As he opened the door to his small rental unit, Court decided that he would begin his new plan on Monday by meeting Jessica's overt flirtations with friendly smiles of his own.

FALSE POSITIVE

LAUREN WAS ANXIOUS AS she puttered about the kitchen finishing preparations for dinner. It turned out that Ted really did have a problem with his car and was off at the shop checking on the car's condition while she waited impatiently for him to return. Highly skeptical, Lauren wanted to know what he would propose and to simply get it over with. As she shoved a pan of frozen lasagna into the oven, she heard the front door of her bungalow open and walked out to greet Ted.

"Everything okay with the car?" she asked.

"Yes, it was just a failed temperature sensor. An easy fix. It will be ready by midmorning tomorrow." He looked at her and smiled. "Is now a good time to talk?"

She nodded and sat down on the couch, gesturing for Ted to join her. She waited, not willing to make it any easier for him.

"Laure, first I need to tell you how deeply sorry I am for the way I left. It was completely wrong of me, and very immature and selfish. I wish I had done things differently," Ted said earnestly.

He leaned over to take her hand in his, but Lauren pulled away before he could touch it.

"I also want to apologize for the decline of our marriage. That was my fault too. I was unhappy…feeling trapped in this small town and trying to please you at the same time. But instead of trying to work it out with you, I just kept it all inside until there was nothing else to do but leave. I can see now that was a terrible mistake." He sounded very sincere.

"Ted, it means something to me that you're apologizing in person *finally*… It really does, but what you are telling me is not new information and it doesn't change anything."

Ted reached out again and this time caught her hands in his. He gripped them tightly and looked deeply into her eyes. "Lauren, I miss you and I still love you. I will never stop loving you. Don't you still care for me at all, not even a little?"

"Of course I still care for you. I'll always care for you after all that we shared, but I've made a new life for myself. While I can't say it's perfect, at least I have some peace."

"Please! Just hear me out!"

Lauren nodded.

"I want you to come join me in Chicago. You can sell the practice here and find a new position there… Something in a small clinic so you'll still have the close patient contact you like. Then you won't have to struggle anymore to make ends meet. And there's no rush to even find a new job, because I make lots of money now, and I can support us both. I make so much that I can even afford to buy a small second home in the country. I know how much you love small towns, and you can be in the country every weekend. See…you can have both worlds… and me too."

"This is so out of the blue. Where is it coming from?" she asked. Lauren realized that she didn't fully trust him. Having him show up after all this time was just too weird.

"I love you! I've never stopped loving you. I've missed you so much, and it's been lonely in Chicago. I know that with you and me together, everything would be perfect."

Ted kept telling her that he loved her, but Lauren couldn't help wondering why he'd needed six months to realize this. Had he really been pining for her all this time, or had he been trying his romantic luck in the Windy City? Obviously he was lonely, but she was not sure that Ted truly loved her. It did not really surprise her that his "plan" was self-serving and one-sided. She turned and looked him straight in the eye.

"You want me to give up everything and follow you back to Chicago? How am I supposed to trust you after you abandoned me the way you did?"

"Please, Laure, just take some time to think about it…just one night. We're talking about your future and the rest of our lives. Think about all the great times we shared in the past, and what a great future we could have together...and all the great sex." He winked leeringly at her.

"Sleep on it," he urged. "I promise I'll leave Saturday morning if your answer is no, but just give it one night, will you?"

"Okay, sure. I'll think about it overnight."

Ted leaned over quickly and snuck his arms around Lauren, clearly planning to kiss her. She pulled away, just before his lips met hers, and jumped up from the couch. "Dinner will be ready soon," she said, hurrying back to the kitchen.

After they finished the simple dinner of lasagna and salad, Lauren went to bed promising to think it over. Ted had attempted to kiss her again, but Lauren had put her hand up to stop him, repeating that she would tell him her thoughts in the morning. Ted definitely wanted her—or at least wanted sex with her—but rather than that stirring her, Lauren felt...nothing.

Lauren couldn't sleep much that night, even though her gut told her the answer before she climbed into bed. In truth, Lauren realized that she didn't think she could ever really trust Ted again. His betrayal had been too great. Although she stewed some over whether he had played the field before realizing he wanted her back, that wasn't really the issue. Lauren knew that while a part of her still loved him and probably always would, she just didn't feel the same toward him anymore, not after all that had happened. Those old feelings were dead, and she knew intuitively that they wouldn't be coming back.

So on Saturday morning she gave Ted her answer. After a quick breakfast, she gathered her courage and said, "I appreciate the effort you made to come and talk to me, but I'm not ready to give up everything and follow you back to Chicago. My life is here."

"Come on, Laure! I can't believe you're going to turn your back on everything we meant to each other! Turn your back on being married to a top Chicago doctor and all that would offer you. Why not just come up and visit for a weekend and see? I love the city and I know you will too."

"I'm sorry, Ted, but the answer is no."

"It's that young guy, isn't it! What is he to you?"

Lauren walked over to the front door and opened it. "Ted, I think it's time for you to leave."

He glared at her, and Lauren realized then that Ted had not expected this answer from her. Clearly, he had thought she would drop everything to run happily away with him.

Before Ted walked out, he made one last attempt. "Laure, why don't you just come for a weekend visit? Think about that idea." And then Ted walked out and down the stairs, glancing back once to wave and smile.

As she closed the door behind him, Lauren felt only relief and a small bit of pleasure. She was now so strong and confident that she could turn down his offer, even when faced with the strong possibility of remaining alone. Things had seemed so empty and sad when Ted first divorced her, but she had managed to pull her life back together and keep going during even the darkest moments. Lauren now realized that she had reached the point of being happy and feeling secure. She was grateful to Ted for his role in helping her understand this about herself, but that was the only emotion she felt toward him now.

For the remainder of the weekend, Lauren allowed herself to savor her newfound peace. She took Rufus on long walks and started really enjoying her independent life, rather than feeling stagnant and stuck watching life pass her by. It was freeing and gave her a new outlook about the future.

As she climbed into bed Sunday night, she realized that while the weekend had been emotionally exhausting, it had helped her to finally let go of the past. If there was a bright spot, it was seeing Ted's animosity and jealousy about Court's visit, which was an enormous ego boost. Lauren smiled, recalling the many times Ted had tried nonchalantly to ask who Court was and why he had come calling.

Playing a private game of misdirection, Lauren had evaded each of his supposedly casual questions, never letting on that Court wasn't her boyfriend. Ted had made some comments about Court's obvious youth, to which Lauren had replied enigmatically that Ted could certainly understand why she was trying so hard to stay fit and trim. Perhaps she had let him get the wrong idea, but so what? She did not owe Ted any explanations about her current life.

After thinking back about how her weekend had gone, Lauren had only one complaint—the unfortunate circumstance of Court now thinking she had a boyfriend. She kept reminding herself it shouldn't matter to her. Court was still her employee, and a much younger man at that. Lauren decided to put it all out of her head and focus her energies on her growing medical practice and the upcoming picnic.

~ 10 ~

WANTING A SECOND OPINION

IN THE WEEK THAT followed, Court behaved toward Lauren with markedly polite professionalism. He made no mention of his weekend visit to her home and was courteous but distant with her. Lauren watched his apparent growing interest in Jessica with despair and tried to forestall her own inappropriate jealousy. Everyone there, staff and patients, couldn't help noticing the brewing office romance between the two youngest members of her staff. Brenda and Kelly thought it was cute. Lauren could only nod in polite agreement to their whispered observations.

If Lauren had any doubts about what she was seeing between her intern and receptionist, Jessica made it abundantly clear on Friday afternoon when she appeared in Lauren's office giddy with delight. After shutting the door, she exclaimed, "Lauren, guess what? Court finally asked me out. We're going to the movies tonight. Isn't that great?"

Plastering a *happy-for-you* smile on her face, Lauren responded, "That's terrific. Lucky you!"

"I'm so excited. You must have noticed that I like him. I hope I wasn't too obvious with all my flirting, but I didn't seem to be getting anywhere," Jessica prattled on. "I was just about to give up and go after Jim, my old high-school boyfriend home from college for the summer. But now I'll—"

Lauren felt the smile freezing on her face. Was Jessica ever going to stop talking and leave her office? And the worst part was that even now thoughts of Court still made her palms sweat and brought tingles to places that shouldn't tingle for him. *Maybe*, Lauren thought, trying not to listen to the young woman anymore, *if I just stand up and start packing to leave, Jessica will get the hint.*

But Jessica didn't. "Really, Court is just tooooo too much, don't you think? I wonder what his kisses are like. I wonder if—"

And so it went, all during the following week. Jessica talked endlessly behind closed doors about Court to anyone who would listen. Lauren recognized she had no claim on the young man, but her pulse still quickened whenever she was in the same room with him. Hearing constantly about his budding relationship with Jessica was a bitter pill to swallow. At least Jessica couldn't talk about it when Court was present, which was much of the time, thankfully.

Still Lauren heard all about their first date—the movies at the old Bijou.

Their first dinner out together—Joe's Place, Plum Banks's only real restaurant.

"I offered to drive to Marion," Jessica reported to the ladies when they all went to lunch at that same restaurant, Court staying behind to man the phones. "But he said it was nicer to walk on such a beautiful night. Isn't that romantic? And then he—"

Lauren wanted desperately to plug her ears. And then she wished that she had, because she learned way more than she wanted to know.

Giving the ladies a conspiratorial smile, Jessica leaned in and shared, "Oh, and we had our first kiss! Wow oh wow, he's a good kisser! It was really sick! But he's a real gentleman. A short kiss was all it was, before saying good night to me at my door," she added with a regretful, pouty tone.

"What?" interrupted Brenda. "What was sick about it?"

Giggling delightedly, Jessica said, "No, no, you don't understand. 'Sick' means that it really kicks. Don't you get it? His lips are like the hottest things you can imagine!"

"Ah, okay. So it was good, then?" the older woman asked, not really understanding.

"Yes, it was *very* good! His kiss was soooo sophisticated. I can tell he'd be a take-charge kind of guy in bed, if you know what I mean," Jessica responded, giggling.

Lauren felt her smile freezing on her face again. Could she please stop talking about Court and his kisses and his lips, she fretted, feeling that familiar burn start as sexy images of him flitted unwelcomely through her mind.

Seeing Kelly watching her thoughtfully, Lauren worried that her feelings were written all over her face. Then Kelly interrupted Jessica with an off-topic question. Being a skilled conversationalist, Kelly easily managed to change the subject without anyone being the wiser—except for Lauren, who wondered how much her colleague had guessed about her private crush on Court.

As they walked back to the office, Jessica threw out one last tidbit that made Lauren groan, silently of course.

"Guess what! Jim…you remember, my old high school boyfriend? Well, Jim has also asked me out," Jessica said gleefully. "At first I thought maybe I shouldn't date two guys at once, but then I decided why not. I'm a modern woman and they're just dates after all, but then again—"

As Jessica continued thinking aloud, the others murmured their agreement. Even Lauren managed a nod, but once back in the clinic, she went straight into her office, calling out a sharp, "Take messages for me. I have some work to do in my office."

"But what about her afternoon patients?" Court questioned the other doctor.

"Oh, that's okay," Kelly responded, glancing over at the now-closed door. "I can fit them into my schedule for the next hour or so."

TELL ME WHERE IT HURTS

THE NEXT WEEK WAS pure agony. While Lauren was mortified to even admit it to herself, she was fuming with jealousy toward the younger woman. At night alone in her bed, she was a welter of aches and emotions. Finally Lauren just gave up on trying to put Court out of her mind and allowed herself to fantasize about making love to him. The Doc and she were intimate friends, even though that didn't help lower her craving for real sex—more specifically, sex with Court—which in turn was making her testy with everyone.

Then toward the end of the week, Lauren got unexpected relief from the daily play-by-play of the great Court-Jessica romance.

"I just don't get it," Jessica whined behind the closed door of Lauren's office. "Court kissed me a few times, but he won't take it any further. I've tried everything…every trick I can think of to get him to make a move, short of making an outright booty call to him."

The surprising news caused a small curl of pleasure to unfurl inside Lauren. The two of them weren't lovers!

As much as she liked and respected Jessica, Lauren realized that any advice she might offer would be disingenuous at best. "Ah, you might want to discuss this with your girlfriends," she muttered.

"I wonder if he's gay," Jessica said, brightening a little. "Do you think that could be it?"

"I, ah, really wouldn't know. Again, I'm sure girls your own age could give you better advice than I can." To make her point stick, she walked over and opened the door to her office.

Jessica nodded, saying, "Maybe you're right. Anyway, remember how Jim asked me out? I think I'll say yes to him now."

"Good, good." Lauren nodded, practically shutting the door in the young woman's face. Leaning her back against the door, Lauren took several deep breaths, telling herself once again...*it doesn't matter.*

However, with the renewed uncertainty about Court's relationship status, the electricity she always felt near him seemed to increase exponentially. Court seemed entwined in it too. At times, Lauren caught him staring at her with a smoky look that made her breath catch. She just knew it wasn't her imagination, but she didn't act on it, applying an iron will to her libido.

Then late one afternoon she found herself alone with him, shutting down the clinic for the night. For days, Lauren had been careful to avoid being alone with Court, given where her mind invariably went whenever she was in his presence. But today she had come out of her office after dealing with several annoying insurance issues to find the lights off and everyone gone—except for him!

"Oh!" Court said. "I thought you'd gone already."

He was in the hallway carrying several stacked boxes of supplies.

"Ah, no, ah...I'm just leaving." Seeing that he was headed toward the supply closet, Lauren offered, "Here, let me get the door for you."

After opening it and realizing how dark the closet was with the office lights turned off, she stepped inside to flip the switch. Turning back, she found her exit blocked because Court had followed her into the small supply room.

"Oh," she breathed, feeling the atmosphere turn suddenly intimate.

"Oh," she said again, feeling hot, her pulse racing. She wanted to exit, but to do that, she had to squeeze past Court. The thought of touching him, anywhere—even her breasts brushing his arm as she sidled by—made her dizzy. Court stared at her penetratingly, seeming to study her reactions. He looked just as hot and bothered, she realized with a jolt.

Breaking the silence, he asked, "Would you help me with these boxes?" His voice sounded hoarse.

"Oh, of course. Let me unload you," Lauren responded, looking for anything to get out of the confining space with him.

Being very careful not to touch his hands, she hurriedly took one box off at a time and put them on the shelves. When she was finished, she reached over and flipped off the light switch. She instantly regretted doing that. The darkness now surrounding them made the room suddenly even more intimate, raising awareness of how close they stood to each other and intensifying the sense that they could feel each other's heated longing.

Then, instead of backing out of the closet, Court stepped closer and reached out his hand to her. At that moment, looking up at him, Lauren didn't feel like his boss, didn't feel their age difference. He was tall, broadly blocking the exit and exuding an adult masculinity that stopped her breath. Court touched her shoulder gently. It tingled, igniting a burning ache that trailed all the way to her core.

He moved even closer, his hand now gripping her shoulder firmly, as if to keep her from fleeing. Looking down at her in the dim light, he stared at her mouth and then leaned down. Unable to help herself, Lauren felt her eyes drift shut and tilted her mouth toward him— waiting for the inevitable, wanting it desperately. And she waited.

Her eyes fluttered open, and she looked at him questioningly. Court seemed frozen in place, his face a cascade of emotions. She couldn't read them all, but he seemed to be at war with himself. Holding her breath, Lauren wondered which side would win.

And then he broke the spell.

Court dropped his hand and stepped back in one fluid motion, mumbling a whispered "sorry" as he looked away in obvious discomfort. Even though he had not actually been holding her upright, the loss of his touch was so sudden and overwhelming that she had to put a hand out to the wall to steady herself. Panting slightly, Lauren felt bereft…but also somewhat relieved. There was danger in kissing Court.

He turned away and she heard him choke out huskily, "Thanks for your help. See you in the morning," as he hurried out the front door.

It had seemed like a dream. As she slowly gathered her things to leave, Lauren wondered if she had imagined that Court had wanted to kiss her. He'd certainly had the opportunity and had not taken it.

Yes, Lauren decided glumly as she drove home, it must have been her overactive imagination. Of course a hot, young guy like that wouldn't be interested in an old woman like her. It was for the best really, she thought, the old refrain—too young, her employee—running through her head like a mantra.

The next day they both kept their distance from each other. When they did find themselves together, they were frigidly, professionally polite, fighting the fiery magnetism between them.

The first annual employee picnic was just a few days away, and Lauren threw herself into the preparations, publicly using this excuse to spend many hours away from the clinic. The other ladies had offered to help, but she declined. Lauren wanted the picnic to be a true thank-you to her staff for all their help over the last draining year, but also, subconsciously, she wanted to be consumed body and mind with absolutely no time for other thoughts...or feelings. And, it had almost worked. But as she shopped for picnic supplies in Marion, Lauren couldn't get her mind off Court and their almost kiss—and whether it had all been in her mind.

～ 12 ～
PLAYING NAUGHTY DOCTOR

FINALLY, THE DAY ARRIVED for the picnic at the Old Iron Furnace swimming hole, and the weather looked like it would be perfect. Lauren, however, felt anything but perfect.

While last-minute details had kept her days occupied, if Lauren woke up at night, she would lie in her bed and ache for Court, yearning for something she couldn't have. The night before had been the worst. Lauren hadn't fallen back asleep until just before dawn, and she awoke with the stirrings of arousal still within her. She felt frustrated and grumpy as she looked at her clothes and tried to decide what to wear.

Later as Lauren waited for the guests to arrive, she had to admit that her mood had colored her wardrobe choice. The bathing suit she wore underneath her tight little sundress was way too skimpy, a barely there number she had picked up in Aruba a few years ago—not really appropriate for more conservative Illinois. "Oh well," she said to Rufus, "I'll probably be too busy to swim anyway."

As the guests arrived, Lauren's spirits picked up. This was going to be fun, she thought as Rufus eagerly ran to greet each party. First came the Walsh family—Kelly with her husband and their two children, along with a pair of grandparents who were visiting. Next came Brenda and her husband, followed quickly by Jessica and... *Well, that's interesting*. Jessica had brought someone else instead of Court.

Lauren hurried over to join Rufus, who was enthusiastically sniffing Jessica's date. Giving Jessica a quick hug, Lauren was vaguely aware that a part of her was way too pleased that Court wasn't with Jessica. As Jessica introduced Jim, Lauren realized that this was the old boyfriend home from college for the summer. By the way they were looking at each other, Lauren guessed they were very close, perhaps even in love. Now her little company picnic was almost complete, but *where was Court?* Ignoring her conscience, she was exceedingly—inappropriately—excited to see him now that he was again available.

Suddenly Lauren realized that perhaps Court had needed a ride out to the park, since he didn't have a car. Scanning the dirt road that led to the small swimming hole and picnic area, she saw with relief that another car was approaching. Lauren started walking over to the parking area but stopped abruptly. Were there two people in the car?

As she watched, Court got out of the passenger side and a young woman emerged from the driver's side. Lauren felt her blossoming excitement about the picnic evaporate, her good mood deflating in an instant. Plastering a smile on her face, she went to greet the last guests to her party.

"Hi, welcome," she managed through a tight smile.

"Hey, hi," Court responded warmly.

He seemed too relaxed, too happy, Lauren thought with dismay.

"Let me introduce Tawny Johnson. She's a childhood friend of mine who's visiting this weekend," Court said as the pretty blond stepped forward to shake Lauren's hand.

"My real name is Tanya, but somehow I ended up with this nickname," Tawny added in an ultra-feminine purr.

"Hope you don't mind me bringing her along," Court added hastily.

"Of course not. The more the merrier," Lauren heard herself saying before turning quickly away to hide her disappointment. Over her shoulder, she added, "We're just starting to eat. Come this way." She gestured to the tables but didn't look at the couple again.

Lauren listened as he introduced his "friend" to the group. She noticed he didn't say "girlfriend," but why else would this woman be visiting for the weekend?

Lauren's annoyance peaked when Tawny shed her clothes to reveal a tight, youthful, bikini-clad body and trilled at Court, "Last one in is a…"

"Tawny! Really!" Lauren muttered to herself. "Are you kidding me?"

Well, she fit the bill, that was for sure—deeply tanned and svelte, with sparkly blue eyes and long, light-blond locks that floated around her. Tawny looked like she belonged on the next cover of *Sports Illustrated*'s swimsuit issue or, Lauren thought spitefully, starring in a porn flick.

Kelly's whispered observation only made it worse. "They look made for each other."

And she was right. Their sun-kissed skin, blond hair, and movie-star looks complemented each other—two angels sent down to mix with the rest of them, all mere mortals. As Court shed his T-shirt, Lauren stopped walking and stared openmouthed. He was a hunk! She had never seen him wearing so little. His smooth, chiseled six-pack abs and strong, young biceps were made to be caressed.

Realizing that Kelly was waiting and watching her speculatively, Lauren responded with feigned nonchalance. "I guess so."

"He didn't introduce her as his girlfriend, you know," Kelly added with an encouraging smile. "I think he would have, if she were."

"Whatever," said Lauren, walking away toward the water.

A small private smile lit her face. *I may not be twenty-two, but I know my body still looks good. Maybe it's not a bad thing I have on such a teensy-weensy suit.*

Stopping on the big rock that people used to jump directly into the deeper water, she slipped off her sandals and waited...and waited...until Court turned and looked in her direction. Pretending not to see him, Lauren casually reached down and slowly pulled the tight sundress up over her thighs, then up revealing her breasts, and finally over her head to toss it on the ground. Glancing at him, she got trapped looking into his hot stare. She wasn't a skinny woman, more voluptuous with sexy curves, and the tiny fabric triangles of her string bikini didn't quite cover the lush mounds of her breasts. Still watching Court as he paddled in place close to the rock, she walked to the edge with a sprightly step, ensuring that the barely covered mounds bounced sexily.

Lauren felt a burning thrill all the way to her core as she watched Court's mouth drop open and heard his inhaled gasp. He had stopped dead in the water, forgetting to paddle. His eyes were still locked on her, but now they were focused about a foot lower on her body. Lauren giggled as she watched Court sink under the water, mouth still open.

Sputtering, he popped his head back above the water, and his eyes immediately sought her out.

Lauren couldn't help saucily inquiring, "Water cold, Court?"

But he wasn't listening. She watched as his eyes traveled further down her body. Court was staring at the little triangle of cloth that covered her mons. She knew the bikini was actually quite sturdy, but its tiny, thin ribbons made it look like it could fall off at any moment. Lauren had originally bought it to impress Ted and was now glad she hadn't tossed it when he left.

Today isn't going to be so bad after all!

Lauren called out to Court, "I think I'll eat now after all, and let the water warm up first."

Turning back toward the picnic tables, she stooped down to pick up her dress, purposely offering him an excellent view of her firm, round backside as she bent over. Spying a beach ball nearby, Lauren scooped that up as well. Turning back, she threw it playfully at Court and watched him leap into the air toward it.

Catching the ball in his hands, Court held it up triumphantly. He would have tossed it back, but she had turned away. He couldn't help grinning broadly as he watched her sexy ass wiggling away. He felt an intense urge to follow right behind and grab her, thinking how much fun it would be to pull her warm, almost-naked body against his cold, wet one for a few long seconds before tossing her headfirst into the pond. But for the moment, he was stuck exactly where he was, hoping the chilling water would cool him down. If he got out now, his raging hard-on would be obvious to everyone.

Court knew she had done it on purpose, but why was a mystery that he pondered while standing in the shallows. Glancing back at his longtime friend Tawny, who was happily paddling around on her back enjoying the cool water and warm sun, he realized that Lauren might think there was something between them. She didn't know that they really were just lifelong friends, more like sister and brother than anything else. But why would Lauren care anyway, unless she wanted him?

Well, he would find out one way or another, Court decided. If Lauren wanted to play games today, so would he...with a vengeance. And while it might not be fair, Court decided not to give up his advantage. He would not outright lie and say he was dating Tawny, but if Lauren drew the wrong conclusion, so be it. Court remembered how jealous he had felt when he met Ted. He'd still be in the dark if he hadn't overheard a chance bit of town gossip that made it clear the older man was just her ex-husband. Court hoped that the jealousy factor would prove useful in this sneaky game of enticement they were mutually, if unofficially, playing.

With that last thought and his penis finally back under his control, Court swam over to Tawny, planning a scene that would be sure to get Lauren's attention.

"Is that her? She's very pretty—the kind of lush handful that I know you like," Tawny said with a laugh.

"Yep," he said with a grin and a laugh loud enough to carry across the water. Glancing over, he saw that Lauren was watching them surreptitiously. Swimming closer to Tawny, he made sure they looked close enough to be touching.

Whispering into her ear and trying to make it look like a lover's tryst, he said, "I'm going to try to make her jealous. One way or another, I want to know if Lauren is interested in me or not. Do you mind playing the foil?"

His friend winked and giggled loudly. Then whispered, "Glad to oblige, but don't forget she is your boss and a friend of your mother's friend. You could say she's a MILF without kids. Do you really want to go there with an older woman?"

"She's not that old actually," Court said, defending Lauren. "And, yeah, I want to go there, you bet!"

Pausing, he noted, "She's usually very professional and probably way out of my league." Smiling impishly at his friend, he added, "But after that performance she just gave me, let's give one back, okay?" And he splashed his friend full on in the face, laughing loudly for Lauren's benefit.

Spluttering loudly to draw attention, Tawny playfully splashed back, and together they tussled in the water until Court successfully pushed her under and swam away.

"I'll get you back, just wait," she called after him as Court glanced over to confirm again that they still had an audience. He felt deep satisfaction in seeing Lauren standing stock-still by the food table and gaping at them. When she saw that Court knew she was watching, Lauren turned quickly away. Court held his breath and watched her pretend to straighten up the food spread. She had not put her dress back on, and her full, sexy ass teased him as she moved about.

Without conscious thought, Court swam closer to her until he was near the big, flat rock. Pretending an interest in sunning himself, Court pulled himself onto the rock and tilted his face toward the sun—but his eyes stayed trained on the woman who haunted his nights. How he wanted to grab her and untie those thin ribbons to watch the fabric triangles fall from her body! That tiny excuse for a bathing suit should be illegal for what it was doing to him. He wanted to get her alone. He wanted to make her writhe with a hunger that matched the ache building inside him.

Court noticed that Tawny had swum closer and was smirking at him. His friend knew exactly what he was thinking, what he was feeling, he realized, and that irritated him further. Without being conceited, Court knew that he was good looking. Girls, and later women, had always made it clear that he was attractive. Sex had always come easily to him—regularly and often. With almost no effort on his part, women would willingly spread their legs for him, and he hadn't ever given it much thought.

This summer, for the first time ever, he had been completely cut off. Court could probably handle that, but every day he saw Lauren at the clinic. His initial impression—that she was the perfect kissable, fuckable, girl next door—remained painfully accurate, and she remained tauntingly out of reach. Feeling sexually frustrated was new, unwelcome, and driving him crazy!

"Go away," he muttered at Tawny. She laughed and swam off.

Glancing around to make sure no one was watching, Court eased himself off the rock and back into the water, waiting for the second time that day for the cold to help bring his raging erection under control. Annoyed with himself and with Lauren too, Court began to swim laps in the watering hole, trying to exhaust himself out of his desire.

With the exception of Court and Lauren, everyone else was having a wonderful time at the company picnic. It was turning into a beautiful afternoon, and the carefree picnickers were having fun. The grandparents sat happily watching the kids as they jumped from the rock into the pond. Jessica and Jim were off in the deep end in their own world, and eventually even the older Theresa and her hubby joined the swimmers in the cool water.

Lauren's earlier satisfaction at getting a reaction out of Court had quickly dwindled as she surreptitiously watched the playful interaction between the golden pair. *Are they lovers?* she wondered. Looking around, she was thankful to see that the rest of her guests were busy swimming or eating. No one else seemed to have paid any attention to the love scene in the pond—or to the lovesick woman wistfully watching.

Glancing back at him, she saw that Court was now swimming toward the picnic tables. As he stood up in the chest-deep water, his eyes sought hers. They challenged her to watch as he slowly emerged, dripping, from the pond. There was no way she could have looked away. Without realizing it, Lauren's tongue slipped out of her mouth to lick her lips as she watched the water sluicing off him. He paused to shake his sexy, wet locks and then continued walking purposely toward her, not stopping until he was directly in front of her, almost touching her.

With Court so close, Lauren had to tilt her head up to look at him.

"Yes," was all he said in a deep, husky whisper.

"Whaa…what?" Lauren gasped, inadvertently taking a step away from his heated gaze.

"Yes," he said again. "In answer to your question, the water is cold, deliciously so, invigorating." Flicking his eyes down toward her barely covered breasts, he added, "I've worked up a big appetite."

With that, Court turned away and went to the spread of food to begin filling his plate.

Lauren felt a monumental jolt of desire, an erotic clenching of the muscles in her vagina that left her dizzy and breathless. She couldn't take her eyes off his wet back and shoulders—how she would love to run her hands over those rippling, glistening muscles right now. She wondered restlessly what he had meant with the innuendo. Was it just her overactive libido, or had he just made a verbal pass at her?

Sighing, Lauren realized there was no way to know for sure what he had meant or whether he was available or not, and anyway she was still his boss. She couldn't—wouldn't—make a move on him, but that didn't mean she had to back off either. With a shake of her head, she decided: if this is a game he's playing, I'm going to play to win it, and the ball is in my court now. Lauren began to fill her plate and plot her next move.

Unable to bring herself to join the golden pair at their table, Lauren ate with Kelly and her family. After she finished, Lauren was starting to clean up some of the mess when Grandma Walsh said, "Honey, you go join in the fun. We'll take care of everything."

Thanking her and turning toward the water, Lauren all but bumped into Court, who was very close behind her. He was once again dripping with water, his glistening, muscular chest right in front of her eyes.

"It's your turn to get *wet*," he whispered to her.

Looking up into his eyes, Lauren was like a deer in the headlights, stopped dead in her tracks and frozen. Her mind was stuck on what he had said. Was it a challenge or an invitation?

"Ahh," she muttered. "Umm."

She unconsciously licked her lips. Court's eyes watched her mouth closely, and she noticed he looked wild and hungry. She wondered if he was going to throw her in the pond or kiss her instead.

Just as he started to reach for her, Kelly's children came running up. Lauren was their honorary aunt, and they grabbed her by the hand, calling, "Lauren, come join us." They pulled her toward the water. Exceedingly frustrated, Lauren realized that the moment was broken and she would never know what he had intended to do. As she joined the laughing group in the pond, she concluded that probably all Court had planned was to take advantage of an opportunity to dunk the boss.

Surrounded by friends, almost like family to her, she knew there wouldn't be another chance for such overt interplay, but Lauren felt his eyes on her often as they all swam and splashed in the water. And in spite of everything—in spite of her constant tingling desire or even annoying Tawny's presence—Lauren thoroughly enjoyed herself throughout the carefree afternoon. Her first-ever employee picnic had been a big success.

Later, as she waved good-bye to everyone—in the mix of packing up and everything—there had been no time to talk alone with Court, even if she'd known what to say to him. He had also hesitated, but then seeing no opening, he'd gotten into the car and waved good-bye before he and his friend drove away. There was nothing to do then but urge Rufus into her car and head home…alone.

~ 13 ~
TEMPERATURES RISING

LAUREN FOUND THE NEXT day utterly unbearable. It had taken hours for her to fall asleep, and even then she had slept fitfully, drifting in and out of aroused dreams until the alarm sounded too early. When she got out of bed, she was irritable, tired, itchy, twitchy—and, damn it all, still hotly aroused!

As she angrily stomped around the bungalow, she realized that the "company picnic" had been a big mistake—for her personally. Seeing Court at the swimming hole in nothing but a bathing suit and with all that tanned, brawny, tight young flesh on display had been torture. Her breath had stopped every time he emerged from the pond, the water cascading off his gorgeous pumped chest. Lauren knew, or thought she knew, that Court had gone out of his way to saunter by or emerge sexily, glisteningly wet every time she was near. Of course Lauren had played that game too. But why was she the only one still tingling and aching—left hanging?

As she dressed, Lauren realized that the game was not yet over— there had been no denouement. So, smiling wickedly, she chose to wear her shortest skirt and skimpiest top to work. She still wasn't entirely sure if this was a game or if the lusting was all one-sided—her sided. Nevertheless, Lauren decided she would continue to play the tease if the opportunity arose. *What could that hurt, really?*

Once she arrived at the office, Lauren pronounced to no one in particular that she could not bear the heat and couldn't possibly wear her lab coat today. So she strutted, or rather stamped, around the office in her sexiest high-heeled sandals and the tight-fitting skirt and blouse. Kelly raised an eyebrow at her colleague's behavior but wisely kept her mouth shut. While Lauren rarely acted grumpy, Kelly knew better than to get in the middle of whatever was going on today, so she spent a considerable amount of time in her office with the door shut.

Nurse Brenda was home sick, and Jessica was also adept at avoiding contact with Lauren when she was in a rare bad mood. So Court got the bulk of Lauren's fit of pique—but that was the point, really. It didn't help that he seemed unaffected by all that had passed between them yesterday.

At lunchtime, Kelly, Jessica, and even Court hurried out to take their breaks elsewhere. Lauren ate at her desk, stewing about what to do with her feelings while absentmindedly paying bills. After an hour, she noticed that the receptionist was taking an extra-long lunch today without permission. In her pissy mood, Lauren was more angered by that than she normally would be. When Jessica finally returned almost thirty minutes late, Lauren marched out to the front desk. Letting her internal angst get the better of her, she unleashed on the young woman.

"Jessica, you know I think very highly of all you do around here, but that doesn't mean you can take advantage of me. If you want to be paid for all your hours, then you need to work them all."

As she returned to her office, Lauren saw Court quickly lean down to smilingly whisper something into Jessica's ear. They both laughed. That was just too much! Court appeared to be showing interest in the receptionist again and was too nice to her by far—too solicitous, too sexy. It didn't seem to matter that Jessica now had a boyfriend, Lauren fumed. Court would rather take another's leftovers than reach out to someone new—*me*. She vaguely recognized that she was being unreasonable; there was really nothing inappropriate in his behavior. She just could not stop the roiling waves of jealousy. Keenly green with both envy and lust, Lauren needed to retaliate.

"Court, would you come in here please?" she called out sharply.

After he entered her office, Lauren ordered, "Shut the door and sit down."

Court looked at her warily as he sat in a chair facing her.

"How dare you undermine me with my staff?" she accused.

"What…what are you talking about?" Court responded, annoyed.

"I saw you with Jessica. She has no right to come back from lunch late without permission, and while I don't know what you said, you clearly were taking her side," Lauren angrily retorted.

"You have no idea what I said to her, and I have a right to talk with anyone I choose," he returned crossly.

"You have the right to work here, not goof off and carry on conversations," Lauren snapped. She stood up and strutted crossly around the desk. Leaning over him, she demanded, "Do I make myself clear?"

Her statement hung in the air. It was really more of a threat than a question. Court looked too furious to speak, and Lauren was practically panting as she anticipated his reaction.

FEVERISHLY HOT

COURT WAS VERY, VERY angry. *Even if she is my boss, she has no right to talk to me like this!*

But Lauren was leaning over him, and he had a clear view down her blouse to her full breasts covered in a sexy, lace bra. His immediate hard-on made it difficult to think or talk, but he managed to mutter a sarcastic "Yes, ma'am!"

Lauren looked affronted at his reply. Then she whirled away, presenting her tense back to him. "Okay, get back to work then," she muttered.

Sitting there, Court was momentarily frozen, staring at her voluptuous ass in the tight, short skirt. He wanted to reach out and grab her ass—or maybe spank it, he realized with a grin. Instead he rose and marched out of her office before he succumbed to either impulse.

He heard Lauren quietly grumble, "Ma'am me, will he!" and he smiled.

As the afternoon dragged on, Lauren seemed to use every opportunity to demonstrate that she was no old lady worthy of the title "ma'am," even resorting to the time-tested method of dropping something and bending over to pick it up. She and Court were walking single file down the hall when Lauren abruptly dropped a pen. As she started to bend over with her high heels and outrageously short skirt displaying her long shapely legs, Court came to a dead stop directly behind her. Even though he knew it was a ploy, Court was fascinated by watching Lauren's pert, tight ass as she bent over slowly. Hardly bending her knees at all, she took her time in reaching down to the ground to retrieve the pen, her tush pushed high in the air.

As he stared, the short skirt inched higher and even higher. Court's breath stopped as he realized, wide-eyed, that he might catch a glimpse of her panties. Suddenly he wondered if Lauren might be bare-assed naked underneath her skirt. He was instantly, almost painfully erect. He turned away to hide the large bulge in his pants, heading back to the closet where he was supposed to be sorting supplies. The way Lauren played him so skillfully annoyed him, as did his uncontrollable hard-on. He swore silently, *Fuck! She really has it in for me today, doesn't she?*

Looking around the storeroom, Court saw that he was nearly done, but he needed time to cool off and sort out his feelings. All day yesterday he had lusted after Lauren in her tiny bikini. That had triggered a long night of intense discomfort. Now here she was, parading around in front of him again and looking like she wanted nothing more than to be taken home and fucked—hard. This was going to be an excruciating day.

He had long since stopped caring that he was inexperienced or younger than Lauren, or even that she was his boss, but still he hesitated to make the first move. What if he was mistaking her interest? There was also the issue of any fallout getting back to his mom. Only two more months and he would be long gone from here, Court reminded himself. *Just leave it alone*, he admonished silently.

Later, with Brenda out sick, Court assisted both doctors with exams, but the intensity when he helped Lauren was wildly different than with Kelly. Occasionally he and Lauren accidentally brushed against each other in the small confines of the exam room, and her sharply inhaled breath punctuated the silence of each encounter.

Court needed a long time to talk down his painful erection while he pretended to work in the closet, and his penis throbbed anew every time the image of Lauren bent over, ass in the air, popped back into his mind. To get even, Court began to purposely brush against her. Sometimes when he was lucky, say passing a patient file, Court was able to graze the back of his hand against her bosom.

Even though he only did it when patients weren't looking, Court found plenty of opportunities to torment Lauren and enjoyed every one of her harsh gasps. Finally, he even managed to bump into her, causing her to stumble. His hands shot out to catch her in a feigned show of coming to her assistance. Grabbing her hips from behind, he let his hands linger a little too long before sliding one down to casually fondle her ass. With a smirk, Court gave her a little pat on the behind before stepping away.

"Would you be more careful!" she hissed.

"You know, if you were wearing more practical shoes—"

"Really, do you presume to tell me how to dress?" she snapped back. Whipping around before he could say anything, she jabbed him in the chest with her finger and said, "No, don't answer that!"

While they were both trying to keep the heated antagonism from showing to the patients, they were failing miserably. At one point, old widow McConnell noted with a sly grin, "Things are getting quite interesting around here, aren't they?"

That remark just added more fuel to the fire. As soon as Mrs. McConnell left the clinic, Lauren stalked into her office and slammed the door. Court paused outside her office, but not knowing what to say, he just went back to cleaning the exam room. Having Lauren angry with him was unsettling, but he felt that she had started it. That it was her fault. Well, maybe not all her fault, he thought, grinning as he remembered the tight feel of her ass under his hand. He wondered what she was doing behind her closed door.

～ 15 ～
CHRONIC SPASMS

LAUREN SLAMMED AROUND HER private office. *It's all his fault!*

She was furious with him…furious with herself too. At the same time, she felt…alive! Gloriously alive and energized in a way she hadn't in a very long time. It compelled her to keep playing at the game, or *whatever* was going on between them. With that thought, she decided to teach him that it is best not to anger the boss. It was an important lesson that he needed to learn and useful for his future, she easily convinced herself. Once again, Lauren ordered him to come into her office.

"Courtney, come here," she called out. "Shut the door. We need to talk."

After he sat in the chair she indicated, Lauren rose and purposefully swaggered around her desk. Leaning her fanny against it, she stretched her shapely legs out just in front of him as she smugly tossed out her first volley.

"Courtney, you really must be careful what you say in front of patients," she said, matching his earlier feigned air of helpfulness.

He looked annoyed every time she used his formal name, which made her smile inside.

He started to open his mouth to protest, but Lauren held up her hand to silence him.

"No, just listen to me. As someone older and with more experience in the world, I want to help you."

Adroitly cutting her off, Court interjected, "Oh, I know you have much, *much* more experience than I do."

"You're missing my point," she retorted. "You need to be respectful at all times."

"Oh, I do try to respect my *elders*," he replied smugly. "But I also believe I might be able to teach a thing or two to someone older, much older," he finished, looking her directly in the eye with a completely straight poker face.

Lauren gasped loudly. *This just won't do*, she fumed, realizing she was losing control of the situation. Well, better to show him than just talk. "Okay, fine! But as you'll recall, when you begged for the internship, you promised to do anything I wanted."

"Yes, I did," he responded, eagerly jumping up from his chair to walk close to her, forcing her to lean back slightly on the desk. Leaning in and staring at her mouth, he murmured, "I'll do anything you want, anything you *need*."

Lauren felt the thrill shoot through her body like an electric jolt, but she was too angry about all his insults to think straight.

"Good! The cleaning staff can't make it today…*Courtney*. I'll need you to the clean the bathrooms and mop the floor tonight after the office closes."

As soon as the words left her mouth, Lauren regretted them. She was being incredibly petty and knew it, but taking the order back would be admitting she had behaved immaturely. She couldn't bring herself to back down, especially when he was glaring furiously at her. Lauren stepped away from Court and walked around her desk, in effect dismissing him.

"Fine!" he snorted before stomping from the room. "And…my name's Court!" he yelled over his shoulder.

～ 16 ～

CODE FOUR

WITH THE DEPARTURE OF the last patient, both Jessica and Kelly swiftly hurried out, cheerfully calling "Have a nice weekend" as they left. As Lauren gathered her things to leave, she couldn't resist offering some helpful advice when Court emerged from the closet with a bucket, a mop, and cleaning supplies.

"Courtney, it's very important that you do a thorough job cleaning. I'm sure you'll agree that we need to eradicate any bacteria that might be on any surface. So you may as well cancel any plans you might have had for this evening. You'll be here for many hours yet."

"Yes, *ma'am*," he drawled mockingly as she turned to go back to her office.

I wish he'd stop saying that, she griped silently. *Stop treating me like an old lady!*

Following close behind her, Court stopped Lauren in her tracks when he goaded, "I know that the cleaning staff are scheduled to come in tomorrow. You're just being spiteful, punishing me for telling you the truth."

Before turning away he added, "Why don't you stay and help me? I know *you* don't have any plans for tonight either...or any night, for that matter."

"How dare you!" she snapped, turning angrily to him.

Staring at her, Court responded, "I never would have pegged you to be such a bitch, with your nice girl-next-door persona and all."

For a second or two his last words hung there in the silence as they both glared heatedly at each other.

Slap! Her stinging hand hit his face so unexpectedly that he didn't flinch or try to duck.

Lauren turned swiftly away again and stood there leaning over her desk, holding herself up in an effort to steady her dizzying pulse. "Get out! Get out of my office and get out of my clinic."

A loud crashing sound made Lauren jump as bucket and mop landed on the floor. She felt Court's hand grasping her arm as he jerked her back around to face him. He looked thunderously angry, she noticed as his other hand raced out and took hold of her free arm to pull her toward him.

"This has gone far enough," he announced with a commanding authority that belied his youthful age. "We both know what this is really about."

Lauren gasped at the zinging, tingling contact she felt on her arms. Watching his eyes lock on her mouth, she realized at the last second that he wasn't angry as much as heatedly aroused. Then his mouth slammed onto hers, his arms sliding around her back as he took charge of the dancing erotic tension that had been swirling between them all day. Locking her into a firm embrace, he used his mouth to begin a new dance that promised a sensual release, finally, for their fiery, intense longing for each other.

With all her senses overwhelmed, Lauren instinctively struggled against his tight hold at first, but then almost immediately surrendered to the raging desire she had been fighting all day—all summer, in fact. Her hands grasped at his sides to hold him even tighter to her as a moan escaped deep from her throat. For long, hot minutes they assaulted each other with their mouths, while their hands roamed wildly about each other's bodies, their mutual moans becoming loud in the small office.

Pushing her backward against her desk, Court slid his hands up her legs, sliding her skirt up, while she felt his chest with one hand and wrapped her other in his soft, corn-silk hair, anchoring his mouth onto hers. With her skirt up, he began to caress her bare thighs before sliding his hands under her briefs. He urgently stroked her vulva inside her briefs as his tongue plunged in and out of her mouth in a similar rhythm.

Feeling on fire, Lauren rubbed her breasts against his chest—her nipples now tight buds aching to be touched. Breaking the kiss, Court lowered his head and latched on to a projecting nipple through her blouse and bra, biting it slightly.

"Oh, yes, please," Lauren urged as she held his head there and her hips began to swivel to the insistent massaging of his fingers at her pussy. She wanted desperately to feel him and lowered her hand to rub against the aroused bulge in his pants. In response, Court groaned and moved himself against her greedy hand.

Needing more, he released her from his embrace to swiftly and roughly pull her top up off her body. Joining him, she yanked his shirt over his head and began unzipping his pants as he reached around, unhooking her bra to free her breasts for his mouth. They were frantic with need as they hurriedly shed their remaining clothing.

As she reached down to pull off her high-heeled sandals, he grabbed her hand and ordered, "No! You paraded around all day in those sexy shoes. You'll leave them on now…for me."

Her hand stopped at once as she acquiesced to his command. She may be his boss and he her employee, but in this new state of affairs he was the one in control, and she willingly ceded the power. Now that they were naked, he resumed his demanding kiss on her mouth as he pulled her against his body, his erect penis hotly pressed between them.

Lauren marveled at the feel of him. His youthful physique was all hard planes and firm muscles, and she couldn't resist rubbing herself against him like a cat in heat. Squirming and swiveling, she continued their silent erotic dance. Lauren was on fire with hunger and pent-up need—months of unfulfilled desire exploding out of her into this one man.

With a hoarse moan, Court swung his arm across her desk, sweeping all the files, pens, and myriad supplies off and sending them crashing to the floor. After taking hold of her waist, he lifted Lauren onto the desk. The feel of her naked ass on the wooden surface sent a titillating naughty thrill through her. Her brain screamed, *This is so hot, hot, hot!*

Court carefully laid her down backward on the hard wooden surface while his eyes burned passionately into hers. Before climbing onto the desk, he pulled a condom out of his pants pocket and looked at her with a question in his eyes.

"Yes, please, hurry," Lauren assented, panting and reaching for him. Quickly Court ripped the package open and rolled it on his long length.

Climbing up to join her, he stared down into her eyes and she could see the intense hunger in them that mirrored her own need. Guiding his thick penis with his hand, he plunged it inside her and she moaned loudly at the wonderful sensation of being filled by him—*finally*!

He then lowered his mouth to begin kissing her again, first on her lips, then her breasts, all the while trailing kisses that explored her neck and chest. Returning to her mouth, he demanded her full participation as he plunged his tongue into her mouth. Lauren eagerly joined this new dance, their tongues plunging in and out of each other's mouths as Court repeatedly slammed his penis into her vagina while she lifted her pelvis, forcefully meeting each thrust.

Together, their bodies performed a horizontal dance of frenzied writhing and moaning. Flooded with glorious erotic sensations, they frantically grasped for the sexual release they had craved for weeks. Crying out his name loudly, Lauren exploded in a towering climax she hadn't felt in years. Her clenching pussy drove Court over the edge, and he came with a deep guttural moan.

They kept the pulsing rhythm going as long as possible as the kisses he gave her turned tender and their breathing slowly returned to something approaching normal. Touching his forehead to hers, he smiled and slowly pulled out of her vagina. Lauren was surprised to realize that she felt a little bereft, that she immediately wanted him back inside her.

Raising his head to look at her, he held himself up on his arms. "That was amazing," he panted, still out of breath.

"That was extremely hot," she echoed, slowly sitting up as he climbed off her and then off the desk.

Lauren ran out and quickly grabbed a couple sheets and towels from a drawer. She wrapped herself in one sheet and offered the other to Court.

"I want to look at you," he said huskily. "You have a terrific body, and I've waited so long to see it. *Please* don't cover it up."

Lauren was thrilled to hear his compliments, but the ramifications of what they had just done were beginning to sink in. She anxiously started to pace, a worried expression on her face.

"Really, if you let me look at you, I'll be hard again in minutes," Court encouraged with a sly grin. "And this time we'll take it slow." Reaching out to her, he added, "You'll like it. I promise you!"

Turning to look at him, she replied, "That was so great, really, but, um, maybe it was a mistake. I mean, what about our age differences and the fact that I'm your boss? Maybe we shouldn't do it again…just call it a one-time mistake and try to forget about it."

With heated anger, Court retorted, "Fuck that! I've wanted to do bad things to you for weeks. It's all I think about…all the time! I know you feel the same way," he challenged.

Then he reached out and yanked the sheet off her body, dropping it onto the floor. Pressing his sweat-slick body against hers, he once again took charge, saying firmly, "I don't care how old you are, and it certainly wasn't a mistake. If there was a mistake, it's that it took so long for us to get together."

Nuzzling her neck, he tenderly planted little kisses behind her ear and trailed more down her neck. Whispering into her ear, "Yes, I'll admit that you are my boss, but when we're here, naked together, I'm in control. Trust me, I'll take us places that will make you beg…for more."

Lauren relished his bold, skillful arrogance, so in contrast with his youthfulness. It wasn't an act of machismo. Court was serious and she believed what he promised. She wanted to go where he could take her, and she felt herself already stirring, desiring more sex with him, right then and right there.

Turning toward him, she raised her face to kiss him, and no more words were needed as their long-denied passion was released again to consume them. This time, Lauren truly let go, screaming gutturally as he expertly brought her to an uncontrolled, thoroughly draining orgasm.

Later, after they recovered, they raided the office refrigerator for leftovers. They didn't say much while they ate, just enjoyed a companionable silence. When they had finished, Court gently touched her shoulder, making small circles over her smooth skin while looking thoughtfully into her eyes. She tentatively reached out and touched his face, then swirled her thumb across his mouth. Taking that as encouragement, Court pulled her to him for a long, deep kiss and Lauren enjoyed the feel of his lips, firm but tender, as they moved over hers. It started leisurely but began to build in intensity.

Pulling back, Lauren asked diffidently, "Would you like to come over to my home? We can continue this there."

In response, Court pulled her into a tight embrace, planting another kiss on her lips and then whispering, "I thought you'd never ask."

HOMEOPATHIC REMEDY

AT HER BUNGALOW, THEY began a weekend of frenzied lovemaking that started just inside the door on the living room floor. They hardly left the cottage the entire weekend. By the time they were done, they had fucked in every conceivable position using every room or surface in the place—the kitchen table, the shower, the living room couch, the bedroom, of course, and more.

On Sunday afternoon they went for a long walk with Rufus in the woods. It was a lovely day, and out of sight of the neighbors, she let Court hold her hand as they strolled along.

"How are you feeling about the idea of going to med school these days?" she asked out of the blue.

He smiled at her then, really more of a delighted leer. "Well, you see, I have this amazing boss who's a doctor, and I've learned so much from her already. I think if my boss continues to provide such in-depth, private tutorials, I might really get a *feel* for hands-on medicine. In particular, I would like to focus on *bedside* manner."

Lauren laughed, a bell-toned carefree sound. Then Court pulled her into his arms and kissed her deeply. When he finally stepped away minutes later, she was breathless. Yes, it was definitely going to be a hot summer, she thought, smiling.

When they started walking again, she urged, "But really, are you going to go to med school? I want to know."

"Yes…yes I am. I can't thank you enough for this chance to experience what it's really like to work in a medical practice. It has shown me that this is what I want to do with my life, and I can now totally commit to med school."

Lauren strolled quietly for a few minutes, thinking about the fact that when Court left for med school, he would also be leaving her. This was to be expected, and while Lauren didn't voice it out loud, she knew that eventually she would want a relationship with someone her equal—her own age and in the same place in life, ready to settle down.

"Lauren," he said quietly. "What do you want for your future?"

"I'm happy to just live in the moment these days," she replied. "Getting over Ted's abandonment was difficult, but I managed to pull myself together and keep the practice going. I feel some pride about that."

"You should," he said, squeezing her hand.

"In a few years, I think I might like to start a family. I think Rufus needs some rug rats to chase his tail." Looking down fondly at her dog, she singsonged, "Don't you think so too, Rufus?"

The dog looked up at both of them and happily wagged his tail. Then Court picked up a stick and threw it. Rufus looked at Lauren with puppy-dog eyes. "Okay," she said, unhooking his leash. In a shot, the dog was off after the stick. Returning, Rufus wouldn't give it up easily, wanting to play tug-of-war before yielding it to a human. They played this game all the way back to the bungalow, but Lauren was careful to let go of Court's hand when they approached Plum Banks proper.

Later, as she lay wrapped in his arms while Court slept off the latest round of lovemaking, Lauren couldn't wipe the silly smile off her face. It was Sunday night, and she could hardly believe they were lying on the hallway floor. *The hallway floor!* Court had come up to her from behind while she was washing dishes at the sink after dinner, and somehow they had never made it all the way back to the bedroom. Funny, Lauren thought, she had never thought of the hallway as sexy before…but she certainly would now.

At her request, Court agreed to keep their new relationship a secret from the office staff during the weeks that followed. Now that Jessica was in deep with her old boyfriend, Lauren wasn't worried about her young friend's feelings. In fact, it sounded like the college boy might even propose before the summer was out. Frowning slightly, Lauren realized that she might end up needing a new receptionist if Jessica followed Jim back to college.

Lauren was still feeling slightly embarrassed about being involved with a much younger man. In such a small community, tongues would wag. Also, they both realized this would just be a summer fling, not something that could develop into a long-term relationship, so why prompt meddlesome gossip for no reason? Having made his decision, Court would head off to medical school in the fall—leaving just two short months for their romance. They tacitly agreed that this was just "summer love," an exciting fling they both planned to enjoy to the fullest.

As is always the case, it seems, the weeks started to pass much more quickly. Days were busy with patients, and nights were filled with steamy sex. On the weekends they went on picnics and once to the movies together, but out in public she didn't let Court even hold her hand. After all, she had a reputation as the town's respectable doctor to maintain, she told him.

And once very late at night during a hundred-degree heat wave, they went skinny-dipping at the swimming hole. At first Lauren was nervous about being discovered, especially since they had snuck into the closed park, but after a while she enjoyed the risqué pleasure of floating around without a bathing suit and feeling the cool water against her bared skin. Seeing the moonlight reflecting off Court's wet body was an added bonus, and they made love right there in the water.

~18~
DOES IT HURT IF
I TOUCH YOU HERE?

LAUREN WAS HAVING AN all-around goooood time! And so was Court. He had kept his little garage apartment but spent virtually every night in the bungalow with Lauren, and somehow even that much access didn't seem to be enough for either of them.

She hardly noticed when their mutual attraction started to seep out at the office. She knew that the staff must have noticed that she wasn't bossing him around in such a bitchy fashion anymore, but Lauren was certain that she was maintaining her professional distance. *Wasn't she?*

Well, occasionally she did ask Court into her office to give him instructions and closed the door, but how could anyone tell if those instructions turned into brief stolen kisses? Although, there was that one time when Jessica had to buzz three times on the intercom to let her know a patient had arrived, but…

She was certain that Court was also maintaining the appearance of professionalism between them. *Wasn't he?*

Well, occasionally he did squeeze her ass when no one was looking, and there was that one time when he wanted her feedback on the organization of the closet. But nobody would have noticed that they were in there with the door shut for a long time. *Would they have?*

Lauren told herself to stop worrying about it. After all, it was all just a fun game and the ladies didn't seem to notice—or if they did, they didn't seem to mind. As long as the patient care remained first rate, what was the harm in a little office romance?

And so it went in the clinic for another couple weeks until Lauren decided to tease Court one morning, perhaps more than she should have. That day she wore the same cotton dress she'd worn his first day there, remembering how he had told her that she'd turned him on when she inadvertently displayed herself in the sunlight.

First thing in the morning, before putting on her lab coat, she called Court into her office for some instructions and made sure to stand in front of a window where sunlight was pouring in, giving him a naughty silhouette of her body. Acting like she was too full of energy, she squirmed around almost posing and giving him an X-rated performance. She had deliberately left the office door open before asking him to sit down, purposely limiting what he could do about the impromptu peep show. Lauren could tell Court was enjoying it, but rather than let him shut the office door and kiss her, she sent him back out to work with a squeeze to his ass.

Court seemed to take that as a challenge and began a game of surreptitiously teasing her that got more flagrant as the morning progressed. He used every opportunity to touch Lauren casually on the arm, brush as if by accident across her breast, and later blatantly return the squeeze to her bottom. Lauren was quickly becoming hot and bothered, when her naughty intention had been to make Court squirm with desire.

He won the round late in the morning when Lauren walked by him in the hallway, and Court grabbed her for a quick, demanding kiss while he slipped a hand inside her lab coat and fondled her breast through her dress. She pushed him away quickly with a laugh, but she was panting and so hot all over that she decided to take off her lab coat. *Anyway, lunch is just around the corner and we have no patients... That's the real reason it's coming off.* At least that is what she tried to convince herself.

As she came out of her office, sans white coat, Kelly gave her a knowing smile.

"What?" challenged Lauren with a smile, realizing she didn't really mind if her close friend and colleague knew her secret. Clearly, Kelly didn't disapprove of Lauren's liaison with an employee—they were both consenting adults, after all—so maybe she should worry less about it.

Lauren wanted to continue playing their little game and get even with Court for his last tease. She was tingling all over and wanted to make sure he was too. *But what to do?* she wondered. What could she do in the office that wouldn't be noticed?

Then she hit upon it.

"Court," she called out. "I remember you were complaining about that sore throat earlier."

"What are—" he started to reply, but she cut him off.

"I've got a few minutes free, since it's almost lunchtime. Let me take a look at you. Come into Exam Room Two please."

Court glanced suspiciously toward Lauren but didn't say anything. After a moment of indecision, he turned and walked toward the room with her following close behind.

Brenda called out, "Do you want me to take his vitals for you?"

"Nope," Lauren said as she walked in behind him. She purposefully left the door standing open. "I can do it myself."

Turning around, she looked at Court as if he were a piece of candy. He smirked back at her, knowing full well the game was on.

With the door left open, Lauren chose her words carefully. "Court, why don't you sit on the exam table?"

"Okay," he drawled, but then whispered, "What are you doing?"

As she stalked toward him with a seductive smile, she whispered, "Giving you a little payback, honey."

Then loudly she said, "Just take a deep breath."

After glancing back to check that no one could see them, she leaned in to him and placed her hand on his crotch while placing her stethoscope on his chest. With the angle of the table, anyone walking by wouldn't be able to see where she had placed her hand.

At his sharply indrawn breath, she cheekily ordered, "No, you need to take a slow, deep breath for me," while she gently massaged his penis through his pants. Smiling down at him, she could see that her tease was working, and she could feel his penis growing under her hand.

"Your chest sounds fine," she continued. "Please open your... mouth," she said while she slowly unzipped his pants. She knew she was playing with fire, but she was having too much fun to care.

As she stuck the tongue depressor into his mouth, she slid her hand inside his pants and squeezed a little harder.

"Ahhh," Court gasped out.

"But I didn't ask you to say 'ah' yet," she said in her most professional tone. Continuing her ministrations to his penis, she watched Court's face grow taut with desire as his hands clenched the table's edge.

Giving him a sneaky wink, Lauren said, "I think you'll be just fine... Nothing a little time *in bed* won't cure." With that, she quickly slipped her hand out of his pants and sashayed back out of his reach as he lifted his hands to grab her.

Sauntering to the open door, she taunted cheekily, "I'll give you a moment alone to take care of your...ah...needs." Then she pulled the door shut behind her.

Score one for me, Lauren thought, giggling as she walked back to the front of the clinic. Turning the corner, she stopped short when she saw Kelly leaning against the wall and looking speculatively at her. More and more, Lauren found she didn't care if her office staff knew about Court and her. She was just too happy to continue hiding it from her friends.

Both Brenda and Jessica threw her a quick smile, but then suddenly the two women became very busy with their paperwork, looking anywhere else but her direction. She saw Kelly's gaze shift to look past her, and Lauren knew Court was standing behind her. Some of her bravado dissipated as she glanced anxiously over her shoulder. Was he really mad? Court was stalking slowly toward her, looking... Oh, how *was* he looking? Lauren couldn't quite tell, but her skin crawled with delicious shivers.

Behind her, she heard Kelly call out, "Hey, Jessica and Brenda, how 'bout we grab some lunch at the diner...my treat."

"Thank you." "How nice." Jessica and Brenda responded simultaneously as they hurriedly grabbed their purses.

~ 19 ~
DEEP TRANSVERSE FRICTION

WHILE THE WOMEN HURRIED out, Court and Lauren remained frozen in the lobby staring at each other—almost challenging the other to do something. Lauren glanced at Kelly and mouthed "Thank you" as her colleague winked at her before stepping outside to follow Jessica and Brenda.

As soon as the door finally shut, Court cleared his throat to get Lauren's attention back on him. Looking at him, Lauren could tell that he was as wildly aroused as she was. Pinning her in place with a hot, seductive look, he walked over and locked the door.

Turning around to face her, he ordered, "Get into your office."

"But it's the middle of the day, and—"

"Now!" was all Court said. He meant it and she knew it.

Turning quickly, she practically ran to her office. Either that, or she guessed he would try to fuck her right there in the waiting room. Lauren didn't think she would have the control, emotional or physical, to resist him once he got his hands on her. She felt wicked but so turned on. Somehow this was so much naughtier than their evening tryst a few weeks ago.

After locking the front door, Court walked slowly but purposefully into her office and shut the door behind him with a decided shove. Lauren was panting with excitement as she watched him stride the short distance to her, and she gasped when his hands grabbed her arms and pulled her toward him. Once their lips met, wildness took over and they started grabbing at each other, hungrily caressing all over each other's bodies. Court roughly pulled her up against his solid length, and she felt the hard bulge of his erection pressing into her belly. Moaning, she squirmed against him and enjoyed the sound of his responding groan.

Court forcefully plunged his tongue inside her mouth before ravishing her with a sensual onslaught of licks, touches, and erotic moans. His physical roughness only drove her arousal higher as one of his hands squeezed a breast and the other groped her ass, each pinching hard.

"Ahhhhhh!" It was Lauren's turn to cry out in surprise.

"But I didn't ask you to say 'ah' yet," he taunted with a decadent smile before roughly pulling her back to him and plunging his tongue into her open mouth—acting as a human tongue depressor! His hand moved to caress her pussy through her dress, turning Lauren into a moaning mass of wanton sensation—squirming, mindless, and incoherent.

Suddenly he pulled away from her. Grabbing her hips, he turned her around to face the desk. Not saying a word, he took her hands one at a time and placed them on the desk, making it clear that she was to lean against the solid furniture. Then he again squeezed her breasts with both hands, eliciting a trilling feminine moan from her. She felt him press his arousal against her buttocks. Burning with a fast need to have him deep inside her, Lauren squirmed and pushed her ass back against his bulge.

It surprised her anew that her young intern could be such a mature and confident lover. He was all man and completely in control of their lovemaking. With him like this, Lauren wasn't the boss. Instead, she felt like the melting ingenue and would have collapsed right there from the raging onslaught of sensations, if not for his strong arms holding her up.

Lauren felt a quick kiss on her shoulder through her dress before he withdrew his arms. Then she heard the sound of a condom package ripping. She started to turn back to help, but he said, "No, stay where you are. You look so hot like that—spread out onto the desk."

Lauren waited breathlessly for him to put the condom on. She wanted to start undressing but followed his orders instead. She liked turning over control to this masterful young man. Then she felt her dress being roughly shoved upward and his hands swiftly yanking her panties down to her knees. Her naughty spread-eagle, on-display position and the pull of her panties stretched between her knees felt wildly wicked, and she moaned louder and swiveled her hips in an erotic display. She was pleased with the sharp intake of air that she heard behind her.

Then she felt him—the rear entry of his cock plunging inside her vagina and his hands grasping her hips as he pulled himself tighter into her. Feeling him thickly filling her, Lauren let out a wild guttural cry, almost coming on the spot.

Court stopped for a moment, wrapped his arms around her waist, and held her tightly to his body. He gently kissed her shoulder.

"You are so sexy!" he murmured into her ear.

Then pulling back, he began to ram into Lauren over and over in fast, potent thrusts. All she had to do was hold herself up with her arms and feel his long, thick penis sliding powerfully in and out, in and out, driving her wild with intense sizzling pleasure. Faster and faster he pounded her until she screamed out in climax. Hearing her orgasm pushed him over the top, and he gave her one more powerful pump before grabbing on to her tightly as he came with a loud groan.

The small office was loud with the sounds of their moans, which gradually turned into heaving pants as Lauren slid her hands out and laid her sweaty upper body on the cool desk. Court followed her down, cradling her back as they both lay there panting.

"Thank you," he whispered, "for the best sex ever in my life!" And she knew he meant all of their lovemaking combined.

"Thank you," she panted, "for making me feel alive again." And he knew her well enough to understand that she wasn't declaring love but rather her gladness to be a sexual being again.

Smiling, Lauren added, "I think...no, *I know* that this is going to be one terrific and very hot summer!"

MAKING A HOUSE CALL

THE TWO LOVERS DIDN'T relax on the desk for long. They knew the rest of the staff would be back soon, along with the afternoon's patients, so they hurriedly put their clothes back to rights. Lauren's lab coat mostly covered her wrinkled dress, and with a quick wash of her face and some fresh makeup, she felt that perhaps, just perhaps, the ladies wouldn't know what she and Court had been doing.

Lauren giggled. *Who was she kidding?* Her staff would take one look at her and know. But what did it matter, really? After Court had pulled his pants up, he kissed her on the cheek. Then he said he would finish the filing in the back, which would put him safely out of sight for the rest of the day. That should help.

However, one thing that she couldn't seem to bring under control was her continuing arousal. Because he had been wearing a condom, she knew the soaking moisture between her legs was all her. That entire afternoon she walked around wet, almost dripping, and the awareness built a raging desire within her that grew to a throbbing, clenching ache by the end of the day.

As soon as the last patient left the office, she went to Court, took his hand without a word, and walked out of the office toward her car. She knew her competent staff would lock up, and she was floating on a thrumming need that didn't have time for words and couldn't wait another moment. He clearly understood and just sat quietly holding her hand for the short drive to her bungalow.

Once home, they made wild love again right there in the foyer, starting the minute the door slammed shut behind them. Afterward, as they lay relaxing on the floor, still near the front door, Lauren realized she was blossoming under the ministrations of her young lover.

She finally also realized that she did not really need healing time as much as the restorative power of great sex. When her ex left six months ago, Lauren had known immediately that the marriage was over. But without the prospect of something new, her situation had felt hopeless. A summer of fun and sex with Court was a perfect panacea.

～ 21 ～

THE PATIENT IS STABLE

BACK IN THE CLINIC on Monday, Lauren no longer felt a strong need to hide their affair, having come to grips with it herself. Anyway, the staff obviously knew about it already. As for the patients, she would let them draw their own conclusions, but her burgeoning happiness was apparent for everyone to see.

She and Court did not make a big deal out of it, but at the same time they no longer pretended that there wasn't anything going on between them. In the clinic, they continued to behave professionally toward each other, actually more appropriately now that they didn't share a hot secret driving them to play naughty games.

Life was good, although the weeks were going by too fast. Looking at her calendar one day, she realized only two weeks were left before Court would leave. With that, she decided to act on a budding desire that she had been unsure about until then. Lauren was going to a medical conference in Chicago in two weeks, and she decided to invite Court to come with her. He might enjoy attending the lectures, and she knew they would both enjoy their nights together. It would be a nice way to end their summer lovin', she thought.

With her decision made, the arrangements turned out to be easier than she had expected. Court was excited about a weekend away with her, and Kelly promised to hold down the fort while they were gone.

"Have fun, you deserve it," she had said with a hug.

Lauren remembered how initially embarrassed she had been at the idea of herself with such a younger man. Not anymore! Now she looked forward to showing Court off at the conference where the anonymity of the big city would give her a freedom she couldn't have in her small hometown.

～22～

THE DOCTOR IS OUT

So Thursday morning they drove away together to spend the weekend in the big city. Lauren was relishing the idea of having a mini working vacation, and leaving town, she felt a sense of freedom that she hadn't in a long time. She even asked Court to drive her car the fifty miles to the nearest regional airport, enjoying the chance to let someone else be in charge, even if just for an hour. Lauren relaxed as she watched the scenery go by, and once onboard for the short flight, Court took her hand and leaned over for a long, sweet kiss. Lauren could hardly wait to get to their hotel room!

When they arrived, they took a taxi to the conference-center hotel. Initially she had reserved two rooms to give the appearance of a platonic relationship with this younger man, but then she decided that was just plain stupid and canceled the second room. Court had agreed, saying that he wouldn't have set foot in the extra room anyway. He offered to wait outside and let her check into the hotel by herself if she felt the need, but Lauren realized that she did not owe anyone an explanation—certainly not the hotel clerk. She took hold of his hand and they walked together to the front desk.

Lauren couldn't help noticing how the young lady serving them ogled Court, and a small part of her blossomed with pleasure and pride. She didn't have to say it out loud, but it must have been written all over her face: *Yep, I'm spending the weekend with this hunk. What have you got to say about that?*

Nothing, of course! The young receptionist just wistfully watched Court walk away with his arm around Lauren.

It seemed incredible, but Lauren realized that she had gotten used to how drop-dead gorgeous Court was. She'd forgotten that her initial reaction to him three months ago was that he looked like a male model. This was going to be fun, she thought. People might think she had hired a male escort for the weekend, but so what? Again Lauren realized she didn't owe anyone any explanation.

As it turned out, Lauren didn't run into anyone at the conference that she knew, but she did have a terrific time. During the day they went to lectures, not necessarily the same ones, and in the evening they went out to dinner. On Friday night they even went dancing, and Lauren felt again the sense of freedom she'd experienced when they had driven out of Plum Banks. She let herself go and moved sexily to the music, offering Court a private dance of seduction performed in a very public place. Later, back in the hotel room, he returned the favor with a seduction of his own on the king-size bed. Life was good, and Lauren intended to grab her happiness when and where she found it.

Saturday had been the last day of lectures, followed in the evening by a fancy dinner and cocktail reception. As she dressed, Lauren gazed out of the tenth-story window of their hotel room. She didn't miss living in a big city, but once in a while it was nice to have the anonymity that a metropolis afforded. She turned as Court came out of the bathroom and stopped dead, looking at him. Wow, did he look handsome in his suit! This was the first time Lauren had seen him dressed up, and it only added to his appeal. Walking up to her, Court told her that she looked beautiful in her tight, silky cocktail dress.

After kissing her briefly, he added, "Let's go get this over with so I can bring you back here and strip this dress right off you."

Glancing once more out the window, Lauren took Court's hand and they headed out.

THE INTERN IS IN

HOURS LATER AND BACK upstairs, Lauren realized she was a little tipsy—too much champagne, she thought dreamily. She stood near the floor-to-ceiling windows of their tenth-story room, looking out at the dark night and colorful city lights. There were no other tall buildings nearby, and being so high up, standing there right up against the glass, felt like flying.

She was happy with her decision to invite Court along for the conference. He had even managed to make the boring lectures fun by whispering naughty things in her ear that he planned to do to her later each evening. Further, she had found this evening's festivities a total blast. Lauren admitted to herself that having Court dancing attendance on her was thrilling. Female colleagues had eyed him hungrily all night and sent envious looks her way. Lauren knew she was still attractive, but at thirty-six she was not an ingenue, and having the arm of a twenty-three-year-old around her out in public felt titillating—racy, even.

Coming out of her reverie, Lauren noticed that Court had turned off the lamps in the room. She was now standing there in the darkness with only a small amount of light glowing up from the city far below. She sensed Court silently walking up behind her before she felt his arms slide around her waist. Gently lifting her hair, he planted tender little kisses along the back of her neck.

Leaning back into his encircling warmth, Lauren moaned in response to the feel of his lips on her neck. Court's hands moved up from her waist to begin gently massaging her breasts through her silky dress. Lauren was aroused and began to push her ass into his pelvis and swirl her hips. She was rewarded with a guttural groan from him as he joined in the gentle swaying of their hips. They continued for many minutes, enjoying the slow sexual dance while watching the movements of the dark metropolis far below.

As she began to turn around in his arms to face him, Court instructed, "No, stay where you are. I want you to watch the city lights while you feel my hands caressing you."

Moaning, Lauren obediently turned back to stand facing out at the big impersonal city. The glowing colored lights were beautiful in the night. Court reached up and slowly unzipped her dress and then skimmed it down over her shoulders. As it glided to the ground, he unhooked the bra and slid it off her arms.

"We should move back," Lauren murmured as her breasts were exposed.

"We're way high up and it's very dark. No one can see us," he disagreed as he took her hands one at a time and planted her palms upon the glass over her head.

Lauren was wildly aroused by the erotic pose Court had arranged her in and moaned loudly. She felt his hands sliding in front of her pelvis to play with her mound through her lace panties, before he pulled them down her legs to drop on the floor with her dress. Court leaned down, gently lifted each leg one at a time to free her clothes, and placed her feet back down so that they were spread far apart. She felt on display for a dark world—wanton, sexy, hot!

Lauren turned her head, looking back over her shoulder to watch him as he slowly pushed her body up against the sheer glass. First she felt the smooth glass press upon her tight nipples, and then her full breasts felt the cold pressure, until the entire length of her body was flush upon the window. His mouth tickled her neck and shoulders while his hands caressed over her back and down along her buttocks as she squirmed against the glass in raging desire, wanting to feel his hands on her pussy. It felt dangerous and scary, so high up, and wickedly exhibitionistic.

Court stepped back and she could hear him swiftly removing his clothes. Plastered naked against the glass as she was, Lauren felt like an erotic window display. Even though it was unlikely anyone could see her this high up, she felt exposed, elevating the arousal coursing through her. The glass felt as impersonal as the big city, supporting her weight but not touching her where she needed to be touched and caressed.

He quickly returned to rest his long, hard, naked length against her, the cool glass at her front contrasting erotically with his hot body behind her. Without talking, he then used his hands to guide her body back so that now just her palms were on the window. She was leaning toward the window and using it to brace herself upright as she stood there spread-eagled and naked.

Surprising her, Court slid down around and under her to sit on the floor at her feet with his back against the glass. Glancing down, she saw that he was staring at her pussy at the apex of her spread legs. A moan escaped her lips as she saw him lean up to lick her there. At the first touch of his tongue, Lauren was on fire, crying out loudly with pleasure. His hands surrounded her buttocks to hold her in place as his tongue lapped at her moist vagina. Groaning gutturally, she ground her pussy into his face as Lauren started to lose herself in the sensations, her eyes drifting shut, knowing that she would come quickly, fiercely.

"Keep your eyes open!" Court ordered, his exploring fingers replacing his tongue for a moment.

"Watch the night…become a fuck toy for the anonymous city out there," he commanded, surprising and controlling her with his hint of wicked mastery. "Perhaps someone in one of those dark, distant buildings is watching you, envying your decadence. Seek them out… perform for them. They cannot know who you are, but they can share your pleasure. You're safe here with me. I want you to imagine desire coursing through them as they covet you, longing to be here with you, hungering to be inside *you*."

Hearing those prurient, alluring thoughts echoing in her mind, Lauren flew into a soaring climax, quaking with intense pleasure and screaming out incoherently. Falling forward, her breasts pressed flat into the glass, Lauren could almost sense the countless, silent, unknown observers out there watching and joining in her intense orgasm.

Court left her no time to recover as he quickly climbed up to stand behind her. He pulled her backward until Lauren was bent over forward and had to use the glass to hold herself up as Court prepared to mount her from behind. She felt his thick penis penetrating between her thighs and arched her back so he could plunge deeply into her soaking wet pussy.

Moaning loudly, Lauren urged him on, "Yes, more, pound me now. Hard!"

Grabbing her hips to stabilize her, Court thrust in and out, over and over, as his grunts and her moans filled the quiet, dark room. She gloried in the feel of him behind her, realizing vaguely that they were making a wildly pornographic display. Suddenly, she hoped that someone was in fact out there watching. She imagined a solitary pair of eyes hungrily observing, enviously watching their erotic performance.

She was achingly aroused, moving wildly against his hammering penis as they slammed into each other again and again until together they reached an exploding climax. Court thrust deeply into her one more time and held her there for a quiet moment. Then he pulled her to standing and once again gently leaned her full front against the cool smooth glass, his hot, slick body providing a counterweight of heat against her backside. The slowing gasps of her panting were the only sounds now in the quiet, dark room, as Court lowered his head to languorously caress her shoulder with his lips and tongue.

After a few moments, he scooped her up into his arms and carried her to the bed, quietly tucking her in under the sheets. Yes, she though dreamily as she fell blissfully asleep, bringing Court with her to the conference had been a very good idea indeed!

~ 24 ~

DISCHARGE

WHEN THEY RETURNED TO Plum Banks it was time for Court to leave. The wonderful, delightful summer was over. Lauren had written a very professional and positive letter of reference, in case Court ever needed one. He said his farewells to the rest of the office staff, and together they walked back to his little garage apartment. Lauren had offered him a ride to Chicago, but Court had already arranged for a college buddy to come and get him. She was secretly glad—it was easier this way, a cleaner break than if she saw him in his new surroundings at medical school where he might feel accessible to her. No, this was the end of their fling, and it was time now for them to go their separate ways.

They both knew it.

At the door to his place, they hugged and wished each other well.

"Thank you for the best summer of my life," Court said sincerely. "I am going to miss you so much!"

"Oh, I think you will be way too busy to miss anyone. Remember I've been through med school myself," Lauren responded. "But I know what you mean. It was a wonderful summer," she added with a slightly sad smile. "I will remember it fondly for the rest of my life."

Court pulled her close for one last deep, lingering kiss. It was a token of farewell, not a prelude to more, and they pulled back to look into each other's eyes one last time.

Nothing else needed saying, so Lauren squeezed his hand and turned away.

"Bye," called Court with a wave. Their summer lovin' was over, now left to live as just tender memories.

DOCTOR, DOCTOR

IN THE WEEKS THAT followed, letting go proved harder than Lauren had thought it would be. Even long walks with Rufus didn't help. She had gotten too used to having Court's company on those evening strolls. Although she had promised herself she wouldn't feel sad, there was still an empty place in her life that was particularly poignant during the long nights alone in her bed.

While she truly cared for Court, she knew the loss of the excitement and romance was what really left her feeling forlorn. *And who am I kidding?* Lauren thought. It was also the loss of the hot sex. She felt bereft, knowing it might be a very long time before she again felt a man's warm body next to hers.

Feeling ho-hum and wondering what to do about it, Lauren walked down Plum Banks's short main street to run a personal errand during lunch. It was then that she noticed activity at a closed medical clinic that had stood empty for years with a "For Sale" sign in front. The sign now said "SOLD," and she could see workmen moving about inside. Lauren started wondering if she going to have to deal with competition, and anxiety replaced her ennui.

The small town really wasn't big enough to support two medical practices, and if she lost any business, the clinic would no longer be profitable. Lauren decided to meet her competition head-on and walked up to the front door. Knocking loudly, she plastered a welcoming smile on her face that she didn't really feel.

The door opened and a man answered. He was fairly good-looking and probably in his mid-thirties, she noted.

Smiling, he said, "Hi, I'm Sam Townsend. Can I help you?"

"I just wanted to stop by and welcome you to Plum Banks," she replied, reaching out her hand to shake his. "I'm Lauren Marks, and I've got the other medical practice here in town."

Lauren was feeling more and more anxious. As he stepped outside into the sun, she could see that he was a *very* attractive man, tall with shaggy, thick brown hair that framed his friendly face. Glancing down, she noticed there was no ring on his finger. Hmmm, single maybe? She could imagine her female patients leaving in droves to get the chance to meet a single, good-looking doctor in this small town. *Heck, I would want to do it too!*

Taking her hand in his, Sam shook it warmly as he closed the door on the paint fumes and noise. "It's very nice to meet you," he said. "My practice will open in about three weeks, once I get the final permits and inspections done. I'm looking for an assistant or maybe just a reception-ist. Can you recommend anyone?"

Oh great, she mused. *Now I'll lose Jessica too!*

But Lauren replied, "Ah, not really, sorry. If there is anything else I can do for you, let me know." She turned to go.

"Well, it was very nice of you to stop by. I knew that moving into a small town like Plum Banks was going to be a terrific change from the big city. Maybe I'll see you around," he said as he opened the door to go back inside. "Oh, wait. I have some flyers for my practice. Maybe you could put them up at your office. Just a minute, I'll get them," he added, disappearing inside.

Lauren was now thoroughly annoyed. *I can't believe he wants me to help advertise my competition! Well, I know a circular file that will hold them just fine.*

He returned quickly and handed her some green sheets of paper. Glancing down, Lauren choked out a surprised laugh.

"You're a veterinarian!" she announced, looking up at him.

"Yes, what did you think?" he replied.

"Oh, it doesn't matter, really. I'm so glad you are setting up shop here. I've had to take my dog, Rufus, thirty miles for his shots and visits. I'll be your first client," she finished, beaming at him.

Inside, Lauren was breathing a sigh of relief. She couldn't help but glance back at his wedding-ring finger. *Nope, still no ring there.*

"That's terrific," he replied, smiling. "Ah, hey, would you like to go out to dinner sometime…with me?" he asked. "Unless you are seeing someone already, that is."

"I'd like that very much. I've got to run, but I'll post these on our bulletin board as soon as I get back to the office…the *human* medical clinic at the other end of Main Street," Lauren said, pointing.

Before she could turn away, Sam stopped her, taking her hand again and giving it a long, unhurried shake. "It *really* was very nice meeting you, Dr. Lauren Marks. I look forward to dinner," he said, smiling into her eyes before slowly releasing her hand.

Lauren walked back up the street, flyers in hand, errand forgotten. She felt fresh hope for the future. The past summer had been a real blast with so much hot, energetic sex—a real summer of bliss. She suddenly realized that all that wonderful lovemaking had also been cathartic, providing a lot of emotional healing. She knew that she was now ready for a deep, loving relationship—looking forward to it, actually—whether it was with the handsome new veterinarian or someone she had yet to meet.

Life is good, Lauren mused as she smiled gaily to herself and looked eagerly toward her future.

My Doctor,
My Husband,
and Me

CONSULTATION

I AM SITTING HERE on the cold exam table, alone in the doctor's office, and waiting anxiously. Maybe I should just get up and leave. I don't really need the foot surgery, do I? I am really scared of all things medical. Jumping a little on the table as the door opens, I watch the doctor walk into the small room.

Wow! My breath catches momentarily. *Wow, wow, wow!* The doctor is tall, dark, and handsome, a total cliché, I know, but that's the only way to describe him. His age is hard to guess but maybe mid- to late thirties. He is trailed by a male intern who is also exceedingly handsome but so young he could be my nephew. But really, I hardly notice the younger man. My eyes are frozen, locked into the eyes of my gorgeous new surgeon.

He is not movie-star good-looking—more dark, almost swarthy, sensual with thick, black hair, a little unruly. Even though I am sitting down, I can tell he must be tall. His presence fills the small exam room. The other younger guy is still here, but almost invisible next to this older, self-assured man.

The doctor gives me a quirky smile and begins talking about my case, but I can't seem to focus on what he's saying. His voice is soothing with maybe a hint of a foreign accent, I notice absentmindedly. So this is my podiatrist, Dr. Luka Czerny.

Shaking off my silly distraction, I make a real effort to pay attention. We agree on a course of action, and even though I'm anxious, his confidence helps me agree to go forward. I had broken my big toe years ago and it didn't heal correctly, causing discomfort for years. When all is done, I'll have a straightened toe with a permanent screw in it. The very thought makes me slightly queasy, but I feel better as I listen to the doctor's deep, calm voice.

"Valerie, my nurse will schedule your pre-op and surgery. It was nice to meet you."

"Great," I respond, plastering an overly big smile on my face.

Dr. Czerny gives me a comforting pat on the hand before he leaves the exam room, trailed by the forgotten intern. Looking down at my hand, which seems to be tingling slightly, I leave thinking, *Wow, wow, wow.*

2
PRE-OP

TOMORROW IS THE AMBULATORY surgery to fix my foot, and I am looking forward to seeing "him" again for my pre-op appointment. A quickening inside me that has nothing to do with surgery fears is making me a little high-strung and anxious. Or perhaps my fear of the surgery is causing me to focus my thoughts on the handsome doctor rather than the operation. Either way, I anticipate his gentle touch on my foot again—and hopefully on my hand too. I can almost feel it already!

"Good morning, Valerie," Dr. Czerny says as he walks into the small exam room. "Are you ready for surgery tomorrow?"

"Umm, yes," I mutter, startled from my daydreams. "Will I see you before the surgery?" I realize that I'm leaning slightly toward him.

Reaching forward while looking deeply into my eyes, the doctor gently pats my hand. "Yes, and it's all going to be fine, I promise," he says in his wonderful, soothing, foreign voice. Ah, the tingling starts inside me again and I am loving it.

I want to grab his hand and hold on tightly, not because I'm scared but because I want to extend the time he is with me and keep him touching me. His bedside manner is probably meant to be reassuring, but for me it feels almost erotic, a guilty pleasure. The rest of the appointment is spent going over my X-rays and the pre-op procedures at Boston's Massachusetts General Hospital. I struggle to pay attention. Dr. Czerny smiles at me as he walks out of the exam room and the smile is dazzling. As I drive home, I can't resist calling my friend Laura and telling her all about the good doctor and his sexy bedside manner.

FOLLOW-UP

WELL, IT IS LATE the next afternoon, and the surgery must have gone well, because I am home now and on some really strong meds. My family is taking care of me, and I have nothing to do for the next two weeks but lie around and eat, watch TV, read, and daydream about the good doctor.

My son's worn high-school copy of *Walden* captures my attention, at least for the moment. Not exactly easy reading for a morphine-addled mind, but Thoreau's ideas of retrospection and self-exploration stir something within me. "'We must learn to reawaken and keep ourselves awake.'" No easy feat when the strong meds keep putting me to sleep, but I know Thoreau doesn't really mean that. While I'm mostly content with my life, somewhere deep inside lies a need that I can't quite identify—*can't quite wake up to*—except that it seems tied to my fascination with the handsome Dr. Czerny.

Maybe it's the morphine, but I'm enjoying some rather naughty fantasies about him as I mostly sleep my days away. Early in our marriage, Elliott and I were more adventurous in the bedroom. Some might even say a little kinky. I can't help remembering some of those nights and wondering what it would be like with the good doctor. The erotic visions are not fully formed, just fleeting glimpses of what we could be together.

They have neither a beginning nor an ending, but rather shift randomly from one shadowy fantasy to another. Dr. Czerny kissing and caressing me in a darkened exam room, his hand slipping under my blouse, frantic groping somewhere private outside the hospital, writhing on a soft bed…all of it in dreamlike nowhere. The images are *hot, hot,*

hot, but strangely Elliott is always there in the room with us…watching, and it only adds to the thrill.

I must admit that mixed in with the sexy feelings is some measure of guilt, because I am married to a kind, attractive man. We have built a life together for more than nineteen years and have two teenage children. However, I've been a good, loyal wife all this time, and he hasn't always been so faithful to me. Certainly Elliott can't begrudge me a few morphine-induced sexual fantasies, especially when he's right there in them.

———

Today is my first follow-up appointment after surgery, and I am looking forward to seeing Dr. Czerny. It's a chilly October day in Boston, which is why I have goose bumps on my arms—at least that's what I tell myself. The plan is to remove my cast, x-ray my toe, and then put on a new cast. My closest friend, Laura, drove me here and is being a good sport about pushing me around in a wheelchair.

She's heard from me about the good-looking doctor and his attractive male interns, and said jokingly, "Of course, I can take you. Do you think they'll mind if I bring my camera?"

Laura is my age, also with teens, and I guess we don't get out much anymore. That's not really true, of course, but being in the vicinity of multiple handsome men is rare for us, actually probably rare for anyone not in the movie industry. She, like me, exercises and takes care of her looks, but as married women in our forties, we're spending most of our time as afternoon chauffeurs or family drill sergeants. And, anyway, I would never go out of my way to ogle younger guys—or any other man, for that matter.

Truly, I'm happily married, even though Elliott and I have had our issues. Who wouldn't, after living two lives together for so long and facing the conflicts inherent in marriage and child rearing? Today, however, I can say we have a good marriage and surprisingly good sex. Sometimes it's hard to come up with new positions after all these years, but even so, we manage to have nights that I'm sure these younger guys would envy.

Before I see the good doctor, the cast comes off in a large room with many beds. The technicians are all men, all with friendly personalities, and several are also good-looking. Back in the waiting room, my foot begins to throb.

I'm in pain, but Laura is having fun and whispers playfully into my ear, "Hey, do they only hire attractive men here? Maybe they have to submit a photo with their job application."

Looking up at her from my wheelchair, I laugh and whisper back, "And you haven't even seen the doctor yet."

Speak of the devil, and he shows up.

"Hi, Valerie," Dr. Czerny says in his caressing, sexy voice as he comes over and smiles warmly down at me. "We'll get your X-rays done, and then I'll see you in the cast room."

Leaning down toward me, he looks into my eyes. He's one of those unique individuals who can seem to focus all their energy in your direction when they are talking to you. The other patients in the waiting room—and Laura standing right behind my wheelchair—all fade away, and I feel like I'm his only patient...ever!

"How are you doing?" he asks. "Is the pain manageable?"

I respond breathlessly that it's okay and I'm fine. He's still bending down toward me, and as he straightens, he soothingly, gently rubs my shoulder for a moment. The spot where he is touching me tingles and I want to lean into his hand. I don't do it, but I surely want to.

"Good," he responds, smiling. "I'll see you in a few minutes."

As he walks away, I become aware of all the people around me and feel like I was openly drooling over this striking man.

Laura leans down and murmurs, "Valerie, would you just roll that wheelchair back over my foot? I'd like a little of his bedside manner directed my way, if you please."

"Didn't I tell you?" I breathe back at her. "I wasn't kidding when I said he was good-looking...and that sexy voice. What is it about that voice?"

"Like warm honey," whispers Laura.

A woman technician does the X-rays, and I realize this is the first female worker I've encountered here. How unusual. They should market their practice that way—a medical office staffed only by attractive men ready to serve.

In the exam room, Dr. Czerny lives up to my expectations once again. As usual, he is trailed by a young male intern who is worthy of barely a glance from me. Dr. Czerny fills the small room with his presence. Even in his staid, white lab coat, my swarthy hero stands out as something earthy, potent, and exotic. With his Eastern European accent and old-world manner, I can easily envision him as a seventeenth-century pirate captaining his own vessel, and yet I think he would be equally at home in the most cosmopolitan of modern nightclubs. There is just something about him that catches my fancy…that draws me in.

However, right now I really don't want him to touch my swollen and painful foot, even as his gentle, reassuring caresses on my shoulder leave me breathless with tiny stirrings of desire. In response to his doctorly inquiries, I smile back at Dr. Czerny and assure him again that I'm doing well. The sensual haze he always brings me is so stirring that I would probably say I was doing fine no matter how my foot felt.

Okay, I'll admit, if only to myself, that it is nice to feel, however briefly, another new man's hands on my body after so many years. It's all very safe and innocent, but still kinda nice. At the age of forty-four, I'm beginning to feel that my life is going to start slowing down, whether I want it to or not. There may not be that many more opportunities for stimulation such as this. So, really, what's the harm in a little sexy flirtation? Nothing's going to come of it anyway.

Later, as Laura wheels me out to the parking lot, she exclaims, "Wow. That doctor gives good bedside manner!"

～ 4 ～
FEEL MY KNEE

A FEW WEEKS LATER, I'm in the large cast room, waiting once more for Dr. Czerny. He's so handsome in that slightly quirky way. My friend Laura is helping me again. She's not missing another chance to see the good doctor and his mostly male good-looking staff, but my awareness of her fades as he walks up to me.

"How are you doing today?" he asks in that slightly sexy, slightly foreign voice that I now look forward to hearing.

"Oh. Okay!" I respond a bit too loudly. Did I sound breathless?

"Well, let's take a look at your X-rays," he says, sitting down on the low stool that always has me looking slightly down at him. Then I remember a question I have, now that my toe has a large metal screw in it.

"Doctor, can I get one of those papers that says I have metal in my foot for airplane travel?"

Laughing slightly, he says, "That's not necessary. I've had a knee replacement after a ski accident and my knee is full of metal. I've never set off the metal detectors."

"Really?" I respond doubtfully. I'm a worrier and don't want to take any chances.

"Sure," Dr. Czerny says. "Here, feel my knee," he says, as if it's the most normal thing in the world. "You can feel the screw through my skin."

Squeamish as always, I reach out a tentative hand and touch his knee with one finger through his green scrubs—and I feel the jolt of attraction down to my core. There is clearly metal there, but that's not what I'm focusing on. Is it my imagination or did the room get quiet suddenly? Glancing around, I see Laura wink at me. The only other technician in the room, a man, is still quietly at work and doesn't look up, but I sense him listening.

My gaze shifts back into my sexy doctor's eyes, and I quickly look away, a little embarrassed and definitely overheated. Was that just *me* or did he feel it too?

The office visit continues, and Dr. Sexy-Bedside-Manner continues to enthrall me with his soothing voice and warm demeanor. He is touching my healing foot with his hands, but it is still so swollen that I can't imagine that the doctor is having any arousing thoughts. It must all be in my head. I cannot wait to talk to Laura about it once we are out of the office.

However, this time when he's done examining my foot, his slow reassuring pat is not on my shoulder but on the top of my thigh. With the touch of his hand, I feel an instant rush of hot desire sweep up my leg, coiling at my center. Then my heart starts pounding, and a pleasurable warmth seeps throughout my body.

Brushing the feelings aside, I tell myself my thigh must be easier for him to reach from his low stool. But my heart is still pounding, and my laughing responses to his questions are a bit too breathless. Even the hands of the male technician as he puts a walking bootie on me feel extra nice today, building the tingling inside me even more. I wonder if the doctor has any idea of the effect he has on me.

In the car as Laura drives me home, we discuss it.

"Oh," she says, "there was definitely something in the air. Didn't you notice how the whole room just seemed to pause when you were touching his knee?"

"I thought it was just me," I reply. "I did take the opportunity to look at his hand, for what it's worth, and there wasn't a wedding ring on his finger."

"But, Valerie," Laura says, "there *is* a ring on *your* finger!"

What can I really say to that?

"I know, but I can't stop thinking about him. I'm starting to fantasize about him. Wouldn't you?"

Laura poutingly retorts, "I wouldn't know. He sure didn't ask *me* to feel his knee."

That night, Elliott and I have very hot, steamy sex, even with my silly bootie on. I'm on fire, but he doesn't know who lit the flame. In the end, I don't think he would care too much, as we both had a rocking good time.

Lying awake for hours afterward, I'm wondering what I can do about this strong attraction I feel toward Dr. Czerny. I want him, but I'm a married woman.

Maybe we could... I let my imagination drift. My erotic fantasy of Elliot watching the doctor and me together transforms, and now it's Dr. Czerny who's watching... Then they are both touching me at the same time. Two men and me at one time? I shiver with a new yearning that I've never felt before. Would they go for it, I wonder. What are the chances... No, that would be too wild, too out there. I wouldn't even know how to ask, where to begin.

Well, I say to myself, it's another two weeks until my last appointment, and then I'll probably never see Dr. Czerny again. I've just got to get it out of my head—easier to say than do, because I get damp every time I think of it.

~ 5 ~

TAKING IT FURTHER

TODAY I EXPECT THIS to be my last visit with the good doctor, and I know I will miss the warm thrill of his bedside manner. I'm almost healed and drove myself here without Laura. I am escorted into a small examination room instead of the big cast room. Excitedly, I realize I may get to see him alone, all alone. But so what? I am married, I remind myself.

An idea has formed in my mind, but it's so daring, so out there that it is hard for me to even fully recognize it as a plan. I'm glad I took extra care to wear a nice dress today and put on makeup so I'd look my best. The colorful dress is on the short side, but my legs are one of my best features. Although it is unlikely that I will have the courage to act on my plan, the titillation of considering it is stimulating nonetheless.

The door opens and Luka enters—we're on a first-name basis now, at least in my mind. Once again, his warm-bedside-manner smile melts my insides and his "warm honey" voice envelops me in a sensual fog. Slightly dazed, I answer all his questions, and he confirms that I can go without even the bootie from now on. Leaning close, he looks carefully at my foot, the lab coat brushing against my knee and feeling like a caress that sends tingles up and down my leg.

I wait anxiously for his physical examination of my foot, for the touch, however brief, that I have come to crave. I watch as he slowly reaches down, my ankle already tingling in anticipation, and then his hand is on my body again. I have to stifle the pleasurable sigh that is on my lips as he gently manipulates my foot and strokes his hand along the skin while he conducts the exam.

Why does everything with him seem so erotic? It must be the smile and the eyes—and the way he looks deeply into mine. This connection feels like a mutual attraction, or is it just my wishful thinking? Reminding myself that he is years younger than I am, I wonder abstractedly why he isn't married.

The doctor seems to be drawing the exam out, or is that also my imagination? As he holds my foot, which thankfully is beginning to look normal again, he gently manipulates the toe, testing flexibility. But he seems to be almost caressing my foot, and it feels so good that tingles are traveling up my leg toward my pelvis. Gently he lowers my foot back down.

Oh, no, the appointment is almost over, and I'm not ready for it to end.

"Doctor!" I suddenly exclaim. "I was wondering. I've been thinking about the metal in your knee and wondering... Can I see your knee? It felt odd, and I am...ahh...wondering what it...ahh, looks like," I finish lamely.

Luka looks at me a little strangely but says, "I guess so," as he pulls up the right pant-leg of his scrubs. I had felt the metal, and seeing the knee now, I can see where the metal is located and the scars along his knee.

Leaning in toward his leg, I reach out one tentative finger and very slowly and gently trace down the outside of his knee. "You really don't feel it?"

"Oh, I feel *that* all right," he chokes out as he stands back and the pant leg drops.

Well, at least that got a reaction out of him! It seems the attraction is not entirely one-sided, I realize as my fantasy of him grows.

My bizarre scheme races back into my mind. An idea so wild that I haven't even mentioned it to Laura, and certainly not to my husband. Why stir up trouble in our marriage or risk hurting Elliot's feelings when the likelihood of Dr. Czerny actually going along with it seems unlikely?

I stare at the handsome, alluring man, daring myself to have the courage. Life is too short and I don't want any regrets. My mind races about anxiously. Maybe I should just let it go, but then I'd always wonder what might have been if I'd had the courage to act. Thoreau's ideas haunt me—to conform to society is safe; to do what calls me might bring greater fulfillment. It's time to open my mind to new possibilities and stop sleepwalking through life. "'Only that day dawns to which we are awake.'"

I gasp. Had I said that out loud? My eyes flash to his.

"'There is more day to dawn,'" Luka answers, surprising me.

We finish together, "'The sun is but a morning star.'"

"You read Thoreau!" I exclaim, utterly astonished that this foreigner knows the quote.

"No," he replies quietly. "Just the one book, just *Walden*. I live my life by it, at least the last paragraph."

"Will you... I...um." Suddenly I'm at a loss for words.

Luka steps closer to me and looks down into my eyes, as if searching for the meaning of my odd elucidation, and then he seems to understand. "I will keep an open mind," he promises.

Taking a stuttering breath, I realize it is now or never.

"Doctor, I have a bold proposal for you." It's barely more than a whisper.

Luka looks surprised, a little taken aback, and I wonder if I've made a mistake about his feelings, but I push forward.

"An open mind," I repeat more firmly, and he nods. "And an interest in nonconformity, or at least following your own drummer."

Luka nods again.

"I feel like we have a connection, and I want to get to know you better. But it would take way too long to explain here, and then I'm sure you'll be shocked into automatically saying no. I want you to have the time to ask questions and explore the idea. Can we meet for lunch or coffee or something?"

After stepping toward me, Luka takes hold of my left hand and raises it up, looking pointedly down at my wedding ring. I shrug but don't say anything.

"You're my patient, or at least you were my patient," he says. "I, ah, I do like you but..." His words trail off to nothing. I can tell he is torn about what to do—his professionalism fighting against his attraction to me.

"Just hear me out," I urge and gently squeeze the hand that is still holding mine. "Won't you always wonder what I wanted to talk to you about?"

Finally, decisively, he says, "Okay, let's meet for lunch tomorrow. I'll text you the name of a restaurant."

I nod my agreement. I'm in a daze. His light hold on my hand is making me breathless and dizzy, and I'm not imagining that he's making little circles with his fingers on the palm of my hand, while he stares intently into my eyes. For a moment I think he may lean in and kiss me, but then he steps back and drops my hand.

"Until tomorrow," he says, watching me as I leave the room.

THE PROPOSITION

THE RESTAURANT LUKA HAS picked is very nice, quiet—just short of romantic. In fact, perfect for this somewhat clandestine meeting. I feel attractive, youthful in my formfitting dress. But I had to give in to wearing flats, because my foot isn't yet up to my usual sexy heels.

He's already seated, and as I walk toward the quiet secluded corner where our table is, he stands to smile down at me. I had forgotten how tall he is. I had wondered what he would look like out of scrubs, in normal clothes. He is even more handsome, wearing a beige mock turtleneck, a brown blazer, and pants that go well with his dark good looks. That thick, black hair of his looks especially tousled today, like he was impatiently running his hand through it just before I arrived. I so want to touch it, to run my fingers through the luxurious locks. I hope that, maybe, someday soon I'll get the chance.

"Hello, Doctor," I say brightly, plastering a more-confidant-than-I-feel smile on my face.

"Please call me Luka," he says. "Even though I don't really understand what you want to tell me, it does seem like we should be on a first-name basis, don't you think? I must tell you I've been thinking about your *proposal* all night but just can't believe it is actually what I'm thinking." Opening his menu, he suggests, "Let's get the ordering out of the way, and then I want to hear what it is you have to say."

After the waiter walks away with our order, I realize it's "showtime," so after taking a deep breath, I lay out my secret desire.

"Luka, what would you think about joining me in a ménage à trois?"

With a startled expression, he leans back away from me, making it clear that this is not what he thought I was going to offer. He looks vaguely uncomfortable or irritated—I'm not sure. Quickly, I hurry to explain: "Sort of a friends-with-benefits thing with my husband, Elliott. Aboveboard, not sordid or done behind his back. I love him too much, and we've had a good marriage and really good sex, so I'm certainly not going to do anything to ruin that. For this to work, we'd all need to become friends. I could never make love to anyone without friendship. So the three of us would get to know each other and only go forward if we're all in agreement."

Not wanting him to cut me off before I'd finished getting everything out, I take a quick breath and rush to continue.

"I know this is unexpected, but ever since you asked me to touch your knee, I've had such intense sexy dreams about you every night. I didn't plan on this, but now I have such a list of fantasies that I want to explore…desires that, well, even an affair wouldn't be enough to satisfy. They will take a third person to fulfill, and I want you to be our third."

Grasping his hand, I lean toward him. "Lastly, I must tell you that I'm not a slut. Really, I've never done anything like this before. Elliott and I are not swingers either, although we've played some naughty bedroom games in the past."

I finish in a husky whisper. "I've been with my husband for nineteen years, and in all that time I've never kissed another man. Never even wanted to kiss another man, that is until I met you. And just kissing you won't be enough. That I already know."

I sit back, out of breath, and there is silence in our little corner of the restaurant. Luka sits quietly, his eyes roaming over my face and down to my breasts as his fingers tap uncertainly on the table.

Finally he says, "But what about your husband? I can't believe he has agreed to this."

He must be a little agitated, or perhaps aroused, because his accent is thicker now, more excitingly foreign sounding, and he is leaning toward me instead of away.

"Well," I respond, "leave that to me. I haven't told him my secret plan yet, but, well, he's had his indiscretions in the past. He owes me." Luka still looks disbelieving.

"We *have* talked about a threesome before, a long time ago. Of course, it always revolved around two women and him, a very male fantasy, but it seems only fair that I can at least ask him. I won't do it if it will hurt Elliott or our marriage, but I'm hopeful he'll agree that it might be fun to make some exciting memories for the future."

Memories for when we are too old, I think but leave unsaid.

As we eat our lunch, I lay out more details, such as that I'm hoping he has a place where we can meet because we can't do it in our home with our teens there. I find out he's been divorced for a few years—explaining his unmarried state—and he is currently unattached. And, yes, he's nearly eight years younger than my forty-four years.

At one point our knees bump under the table, and we both just leave them there, lightly touching as we continue talking. It's titillating, and I lean closer to him as he looks deeply into my eyes. I feel warm all over and slightly turned on—not quite aroused, but so close.

He asks a few questions but is mostly quiet, and I cannot tell how he feels about my idea. Perhaps it's just too wild for him.

I want to try to build on the connection I know exists between us, but I'm not sure how until I remember yesterday's surprise. "Luka, I know you said you only know *Walden*, but still I'm so curious about that. It was such a slog when I had to study it in high school, and I wonder where you picked it up."

He responds with a smile, a sort of self-deprecating one. "Believe it or not, I studied it to learn English better. I think perhaps my tutor was a sadist because he said I would know the language when I could understand Thoreau's *Walden*."

"You're joking." I laugh.

"Unfortunately, it's no joke. Obviously I knew it was written more than a hundred and fifty years ago, but I had no idea, really, that it was so far removed from how Americans actually speak. However, my teacher was right. The painful task of learning to understand it was useful in learning to read English, which of course I needed to do to read medical texts. Then, surprisingly, I came to like the book. I even try to live my life by some of Thoreau's ideals."

"Well," I murmur, feeling like I am glowing with excitement, "I only recently rediscovered it, but I like its message of self-discovery and nonconformity. To go through the rest of my life wondering what if… I hope you'll think about my proposal."

Luka nods in general agreement but still doesn't give me an answer. Our knees are still touching, and the tingle remains, seeping upward along my thighs and higher. I wonder if he still feels it. If it is as arousing to him as it is to me.

Realizing that Luka may ultimately say no, that this may be the last time I get to speak with him alone, privately like this, I want to continue the conversation—want to continue the intimate touch of our knees. Searching for something to say, I ask Luka about his homeland and when he came to the United States. I find his foreignness romantically exotic, and I realize that must show on my face.

"It's no great story, really," he says with a slight smile. "I came here in my twenties to attend med school…after a crash course in English, of course."

"What made you come all the way here for med school?" I ask, curious.

"I'd won a scholarship to study abroad and so applied to several schools in America. You know…the land of opportunity. Afterward, I served as a doctor in the U.S. military for a number of years and earned my citizenship that way. Eventually some other members of my family, including my parents, followed me over, but most of my extended family is still in Czechoslovakia, or the Czech Republic as it's called now."

"I've never been to that part of the world. What's it like? Do you get back often?"

"Not too often…maybe every eight years or so. It is a small but beautiful country, with lots of historic places and tiny, ancient villages. It's greatly changed, of course, since when I was a child and the Soviet Union was Big Brother watching us. When I get back—"

"Are there castles?" I interrupt, imagining dreamy fairy-tale places.

Smiling indulgently, he offers, "Yes, many glorious and ancient fortresses and palaces. I particularly like an area called Bohemian Paradise. It's pretty there with towering rock formations and extensive pine forests, and many remote castles and ruins to visit in the hills. I think you would like it very much."

"How exciting to be able to call two countries home," I murmur. I had never thought of myself as a Europhile before, but I can see now that a part of me is drawn to him specifically because of his exotic allure.

"What about you?" he asks. "Where are you from?"

"Nothing exciting like you. I was a suburban child, born and raised right outside Boston in Melrose. Went to college in Boston and ended up staying. The farthest I've been is Paris on my honeymoon."

"*Paris…*" he breathes out in hushed tones. "They call it the city of lovers. I've never been, but I want to see it. So you see, you've been somewhere I haven't."

Suddenly I don't feel quite so provincial, and just as suddenly thoughts of "lovers" fill my mind. I glance away, slightly self-conscious, before boldly returning my gaze to him. Silly of me to feel shy after the wild proposition I have laid before him.

Luka stares intently into my eyes and my breath catches. I know then he is thinking of lovers too, of us as lovers. My pulse races and I can't resist reaching over to touch his hand resting on the table. Several long moments pass like this in our quiet corner of the restaurant, but the air surrounding us is ripe with hot anticipation.

Then, all too soon, lunch is over. Luka insists on paying the bill. As a modern woman with a very cosmopolitan proposition, I had planned to pay it myself, but I'll admit I like that he is proving to be a gentleman.

Since Luka hasn't revealed what he is thinking, as we stand to leave, I say, "I know you'll want to think about it, and—"

"No need!" he interjects firmly. "I'm in, *all* in—that is, if your husband goes for it, which I doubt he will." Then he leans in and whispers hotly, "Too bad, really, because taking your clothes off is all I can think about right now."

His declaration slams into me with an almost physical force. Swaying a little from the intense, rolling waves of desire, I grab the table for support and our gazes lock.

"I want it too!" I whisper back.

~ 7 ~
TAKING IT HOME

WAITING UNTIL THE RIGHT time to speak with Elliott was nerve-racking, but obviously I couldn't do it with the kids around or over the phone when he was at work. Now, finally after several days, the kids are asleep and we have some time alone.

Speaking quietly, I begin, "Darling, do you remember when we talked about a ménage à trois years ago?"

"Yes, sort of. That was a long time ago," Elliott replies.

We're on the living-room couch holding hands, relaxing. Looking at him sideways, I notice once again how charming he is. After nineteen years it's easy to just look through him, seeing the whole person combined with our history together, rather than noticing how he actually looks. I'm surprised to note that he's older with a few wrinkles and a little graying hair. I guess I appear older to his eyes too. However, his face is still that special combination of chiseled masculinity and warm friendliness that drew me to him all those years ago.

I realize I've let the conversation lapse as I look at him and try to decide if I'm doing the right thing. How will he take even just being asked the question? Elliott may have fantasized about two women and him—I would guess most men have at some time in their lives—but I worry that he'll be jealous of the idea of me with another man. I'm uncertain but know that this is something I want very badly. So sitting up, I turn toward him and spill it all—that I want to try a threesome now but with a twist, with another guy, not a woman.

Pulling his hand away, Elliott asks emphatically, "Who? Who do you want this with?"

"Well," I hedge, "not with anyone you know. I really don't know him well either."

"That doesn't make any sense," he says testily.

Quickly, I lay out my secret plan and tell him the person is my surgeon, my *former* surgeon.

Interrupting me, Elliott growls, "That letch, coming on to a patient. I'm going to report him and have him disbarred. How dare..."

"No! No, Elliott, it wasn't like that, really! And you can't have him disbarred. He's a doctor, not a lawyer."

Leaning toward my husband, I make him look me in the eye and carefully explain it all again and that it was entirely my idea. I reassure him, "I won't do it, if you don't want to, and we'll become friends first, take it really slowly, and we can stop moving forward at any time."

Looking somewhat angry, he seems like he's going to say no. I'm not sure it's wise, but I remind him about his affair years ago. "Remember how hurt I was and how I said that I should be able to have one too, sometime? You didn't disagree with me then, but I never thought I would actually meet anyone who interested me. I don't think you thought I'd meet anyone either."

Elliott sort of shrugs, and I can't tell if he agrees or disagrees, so I rush on.

"But I don't want to have just an affair... I want more than that. I feel myself getting older, Elliott. Suddenly there's this surging sensuality that wants to flow out of me, and I feel freer than I did when I was younger, freed even to risk something new and exciting. I want to explore all of this before I'm too old."

"Valerie, I don't think you're old at all," he contradicts. "Not to me anyway."

"Don't you see? Soon it would be just absurd to have a ménage à trois with gray hair and wrinkles. And wouldn't it be, you know, exciting to make some erotic memories that we can share in our old age? I have lots of naughty fantasies, Elliott. I promise you it'll be lots of wild fun!"

"If I were to agree, and I'm not saying I would, but for argument's sake, why would we have to become friends with the guy? Can't you just have a one-night stand and be done with it?"

"I'll never do something behind your back. I love you too much and value our family. And I'll only go forward if you want to also," I promise him. "But I just can't hop into bed with a stranger. I would need to be friends with the person to be comfortable…and if I'm not comfortable and enjoying it, then, really, what would be the point?"

Then to show my husband how much I love him, I lean over and start kissing him gently and seductively on his lips, then around his face, and working down his neck. Elliott doesn't object, and while I may have started this to distract him and to prove my love, I quickly begin to get very excited. Just talking about a threesome is already adding juice to our sex life.

We finish the discussion in the bedroom after some rocking good sex. After thinking about it for a while, Elliott agrees that we can proceed. He will at least meet Luka and then see how it goes. He's not promising anything else.

8

GENTLEMEN'S AGREEMENT

TONIGHT'S THE IMPORTANT FIRST meeting. Both men have to like each other for this to work, and Elliott has a bigger stake in it. With this many years of commitment to me, he must realize the risk he is taking in letting me pursue the idea of sex with another man. I'm confident that I'll remain committed and in love with Elliott, but for him there must be questions.

My hubby must think I've overdone it with my choice of clothing for tonight, but I want to wow both men—make them want it as much as I do. I chose a skintight black dress that has long sleeves with sexy cutouts that leave my shoulders bare. The dress is very short, reaching about mid-thigh. The pièce de résistance is my footwear, gray-and-black zebra-striped platform pumps described once by my appreciative husband as "fuck-me shoes."

My long, lean legs are my best feature, and I want the men to get a good view of them. I'll admit the shoes are just a little painful after the surgery, but we're just going for drinks, sitting down, so it should be okay. I am slightly giddy with excitement, and my sexy clothing only adds to the edgy thrill. I know I look good, and tonight I'm going to show off. *Otherwise, why bother with all that hard work exercising?* I tell myself.

"I see you want to cement the deal, don't you?" my husband says as he slides his arm around my waist.

"Do you like it?" I taunt with a sexy smile and get rewarded with a hot, demanding kiss.

This is going to be an exciting evening!

We are meeting Luka at a popular club in downtown Boston.

Called a "superlounge bar," it has loud dancing in one room and a quieter lounge section in another. We've made a reservation, so I know we'll be seated in a dark, quiet corner. As we ride the elevator up, I squeeze Elliott's hand and offer him a quick kiss.

"Thank you for being so open to trying something new," I say for perhaps the third time tonight.

The hostess tells us that Luka is already waiting and leads us toward the back. Butterflies jump in my stomach as I wonder if the guys will get along. I realize that I'm already one hundred percent committed to fucking them both, but it all depends on tonight. Watching Luka intently as we walk over, I can tell that both men are sizing each other up. But then Luka's eyes light on me, and he obviously likes what he sees, looking me over from head to sexy toe.

To Elliott, Luka says, "I hope you don't mind my saying so, but you have one sexy, beautiful wife. As a podiatrist I shouldn't like the shoes either, but they're hot!"

Elliott seems pleased, rather than annoyed. I guess he's enjoying showing me off. The guys shake hands and we sit down on a comfy lounger, with me in between them. At first we busy ourselves looking at the menu and ordering drinks, but then we fall into an awkward silence. Not knowing what else to say, I ask about his kids—a boy and a girl— and we talk ages and exchange photos before the conversation drifts off again. I realize I'd better take things up a notch, or this threesome plan is going to turn into a big dud.

"So, Luka, what's the wildest thing you've ever done in bed?" I ask.

Both men start a little in surprise, but that gets the conversation going, and we play a game of besting each other's tall tales. In truth, although Elliott and I have played some kinky games in the bedroom in the past, none of us has done anything quite like this. But my question does get us talking and joking and laughing. Ordering second and third rounds of cocktails, we move on to talk about our jobs and hobbies. We're now having fun—which is the whole point of this plan, isn't it?

I'm careful to keep planting kisses on Elliott and showing him lots of attention, but I can't resist casually, as if by accident, dropping my hand onto Luka's thigh. I guess it was not casual enough because both men glance down, but no one says anything, so my hand stays where it is. The bar has filled and others have joined our seating area, but we're not out to make new friends, so we just keep talking among ourselves.

I'm loving it!—openly flirting with two men at once and seeing curious looks from the three women sitting near us. I am not going to share my toys, and to make that clear, I turn and give Elliott a long, adoring kiss on the lips. Immediately after, I turn to my right and give Luka a little peck on the cheek. The ladies are openly watching us now, so Luka winks at Elliott and then gives me a quick but passionate kiss on the lips. Afterward I purr and lean into him, throwing my legs up onto Elliott's lap and lounging against Luka.

We are all enjoying a little exhibitionism, so I ask without looking at the women, "What are they doing now?"

"Well," Elliott responds, "a number of people have noticed us, and it's a mix of curious glances, disgusted glares, and even two guys smiling and giving us a thumbs-up. The ladies can't seem to decide if they are outraged or think it's funny, but they keep looking over."

I'm a little tipsy and laugh loudly about it. How often in my life have I been the envy of other women? And as good-looking as my two dates are, those women must be more than a little envious.

It's quite late now, and Luka says, "This has been fun. How about we meet for drinks again or maybe dinner sometime?"

"That sounds great," I respond, looking at Elliott for confirmation.

"Well," he says, pausing a little as I hold my breath, "I'm thinking that I'm okay with taking it to the next level, if you are?" he asks Luka.

Luka nods agreement, and Elliott continues.

"Perhaps you and I should shake hands on a gentlemen's agreement that the three of us are going to keep getting to know each other, hopefully becoming friends, and eventually maybe I'll be okay with sharing her. But she stays my wife."

As I sit between them, I feel the undercurrent of excitement but also some tension. Looking back at Luka, I wait for his reply.

"That sounds good," he says, reaching his hand over me and

extending it to Elliott. I sit quietly in a sort of amazed stupor as the two men firmly shake hands over my body, both literally and figuratively.

Thus ends a good evening and officially begins our ménage à trois.

9

BECOMING FRIENDS

ELLIOTT AND I ARE both excited—or on edge maybe, I'm not sure. Nevertheless it's the following Saturday night and we are at Luka's apartment door, ringing the bell. Curious what his doctor's bachelor pad would look like, I am pleased to see that it is the perfect place for a risqué liaison. The new, modern complex consists of townhomes with their own outside doors, which means no doorman would be into our business or smirking behind our backs.

Inside, the place has an open floor plan with a kitchen and dining area on one side and the living room on the other. The glow from a fireplace along one side of the wall lends a seductive ambiance, and the modern black leather sofa and chairs look inviting. Rising from the middle of the great room is an open staircase, creating a natural break between the dining and lounging areas. The staircase leads up to what looks like a loft bedroom. Hugging Luka hello, I can't help wondering what size bed he has.

"My bedroom's upstairs," he volunteers. "And it just so happens that I recently bought a king-size bed."

Giggling a little, I respond, "Oh, that's nice!"

Was that about the stupidest thing I could say? I guess I'm a little nervous.

"There are bathrooms upstairs and down," he continues, gesturing behind the staircase. "Along with an office, but I'm using it as the kids' room when they sleep over."

Will we ever meet his kids or vice versa, I ponder, but really it is just fine to keep this wild part of our lives completely separate from the children.

I see that the table is set for three. After opening the wine we brought, we sit down to a simple dinner of pasta and salad. It's good, but sometime it might be fun to make a nice dinner for them—play wife to two men.

I dressed in a tight, fairly short sweaterdress along with my one pair of Japanese schoolgirl socks that reach to my thighs, leaving just a hint of skin showing between the hem and socks. Dark fall colors and warm enough for a Boston autumn, but still I hope seductive looking. I feel attractive and just a little sexy when Luka's eyes travel up and down my body. Expecting a rebuke from my surgeon, I have on fairly high-heeled shoes—I just can't surrender to flats anymore—but he doesn't say anything as he smiles at me.

Underneath my more modest street clothes, my desires truly rage on. Although I'd be embarrassed to admit it to them, I made a special trip to a fancy lingerie store and tried on lots and lots of sexy, skimpy things, keeping the staff busy bringing me this and that different size until I found the perfect set. So tonight I have on lacy, China-red boy-style hip-hugger panties. Just knowing I have them on makes me feel ever so sensual. My matching push-up bra gives my bosom an extra boost, and I know that at least my husband will appreciate my seductive lingerie later this evening. Lastly, in my purse is a deck of playing cards—a woman wants to be prepared, just in case!

We are taking our time eating and getting to know each other better. Elliott doesn't share Luka's interest in television sports, but we all like to ski and we discuss the merits of various Vermont ski resorts. After finishing dinner, we bring our wineglasses with us to the sofa and talk for a while longer. The more I get to know Luka, the more I like him. I hope the feelings are mutual all around.

Certainly the men seem relaxed, laughing, at ease. They're engaged in the conversation, as I absentmindedly join in now and again. I am distracted thinking about my fantasies and whether or not there is the chance they might actually come true at some point.

The whole scene, my sexy underthings, and the company of two handsome men make me feel hot and touchy-feely. As the evening progresses, I find myself caressing Elliott's arm or dropping a kiss on his cheek or neck. And whenever I have the chance, I can't resist quickly touching Luka on the shoulder or arm. I miss his gentle touches from the office visits.

Don't they have a clue how turned on I'm getting sitting between them? When I get the chance, laughing at some joke I didn't even listen to, I "innocently" touch their thighs or slightly higher on their legs. But they seem immune to my little overtures. After another hour, I can't stand the building sexual tension inside me one minute longer. I need to get home so that Elliott and I can act on those feelings. With a throaty, husky voice, I murmur, "Well, gentleman, I enjoyed our evening very much. Should we do it again to, umm, build our friend-ship further?"

Is there too much hope sounding in my voice? I wonder. Both men are silent, observing me for long moments. Their faces show speculation or annoyance—I'm not sure. Their quietness leaves me wondering what they are thinking. I am really not ready to give up on my fantasy, but maybe this is the turning point when either man will say he just isn't into it. I guess I am asking a lot. Men joke about a ménage à trois, but I know a straight man's version usually involves two women and only one of them. The silence drags on. I am wondering if this is a standoff over who will speak first.

Finally, Elliott clears his throat and says, "Well, I think I'm ready to take it to the next level…"

Luka leans in and says, "Yes, I am too. And, with your permission, Elliott, ah, why wait?"

Happily I plant a quick kiss on each of their faces and offer, "I have a deck of cards in my purse. Anyone up for strip poker?"

They look at me and laugh.

"Why not?" one of them says as I dig through my purse for the deck.

I quickly explain the rules—my rules. We'll play Five Card Draw, and the loser of each round will have an article of clothing removed. The winner gets to undress the loser, but only I will undress the men and only I will touch them, ever. We'll have one chance to draw better cards, and then we show our hand. The loser is the one with the worst hand. Then I showed them a list of winning hands, easier than explaining it.

I'm so pleased I have on my new sexy lingerie, although there is a chance I will win and they'll never see it.

We play a quick practice round and make sure we have roughly the same number of articles of clothing. After playing six rounds, we've all lost our shoes. Then Luka loses with a lousy two-pair hand, and I reveal my full house. He dutifully lifts up his leg, and I slowly strip off a sock, giggling as I toss it aside. We're enjoying our wine and it shows.

My husband wins next and I'm the loser. I move in front of him, and he slowly strips off one of my schoolgirl socks as I sit on the coffee table with my leg raised. How can my one naked leg feel so exposed? Both men have seen this leg before.

After I return to the couch, Luka wins and I seem to be on a losing streak. I'm tingling all over with excitement as I move in front of him and sit again on the low table, raising my leg for him to take off the second sock. But instead Luka gently pulls me to my feet, with his knees on either side of my legs. He reaches out and slowly grasps the hem of my knit dress.

"Wait…you're supposed to take off my other sock!" It comes out as a surprised squeak as I look down to see him raising the hem.

Luka glances at Elliott, almost apologetically, and says, "I may not win again, and I won't give up the chance to unwrap this sexy package." There's an unspoken "Do you mind?" directed at Elliott. I'm hot all over, realizing we may have reached a point of no return.

Ever so slowly, Luka pulls up the hem of the dress. The soft sweater material wisps up my legs, and my red lacy panties are exposed. I hold my breath, my insides tingling—I'm actually trembling with excitement. The men's eyes are riveted on my body, and the dress is bit by bit pulled over my head. I hear their low moans of appreciation as the dress is tossed aside. Luka's hands come back to me, unhurriedly sliding up my body, gliding over my panties, up my hips, and just passing by the outsides of my breasts. The tingles in my belly move lower, and looking down at him, I also see my nipples peak underneath the lacy bra. Luka sees them too.

"Well, okay, well," I say to no one in particular. "I guess it's your deal," I say to Luka as I move to sit back down between them.

I'm a little anxious now, as I am forty-four after all. At his age I'm sure he's used to much younger women, but after coming this far, I am not going to give in to nervousness. I'm not going to give up—one of them will have to stop this risqué game. I glance over at Elliott, then lean over and kiss his cheek.

"You are the best!" I say, and he kisses me back hard on the mouth—so far so good on that front.

Luka states, "I *will* win the next round with you, Valerie…somehow I'm going to win."

Well, he didn't win the next two rounds. I did! And I happily enjoyed my opportunity to take their shirts off. Forget the socks—I wanted to see skin. Elliott had a pullover, so that was quick, but with Luka, I leisurely undid each button starting from his neck and working down, using my hands to slide the shirt off his strong shoulders and down his arms. It was my first long contact with his body and I took my time, enjoying the feel of his skin and firm muscles. He sucked in his breath sharply as I finished caressing down his arms.

My head is beginning to swim. I'm so aroused, sitting here with practically nothing on, knowing that Luka is constantly watching me, looking at my breasts and lower. Another round of wine and we're all a little tipsy, but not really, more like wired. The room sizzles, or is it just me?

Luka wins the next round with the best possible hand, a royal straight flush. I turn my hand over to reveal a two pair, and only Elliott's hand remains now. I know Luka will win, but who will be the loser? I have butterflies in my stomach, and my nipples are tight, hard buds.

All eyes are on Elliott's cards as he slowly rotates his hand—he has a straight flush, the second-best hand possible. I freeze when I realize I've lost, wondering what Luka will take off next.

Elliott tosses his cards down on the table and leans back to watch the show, wineglass in hand. Swirling the wine in his glass and inhaling the aroma, he's clearly enjoying himself. Glancing at Luka, I see he's leaning back, watching me hunter-like, with a small predatory smile on his lips.

It has all come down to this. It's time for me to back down and call it quits, or to surrender to him. I can sense tension in the room as we all wonder what will happen next. I'm nervous but I know what I want.

Dutifully I get up and move to stand in front of Luka. I'll make it his decision. What will he do? Maybe he'll be the one to back down and just take off the other sock. It does feel silly having on only one sock. Looking down at him, into his eyes, I can see how steamy they are—intense, blazing—and there is no indecision there.

He gently but firmly pulls me forward until I'm crawling onto his lap, straddling his thighs, my breasts now directly in front of his eyes. I can't breathe, and it seems no one is breathing; it's so still and quiet. Sitting over his crotch, I can feel now that he desires me. I am becoming wet too and feel light-headed. As he reaches around me and masterfully unhooks the bra, there is no fumbling and no hesitation.

Trembling on his lap, I gasp when I feel the hooks come apart. This is so much more intense than the dress. Locked in his gaze, I am frozen, looking into his intense stare as I feel the straps sliding forward over my shoulders. Then his eyes drop to my breasts and the silky bra falls away.

These aren't young breasts—they've fed two children. What will he think? What is my husband thinking?

The bra is tossed aside as I watch Luka slowly lean toward me. His sensual mouth opens, and he takes my nipple and areola into his mouth. I am helpless now, moaning and leaning into him, the exotic feelings of having another man's mouth on me making me quake.

Holding his head to my breast with both hands, I moan louder. I can't let this stop. It can't stop; it feels too good. Luka continues to suck and lick my nipple, and I tremble. I know what I need, what I must have.

I raise my head and turn to look at my husband who is frozen, still watching intently. Does he like it or hate it?

I reach one hand toward him. "Please, Elliott, please," I say as I reach for him and turn to expose my other breast toward him. "Please!" I reach and crook my fingers, gesturing and pleading.

I know he knows what I want, what I need. Elliott slowly puts his glass down and half crawls across the space on the sofa until he is right next to me. I watch the mouth that I have loved for years slowly lowering onto my other breast as I gasp and moan loudly.

This is heaven, so much better than I could have imagined. This sexual fantasy that I hadn't even known I wanted a few months ago is astonishingly fulfilling. I hold both men's heads to my breasts and give in to the wild feelings coursing through my body. The excitement I'm feeling is obvious, and it inspires the men as they suck harder on my breasts and begin using their hands to caress all over my body. My whimpers and pleading grow loud in the room. I'm on fire. It feels so good!

The large room is filled with my gasps and moans and the slight sucking sounds of two mouths. I am so wet and hot, and there is tingling everywhere, swirling sensations filling me and taking over as I mindlessly surrender to an orgasm centered in my breasts. As it overwhelms me, I feel so good, so alive, so right.

Gradually my breathing slows, and I relax into Luka's arms, resting my head on his shoulder while looking at Elliott. I'm too comfortable to say anything.

Resting his chin on my head, Luka looks over at Elliott and asks, "Did she?"

With a small smile, Elliott says, "Valerie sometimes has very sensitive breasts. Lucky for her, lucky for me."

After reaching out one hand, I gently caress Elliott's arm, love for him and wonder at my good fortune filling me. Could any woman be this lucky? After a while, I lean back, acutely aware of how exposed I am with practically no clothes on and the men almost fully dressed.

"Well, I guess we should get back to the game," I say with a slightly embarrassed smile.

Luka gently pushes me to my feet and back further, until he stands up and is very close looking down at me.

"The game's over. We're done!" he says as he scoops me up into his arms and starts for the stairs to the loft.

So, I guess there's no turning back. I know I wanted this, and I do want it, but I haven't been with another man in nearly twenty years. Almost frantically I reach back toward my husband. "Elliott!" I plead, feeling he has to be there too. Elliott is quiet but doesn't seem angry—at least I hope he's okay with this. I wait for something from him, some response.

"I'm coming," he drawls. "Just let me refill my glass. If I'm going to enjoy the show, I want some good wine to go with it."

Even though I just had an orgasm, I'm already burning all over. Anxious and nervous about what's coming next, but oh so hot, hot, hot!

10

WITH BENEFITS

Luka lowers me to the floor at the foot of the stairs, and we walk hand in hand up to the loft bedroom. My trepidation grows with each step. What will it be like after so many years with the same person? What if I don't like it, or worse, what if he doesn't like it? My forty-four-year-old female ego will suffer badly if it's a bomb. Shivering slightly, I know it's not because I'm cold.

I hesitate anxiously in front of the bed, looking down at the sheets and realizing it truly is showtime. What we did downstairs was just a prelude—the real performance begins now. Or I could just call it quits like a coward. Glancing over at Luka, I see that he is watching me intently. He doesn't look inclined to gracefully give up on the plan. Instead, he looks really turned on and wanting, his hold on my hand tightening.

I know Luka would stop if I asked him to, or Elliott would intercede if he didn't, but nervousness aside, I also know that I truly want this. At this point in my life, before I'm too old, *I want this!* I want sex, lots of exhilarating erotic intercourse. I need new experiences and a new lover who will bring exciting freshness to Elliott's and my sex life.

Before meeting Luka the doctor, the unexpected new man in a life that rarely meets single men, I had not even realized the wanting was there inside me. It burst forth like an exotic autumn bloom. Now I have a choice to make. I can pluck that flower, enjoy its heady fragrance, feel the soft petals' caress, and discern its rare beauty. Later, I will have the memories to cherish even as my flower fades. To walk away and leave it all untouched would be a waste of such an extraordinary gift. Something that won't ever come again, this I know deep in my being. So, taking a steadying breath, I give myself over to the moment, to consummating the agreement, to not turning back.

Elliott had followed close behind with his glass of wine. After seeing my hesitation, he gives me a quick encouraging kiss. Then turning away, he goes to the only chair in the room, a comfortable chaise, and settles back to watch.

Luka senses my consent and takes control, demonstrating that he is a self-assured, confident man.

"Lie on the bed, Valerie," he instructs as he begins removing the rest of his clothes. I watch fascinated as he removes first his socks, then his pants, and last his briefs. He's already rock hard, jutting out strongly, and I can't help gasping. Once again, I'm struck by the newness of seeing a different naked man after so long.

After joining me on the bed, he kisses me passionately while caressing my breasts and belly. My hands slide into his thick, black hair—finally mine to caress as much as I want. It is smooth and luxurious, and I playfully tousle it. I run my fingers through the silky locks, teasing the sensitized skin on the palms of my hands. I want to crawl into that head of hair—crawl into him!

At the same time, I rub my breasts against the dark hair on his chest. It tickles, rather than caresses, the wiry curls a tantalizing torture on the ultrasensitive points of my nipples. My hands then begin to tentatively roam over his back and shoulders, and lower. I cannot get enough of touching him, anywhere and everywhere I can reach.

He is all new to me and it's extraordinarily erotic, a whole new body to explore and to discover how he feels and what turns him on. Between kisses, he murmurs encouraging sounds and moans. I guide his hand lower and he massages my clitoris through the red lace of my underwear. My moans join his and we're enjoying exploring each other's bodies.

I'm in a thick, warm fog, but I remember that I'm not alone with Luka, that my beloved husband of nineteen years is quietly watching us. Luka continues loving me while I raise my head and look at Elliott. He is staring at us intensely, watching Luka suck on my breast, and it almost looks like he is holding his breath. He stirs a little, as if uncomfortable, and I can see the bulge indicating that he is also hot and ready for me.

I had no idea this would be so incredibly erotic, being made love to while being watched by another man. I've never been into exhibitionism, but giving a private show is turning out to be a real turn-on for me.

As my attention returns to Luka, I take his hand and slip it under my panties and feel a jolt of pleasure as I feel his finger slide into me. I'm about to go over the edge again but want to take him with me. Writhing and moaning, I am ready to surrender to him.

"Luka, I want you inside me, please," I murmur into his ear.

He slides my panties down and then reaches for a condom. We've agreed that we'd play it safe, of course. I take it from his hand and relish the opportunity it gives me to touch his penis. Carefully, I roll it down over his long, thick shaft and then wrap my fingers around him and slowly slide my hands up and down, holding tightly. Luka rewards me with a loud groan, before pushing me back down onto the mattress and raising himself over me.

Holding himself on his arms, he asks, "Are you ready?" and I know him to mean, are you sure?

In answer I raise my hips and rub against his cock, inviting him in. As Luka passionately kisses my mouth, he slowly enters me an inch at a time. Moaning, I rock into him. I am so turned on that I want it fast…now!

"Shh," he says. "We're going to take this slow and build it. You will like." His accent is now very thick with his excitement.

So I settle back and let Luka guide me. We luxuriate in fucking ever so slowly, and I feel so wicked observing my husband watching us. Elliott's pants are unzipped now and his hand is working his cock, matching our tempo. Luka's mouth settles on my nipple, and he bites down sharply.

"Ahhh," I squeal more from surprise than pain. My eyes shift back to Luka, and he is grinning naughtily at me. It seems he wants my full attention on him while he slowly builds the tempo. I am wildly turned on by the novelty of a new lover after so many years and eagerly match his pace.

Luka continues to increase the speed, pumping me more rapidly and harder, until I'm gasping and holding on to his back, urging him on. Then I feel myself exploding, a climax so strong I scream out my moan. Luka joins me with a hard rapid thrust, and I raise my hips to meet him one last time.

Slowly I come down to earth. Luka has collapsed onto me and is breathing hard. "That was amazing," he whispers.

"Yes, it was," I reply, but I'm already thinking about my husband and what will come next.

Elliott stands up and walks over to the foot of the bed, looking down on our wet, panting bodies.

"I believe it's my turn now," he groans out. I can see he's still rock hard.

Luka drops a kiss on my chest, pulling out and rolling away in one fluid movement, heading for the bathroom. Elliott removes his clothes while I watch, and Luka returns with a towel wrapped around his waist ready to take his turn as voyeur.

Feeling overwhelming affection for my husband, I reach out and entreat, "Join me, Elliott. I love you. I want you."

There is an intensity about him, not exactly anger, but something. It is clear that he is in the grip of strong emotions, and I'm hopeful that he doesn't regret our ménage.

Climbing on top of me, he looks down into my eyes and says, "That was, perhaps, the most fucking hot thing I've ever seen! I feel some jealousy too, I guess, but all I want now is to fuck you hard and long." His eyebrows rise in question.

"Yes, right now. Do it now," I urge him. I can't believe I'm already hungry for more.

Over the years we've done it many ways and at many tempos, but tonight he's driven to work me over, and I'm ready for it. Firmly grasping my body, he swiftly rolls me over onto my knees. Panting and grunting, we fuck hard and long doggy-style. Perhaps he's working out some angst over my assignation with Luka. Or, maybe he was deeply turned on by watching me with another man. I don't care as long as he continues to love me.

Even as we rock the bed, I feel added excitement knowing that I'm being watched again by Luka who is standing right next to the bed looking down at us. Surrendering to the intense feelings, I climax for the third time this evening, followed swiftly by Elliott's cries of release.

Slowly coming back to awareness, I lie down as Elliott cuddles my backside. Luka's still by the bed so I reach out and pull him down in front of me. Together we three lie there in what I later name the "Valerie Sandwich." Shortly, we'll need to go home, but for now I'm enjoying feeling like a woman well loved.

Later, as we are turning to leave, I laughingly say, "Guess what, boys? My fantasy bucket list is getting remarkably shorter, thanks to both of you."

Playfully I reach out and give each of my guys a quick thank-you kiss. Leaving with my husband, I am truly looking forward to experiencing all that our "friends with benefits" liaison may bring in the months to come.

~ 11 ~
THEIR TURN

IT IS A COLD January in Boston, and we're in the third month of our ménage à trois. I'm well pleased with the arrangement, and the guys sure haven't complained. I've crossed off several more items from my unofficial fantasy list. We've settled into a routine of meeting about every other Saturday at Luka's apartment when he doesn't have his kids. It's exciting but also freeing—a night with no kids, no obligations, and such wild sex that I couldn't have known I would ever experience in my life.

I'm excited because it's Saturday night again and we're about to knock on Luka's door. Now that my toe is all better, I'm never out without sexy high-heeled shoes. Tonight they are red platform pumps that advertise, "Fuck me." Both Elliott and Luka have been so accommodating, doing anything I've asked of them, and my tentativeness and mild embarrassment are a thing of the past. Tonight is going to be lots of fun!

As I'm ringing the doorbell, I ask Elliott what is in the bag he is carrying. I hadn't noticed him putting it in the car earlier.

"You'll find out soon enough," he says secretively.

Luka greets me with a warm embrace and offers me a sip from his glass of ice-cold white wine. I kiss him passionately and don't want to stop to even shut the door. He leads me by the hand to the couch, and both men sit down, looking at me with conspiratorial glances at each other. After dropping my coat on a chair, I turn to join them, but Luka holds up a hand to stop me and looks over at Elliott.

"Should I tell her or do you want to?" he asks.

Standing there, I'm beginning to get anxious. Are they calling it quits? Have they had enough already? I haven't, not yet!

In his refined Bostonian accent, Elliott says, "We have done everything you have asked of us. And we are not saying we haven't enjoyed it, but tonight we think it is time we turned the tables. Tonight it is our turn. Tonight you are going to be our sex slave and do whatever we say the entire evening. Do you understand?"

All over my body, my skin begins to tingle, and standing there in my very high heels I begin trembling, wondering if I'll be able to remain standing with my legs feeling like mush. Wow, this was a complete surprise, and so, so hot!

After all these years, I completely trust Elliott. I know he'd never hurt me or do anything to humiliate me, but he can also be exceptionally adventurous when it comes to sex. We've done lots of things in bed that I've never told anyone, and I wonder what Elliott's clever mind has planned for me tonight.

"Well?" he says.

I can tell Elliott is completely serious as he relaxes on the sofa. Glancing at Luka, I see that although he is smiling, almost apologetically, he is also looking too eager by far.

I nod yes to the two men, not sure if I'm acknowledging my understanding or my compliance. I am already feeling like an object on display as they look me up and down in my tight-fitting blouse and short skirt. Perhaps the platform pumps were not such a good idea tonight.

"Good," responds Elliott, clearly in charge of tonight's festivities. "Take your clothes off...slowly."

"Whaaa, what?" I mumble. I can't seem to get my mouth working.

"No talking. Slaves don't question their masters. They just do what they are told. Now strip for us. Tonight you will serve us without comment and without clothes."

Nodding again, I feel both excitement and trepidation. This is so erotic, but doing the bidding of two men all night and without clothes, while they remain fully clothed... And, not being able to talk, to voice any objections or wants—that makes me feel helpless, at their mercy.

This is not something on my fantasy list! This thought pushes into my consciousness as I stare at the two men like a deer in the headlights.

It's a game surely, I think, as my mind slowly acquiesces. I'll go along for the ride, hopefully a very sizzling, erotic ride!

To get better balance, I spread my trembling legs apart a little and quickly regret the more provocative pose, an upside-down vee that leads straight to my pussy. But rather than appear inanely modest at this late stage in our threesome, I keep my feet spread and reach up and begin to slowly unbutton my blouse from top to bottom, letting it drop open to reveal my sexy black bra. The men nod for me to keep going, so I let the blouse slide off my shoulders to glide to the floor.

Reaching behind me, I unzip my short skirt and push it down over my hips, slowly revealing my lacy black bikini. Stepping out of the skirt, I look at the men and stop moving. Maybe this is all they expect, not so bad really, since it's as much coverage as a swimsuit.

Both men are enjoying their cold chardonnay and watching my every move like two predator cats, male ones. Licking my lips, I think I'd really enjoy a sip or two. Maybe I'd down a whole glass as fortification. I start to walk toward Luka and raise my hand to take his glass.

Luka shakes his head no.

"You haven't finished yet. Everything goes"—he pauses to look me over—"except perhaps those sexy shoes. You can keep those on."

I guess he's not just going to be a bystander this evening after all. Well, if I'm going to do this, I might as well make it the best show I can. I'm slightly nervous, but the appreciative smiles and nods are encouraging me. Throwing both men a big compliant smile, I reach behind and unhook the bra. Then almost caressing myself, I pull it off my breasts and toss it at Luka. Catching it with his free hand, he then raises his glass to me in silent salute.

I'm in no hurry, so very slowly, bit by bit, I slide my hands under the sides of my panties and push them down my body until they fall to the floor. After scooping them up, I flip the undies toward Elliott and stand facing the men, legs spread provocatively apart, hands on hips—stark raving naked except for my flaming-red "fuck me" platform pumps.

The men look well pleased with themselves lounging there, ogling me up and down and all but licking their lips. My stomach is doing flips, and my snatch is so hot it almost hurts.

As he puts his glass down, Elliott says, "That's good. Now come here," pointing to a spot just in front of him. "That's right. Kneel before me."

As I submissively go down on my knees, he reaches for the mysterious bag and takes out a hair clip. So I guess slaves get their hair done by their masters? Taking my hair in his hands, he fashions a sort of French twist and clips it up off my shoulders. After pulling a few strands out to curl around my face and neck, he nods and reaches for the bag again. Now what? All the while Luka is watching me and sipping wine that I now really want as my throat has suddenly gone dry.

As Elliott pulls out another object, I gasp and my eyes flare. Is that really a slave collar in his hand? It's black leather with sparkling rhinestones and a ring attached to it. My breathing is coming in gasps now, and I'm not sure if it is excitement or panic. Reaching around me, Elliott straps it onto my neck and then takes out a long, thin, almost pretty, silver chain that he clips onto the loop on my collar. I'm really breathless now, and desperate to know what comes next.

"There," says Elliott. "I think you are now dressed appropriately as our sex slave. Don't you agree, Luka?"

His voice sounds tight, and I realize he's really turned on. A quick glance down as I stand up confirms a ready bulge in his pants.

Talking to Elliott but looking at me, Luka says, "Shit—that's hot, really hot!"

That is so unlike Luka, with his slightly formal foreign way, that I laugh and smile.

As I feel the chain being tugged gently down, Elliott says, "I don't think I'm done with you yet. I have a need, and my slave's going to take care of it."

Slowly he pulls the chain down until my face is inches from his crotch. "Suck me off, slave, and don't spill a drop," he commands.

The tingling excitement I've been feeling since we started this game is now a boiling fever in me, and I readily comply. After kneeling between his legs, I unzip his pants. He's got the leash coiled firmly around his hand with my face held just inches from his long, hard dick. I know it's a game, but I also know he's dead serious that I'm commanded to suck him dry, and he won't let me up until I do.

Elliott knows that while I like licking him, I'm not usually into swallowing his cum. But I think this game has him feeling in control, making his deep desires known, and in my submissive role I'm actually excited to see this through.

His hold on my chain loosens a little to give me some room to maneuver, and I take his penis in my hands and begin to lick him. I start with a small swirl around the tip, gradually licking him up and down, over and over. Elliott relaxes back against the cushions and sighs his appreciation.

I wonder if Luka is watching, but my husband's tight hold on the leash prevents me from lifting my head. Being in this subservient position—servicing one man, while another man waits his turn—is so erotic that I'm becoming damp and so turned on that I need relief now. I reach my free hand down to touch myself between my legs.

"No," orders Elliott. "Slaves get their release when their masters say they do. Right now, you are commanded to service me."

This only turns me on more as I burn to fondle myself or have either of them pet me. *Yes, pet me, treat me like your pet, anything! Please just touch me!* Elliott rests his hand firmly on my free hand; he means to withhold my pleasure, to tease me. I groan in desire and my body is starting to writhe in want.

Returning my attention to Elliott's cock, I take him fully into my mouth and slowly slide up and down, gradually going faster and faster. His answering moans and pants tell me I'm doing it right. Then he grabs my head, more forcefully than ever before, and pumps my head up and down on his penis. I moan in answer to him, and suck and lick as fast as I can, until his body goes firm and he gasps and shoots warm, thick cum into my mouth. He holds my head firmly in place, his commands in my thoughts. It tastes salty, and I follow my master's order and gulp it down. Elliott lounges back while I dutifully and submissively lick him clean.

Once done, he releases my leash and pats me on the head. "That's a good slave. Now see to your other master's needs."

Leaning back on my heels, I look at Luka and he shakes his head no.

"I'm hungry for dinner now, but you'll take care of me later," he promises. "Go get the dishes of food in the kitchen, slave," he instructs.

Looking at Elliott, Luka says, "I thought we'd go a little Middle Eastern tonight to go with our slave theme."

As I bring out the platters stark naked to serve the clothed men, I feel so hot and bothered, wondering when or if I'll get to have an orgasm this evening. The food is an assortment of dips—hummus and such—along with olives, pita bread, and stuffed grape leaves. As I set them down on the low table in front of the couch, I see Luka pour a small glass of clear liquid from a small decanter.

"This is for you," he says, handing it to me. I've been coveting the cold wine, so I eagerly take a big drink, and choke and sputter on the liquor as it burns down my throat. I don't know what it is, but it's both sweet and strong—something foreign. I guess they want to get me drunk before they do whatever they plan to do. That thought both excites and unnerves me at the same time. Liking the warm feelings the drink engenders, I quickly raise it back to my lips, but this time take just a little sip and enjoy the sensation of warmth trickling down my throat.

"Sit here at our feet like a good slave," orders Elliott, taking the glass and putting it on the table.

Wow, they are really getting into this slave business, aren't they? I think. He pats my head like a lap pet, but then Luka leans forward and gives me a long, passionate kiss while dropping his hand down to fondle my breast, which sets my head spinning. *Can we just skip the meal and get on with it?*

I sit quietly sampling the delicious, sensual food, while the men talk about their week and eat. I have drained the small glass of liquor and want more, but maybe not, as my head is already foggy. Occasionally as we eat, either Luka or Elliott reaches down to fondle my breast or to feed me an olive or something. I know it's obscenely subservient, but I'm so turned on that I just can't help leaning into their hands and practically purring each time they deign to give me some attention. I open my mouth to ask for more of the drink, but Elliott puts his finger to his lips. They are set on having me silent and compliant this evening.

Dessert is an assortment of small little baklava sitting in honey,

Turkish delight, almond cookies, and other foreign treats. Bite-sized, and they order me to feed them dessert. Each time I place one in their mouth, they suck on my fingers, pulling them into their mouths and sometimes licking down to the vees between my fingers. I can't help moaning loudly. I want to rub myself along their legs, anything to relieve my building sexual tension. They are taking turns feeding me small pieces of the sweet desserts, and I suck strongly on their fingers too. Soon there is nothing left but a little puddle of honey on the dessert plate.

After Elliott gets up for more wine, Luka stands and orders me to lie down on the sofa. The leather feels warm along my naked back and legs, and my nipples tighten as Luka looks down at them. After kneeling and picking up the empty plate, he swipes some of the remaining honey onto his finger and then swirls it around my nipples and areola. He leans down and takes my nipple, then my whole breast into his mouth and swirls his tongue languidly around and around the breast. It's so intense that I gasp and moan and hold his head to my breast. Luka then begins on the other breast, while placing a finger full of honey into my mouth for me to suck too. I'm so close to coming, just a little more and I'd be there—please, please, please—but Luka raises his head and slowly stands up.

"I think it is time our sex slave continues with her official duties," he says thickly to Elliott.

After taking the end of the chain that is still attached to the collar around my neck, he slowly pulls me to standing. I wobble quite a bit from the liquor but also from the intense desire, and holding me upright, Luka reaches down and takes off my shoes. Turning without a word, he takes the end of my leash and begins walking to the stairs to the loft. I follow docilely behind, still naked and now barefoot. I notice Elliott has scooped up the mysterious bag and is coming too. What more could still be in there I wonder?

In the loft, Luka orders me to lie down faceup on the center of the large bed. Then Elliott takes a rope out of the bag. A rope!

"We will not tolerate any resistance from our slave," he says as he binds my hands and ties them to the bed above my head. Then he takes out a blindfold and covers my eyes. Now I really feel helpless. I can't move my hands, can't see, and they won't allow me to talk. I trust Elliott after our many years together, but Luka adds an element of uncertainty, and my senses are heightened.

From the foot of the bed, I hear Luka say, "Tonight you won't know which one of us is touching you. We'll do anything we want to you, but you won't know who is doing it."

I shiver wildly and can't help the loud moan that erupts from my throat. They are silent now, and I can hear that they are moving around. I hear the bag being opened again. What now? Then I feel a softness glide over my body—is it a feather? The gentle feathering caresses my whole body on both sides as I lay shuddering and softly moaning.

Then I feel a mouth on my breast, sucking and even biting. I arch into the mouth, moaning, and try to grab the head to hold it to my breast, remembering as my hands are jerked back that I am tied to the bed. Now my other breast is being suckled, and I moan, rolling my head from side to side. I'm on fire. *What next?* I wonder wildly.

I feel a toe being suckled, and a hand reaches between my legs and flicks my clit. Too quickly it goes away as I try to rear into the hand for more. Then a tongue replaces the finger at my pussy. I'm almost mindless now as the mouth suckles my clit, but I wonder who it is. Luka and I are such new lovers that he hasn't yet kissed me down there. I'm frantic to know who is doing what to me, and it's overwhelming as I writhe and moan on the bed. Now someone is squeezing my breast, then pinching my other nipple. Four hands are caressing my entire body as two tongues lick here and there at the same time.

"Please," I can't help moaning. "Please!" which is cut off as a tongue stabs into my mouth. Whose tongue is it? Now I'm being passionately kissed both on my mouth and my pussy at the same time. This fantasy may not have been on my list, but this is more erotic than I could ever have imagined. I'm so close, reeling with abandon and excitement, moaning loudly, almost crying from want.

And then it all stops cold. All hands and mouths are gone from my body, nothing but darkness and isolation and my raging desire.

"Wait, please. I need…" I plead with them.

"Do you need us?" asks Luka in a husky, deep voice, the accent really strong now. "Do you want us to finish you?" he taunts.

I can tell both men are at the foot of the bed as I lay there panting, wanting them back.

Elliott speaks now: "We want you wild with desire, begging and pleading for more, and we'll ensure that you are well pleased, we promise. But, will you take whatever we offer? Do whatever we want? No resistance, slave?"

"Yes. Yes, please, anything," I beg. "I'll do anything you want!"

I'm on fire and I don't really care now what they ask of me, just finish me. There is movement as the men crawl back onto the bed, and the roaming hands and tongues resume their thorough exploration of my body. I don't care who's doing what now, I just want more. My body is bucking and I'm pulling at the bondage.

Then I feel a warm male body climb over me and a gentle probing penis at my mouth. I welcome the large cock, sucking it deeply into my mouth, hungrily licking and suckling. Yes, more—I want more.

Now another man is climbing over my hips and there is the same gentle probing between my legs. I spread my legs wider and the unnamed lover plunges in, spearing into my cunt strongly. I'm well and truly a sex slave now, with two men getting serviced by me at the same time. And I welcome the invasion, moaning and hungrily working my mouth and hips for more.

The men's moans and pants have joined my passionate cries as the tempo gets faster with the two men wildly ramming their cocks into me at the same time. Faster and faster, until together we scream out our release as mindless orgasms overtake all of us at the same time.

Slowly I return to earth as I feel my hands untied and the blindfold removed. The men are lying on either side of me and smiling down at me. I can tell they want to make sure I'm okay with it, and I give them both quick kisses before languorously lying back into the bed. We make our usual "Valerie Sandwich" with me in the middle snuggling on the bed while we lazily relax together. Soon it will be time to go home, but for now, I smile dreamily and wonder at the sexually free woman I've become. Life is good!

Before we leave, Luka takes me aside, hugging me warmly, and whispers into my ear, "Next weekend is my birthday. Don't get me wrong. I love, and I mean *love* our ménage-a-friends-with-benefits. It's certainly not something I ever expected to have in my life. But I was wondering, do you think Elliott would mind or would allow me to have one night alone with you as a present, maybe?"

"Your birthday wish thrills me," I whisper back, "but only if Elliott is totally okay with the idea. If we mess up our new ménage friendship, then we all lose."

Luka nods, and I give him a quick kiss on the lips.

"I'll call you and let you know, and happy birthday!" I say.

Luka stops me and murmurs, "If you do come, wear your black fuck-me shoes, would you?"

~ 12 ~
BIRTHDAY WISH

AS WE DRIVE HOME, Elliott wants to know what we were whispering about. I explain and make it clear that I will not do anything that he doesn't want me to. Elliott's adventurous and giving spirit is allowing the three of us to have the time of our lives, even if we know it's only a short-term affair. Probably by next year this momentary interlude in our lives will be over. But I don't want to end it prematurely by causing jealousy or hurt feelings.

Elliott is silent for a few moments. "This isn't really what I agreed to."

I open my mouth to say never mind, but he cuts me off with, "But as a birthday present, sure, but only this once."

What an amazing guy! I make a mental note to shower him with even more affection this week. Elliott will have no doubt how very much I love him.

The week passed oh so slowly, but finally tonight is my solo date with Luka. I'm driving there alone—a first. If I'm honest with myself, I have to admit that I'm already incredibly turned on. I have on the same red lacy underthings as our first night as a threesome, a sort of surprise for him. I'm also a little anxious, because I haven't been alone with another man for more than twenty years. Of course, we've had lots of wild sex together in the last few months, but knowing I'll be all alone with Luka for the first, possibly the only time, makes it seem more intimate, more personal.

Luka opens the door and pulls me into a warm embrace, his deep, husky voice whispering that he's been thinking of nothing else all week but having me here alone.

And he thanks me for wearing my fuck-me shoes. "I think I could lose my license for encouraging you to wear those sexy things, but they really are hot and with that tight dress…"

Luka pauses to caress his hands down my body before continuing, "That first night we had drinks, I just sat there thinking how I wanted to slowly peel that dress off you and then make love to you with just your shoes on. You must have noticed I was a little tongue-tied."

Eyes locked on mine, Luka slowly lowers his face to me and gently brushes his lips across mine, almost reverently. They taste warm, with a hint of wine. Deepening the kiss, he crushes me to his body, and our tongues swirl around each other's until I hear myself moaning deeply in the back of my throat.

Breaking the contact between our lips to look me in the eyes, Luka says, "Tonight, for this one night, you are just mine. I'm going to love you thoroughly, just you and me. I'm going to take my time arousing every inch of your body till you cry out my name, till you are begging me, Luka, to enter you and fuck you."

I am instantly wet, hungry, burning, and my body sways toward him. He slowly takes my hand and leads me farther into his home. As I look around the room, it's clear he has spent time making it a romantic, intimate place. There are candles everywhere giving off a seductive light. Soft music plays and he has set a place for two on the low table in front of the couch.

"Luka!" I exclaim. "Wow, this is amazing, but I'm here as your birthday present and you've done all the work!"

"I want this to be special, different," Luka says as he tugs me down onto the couch.

Dinner is an assortment of finger foods and dips that we feed each other, licking each other's fingers clean. Quickly, this evolves into full-blown foreplay—kissing, touching, and nibbling. Forgetting about the food altogether, we realize it is time.

Luka stands and offers his hand to help me up. I am so aroused, so weak and trembling. Will I be able to walk in these super-high heels up the stairs to the loft? With a whoosh I find myself swung up into his arms, cradled there against his strong chest as he carries me to his bed.

In our time as a threesome, our sexual experiences have swung back and forth from wild to playful to really out there. But tonight with Luka is going to be different, I can tell. As he carries me, he is looking down at me with the same self-confidence I saw in him at that first doctor's visit. His deep, dark eyes are locked on mine, and I know he's masterfully in charge. Any anxiousness I felt earlier is long gone. We truly know each other as friends and lovers, and tonight we'll build on that relationship.

Gently he sets me on my feet and slowly slides his hands down my dress. After grasping the hem, he begins to pull it up over my head while looking intently down at my body. Luka gasps as he sees my red panties and smiles wickedly down at me.

"I like the gift wrapping on my present," he says. "But the shoes stay on."

Now I'm lying on the bed with just my red underwear and sexy pumps. His eyes, which haven't left mine as he lowered me down, begin a slow, languorous perusal of my body. His look is almost tangible—I can feel it on me like a gentle presence. A moan is wrung from my throat; I can't help it as his eyes pause on my breasts. *Oh, touch me, please.* Did I say that out loud or just think it?

His eyes continue down across my stomach, over my mound, and across my inner thighs, and finally down to my sexy pump-clad feet. Unaware, I am moving restlessly on the bed, undulating slightly. Feeling urgency, I reach out to him, pleading for him to join me.

"Shh," he breathes as he quietly but firmly shakes his head. "We have all night. I'm not going to rush anything."

His eyes begin a slow trip back up my legs to settle at my mound, still covered in bright red lace. The rush of heat to my pussy practically sends me over the top, and I moan loudly this time.

"Please, Luka, please. I need you. Now!" I gasp out.

Once again I'm reminded of our first meeting as he gives me that quirky, charming smile of his. I can tell he is rock hard inside his jeans, but he just winks and shakes his head. Then he does a striptease for me, slowly pulling his sweater over his head, followed by his jeans and briefs. He is so handsome, so strongly masculine, with curly black hair on his chest that trails down to his penis.

I feel like I know Luka very intimately after these ten weeks, but tonight seems different. We're alone together, without Elliott there looking on or joining in. Even without ropes or blindfolds the air is charged with sexuality. It is more private, more intimate. I'm extremely turned on, but also wonder if maybe this should be taboo. Are we crossing a line that shouldn't be crossed?

After crawling onto the bed with me, Luka slides his arm under my shoulders and kisses me on the lips. I feel his tongue enter my mouth to play with my tongue—a warm, quiet dance between us. Then his mouth drops little kisses on down my neck as he makes a trail to my breasts. There he begins licking me, swirling his tongue around my nipples until I'm arching into him and my nipples are hard little buds. As he sucks a breast into his mouth, I moan and thread my fingers through his hair.

I feel truly wonderful, and I realize that I have great affection for Luka, maybe even a little love. This is dangerous ground, so I stop letting myself think and just respond physically to what Luka is doing to me, with me. My hands start roaming over his back, down his arms, over every part of his body I can reach. I can tell he likes this from the little murmurs he's making. Slowly I reach between his long legs and grasp his penis with both hands to squeeze and caress him. His guttural moans encourage me to rub harder and faster.

He moves lower out of my reach, and I feel him kiss my pussy. This is almost too much, so intimate. I haven't allowed this with him before, although what he did when I was blindfolded—well, who knows?

Sensing my reluctance, Luka moves lower, licking my inner thigh and making small nips with his teeth. My legs drop open to encourage more, and I find I'm reaching my hands to bring him back as my traitorous pussy arches up to him, wanting his mouth back on me. My mind might say stop, but my body wants it badly. Laughing, he murmurs that I'm not sure what I want, but he won't stop until I'm begging him.

He kisses my ankle and then slowly removes a shoe. I gasp loudly when I feel his tongue sweep up the sensitive, ticklish sole of my foot. Then Luka suckles my toes, before moving to my other foot. Again, the shoe comes off and he repeats his teasing torture. Then Luka licks his way back up the other thigh toward the apex of my legs. I'm writhing and whimpering in anticipation as his face gets closer.

But he skips over my mound and tickles my stomach with his tongue. No, no, I want his mouth on my sex, as I try to gently push him back down. He laughs quietly at me as his hands and mouth continue to roam everywhere on my body, except where I want it most. Tweaking my nipples with his fingers and then kissing my neck, he places a finger in my mouth for me to suck, which I do eagerly. His tongue continues to lick all over my torso but doesn't go lower again. Instead his other hand begins teasing my clitoris, until I'm moaning and on the verge of coming.

But just before I go over the edge, his hand glides away and he murmurs, "You know what I want to hear."

"Luka!" I cry out. "Please, Luka, I want you to make love to me. Only you tonight. Please, Luka. I need you now."

After practically throwing himself onto me, Luka kisses me with a demanding force. He hands me a condom as he orders, "Put this on!"

Once I'm done, his mouth lands back on mine, demanding a passionate response, at the same time that he powerfully rams his penis into my vagina. I'm still crying out his name over and over, and we mate forcefully, both of us rocking our hips to slam into each other until we explode with a delicious orgasm, mine followed swiftly by Luka's. After drifting back to reality, I gently kiss him on his cheeks and nose and then mouth.

"Happy birthday," I murmur before we both fall into a restful sleep with our arms wrapped around each other. Any ramifications of our actions or my growing feelings will be dealt with later. I wake in a couple hours, feeling utterly relaxed and peaceful, and the slight smile on Luka's face while he sleeps tells me he feels much the same.

~ 13 ~

THREE FRIENDS WITH BENEFITS

"Our truest life is when we are in dreams awake."
—*Henry David Thoreau,* Walden

THE THREE OF US are taking a short friends-with-benefits vacation together, getting away from a frigid February in New England. The grandparents are watching our teens and his ex has theirs, but none of them are aware that it is vacation for three—that's our little secret. At this moment, we are lounging on a beach enjoying the sun after an energetic few hours fucking on the king-size bed in our hotel room. I have a hand resting on both my guys, something that can only happen here in this tropical island locale, away from prying eyes of friends and neighbors.

I'll admit that I secretly enjoy the occasional curious glances, some from women who obviously envy me. Some are clearly disapproving, but that is their problem. The three of us are comfortable with our arrangement. We are, after all, consenting adults in an open and equal relationship.

I have no idea how long it will last, but we've already enjoyed four wonderful months. I know this liaison will end in due course, perhaps when Luka gets a girlfriend or maybe Elliott will tire of sharing, but for now all is good. Certainly my middle-age libido has had a wonderful reboot, which has had a nice impact on our marriage, even when we're home alone. So, for now, I'm just going to enjoy my good fortune and store up memories for later.

We only get one life to live, and we have to seize opportunities when they come along. I am living my dreams with courage, stepping to a beat that is mine alone, and truly living my life to the fullest with no regrets, I realize, as I drift off to sleep in the tropical sunshine.

Seize the Doctor

1

SAYING GOOD-BYE TO THE OLD

NIKKI HURRIED TO JOIN her three friends for lunch, something they did at least once a week to catch up on gossip and help each other through girl stuff. They always met at their favorite lunchtime dive, a place they'd frequented often since they graduated from NYU a few years earlier. They were all starting out at the bottom with entry-level jobs, but they also knew that they were going places. After all, they worked at world-class companies in the center of the universe, New York City—or at least that's how *they* felt about it.

Walking into the joint, Nikki knew it was her turn to accept some boyfriend advice, but she didn't really want to talk about it. She was running late and saw that her roommate, Kim, and friends Rachel and Amy were already there.

"Hey, Nikki, glad you could find the time to join us," Rachel noted in her usual sarcastic manner.

"Sorry, really," Nikki responded. "My boss grabbed me at the last minute."

"Cut her some slack, Rachel," said Kim. "You know she had a rough time of it last weekend."

"Yeah, I heard that you broke up with that a-hole you called a boyfriend." Rachel jumped at the chance to talk about the latest gossip. "Spill it. What happened?"

Timidly Amy interjected, "Umm…maybe Nikki doesn't feel like talking about it." After giving Rachel a pleading look to let it drop, she added, "It's okay, Nikki. It's none of our business really."

"Let me order some food first, okay? I'm starving," Nikki said as she opened the menu.

"You know what I'm thinking? Let's go out later tonight for drinks and dancing. It'll be a good chance to take our minds off work and, you know, other things," said Kim, giving a slight nod in Nikki's direction. "Maybe Club X… It's fun."

"Boo-yah! That's a great idea," Rachel agreed. "It'll be packed tonight, and I'm ready to hook up with someone new."

"Don't you think it's a bit of a pickup dive?" Amy asked. "Maybe not the best place to go, given—"

"Yup. All the guys there are on the make, looking for someone new to bone," retorted Rachel, smirking at the three girls. "Perfect for me and for all of you too."

"Really, Rachel, where do you get this stuff…'someone to bone'?" Amy commented with exasperation.

Joining the fray, Nikki said quietly, "I don't know. I'm not sure I am ready for a meat market. Why don't you all go, really. I'll enjoy a calm evening at home."

"Not a chance," said Rachel. "We'll make sure you have fun, maybe dance a little. You don't need to actually try to meet anyone, just enjoy a little window-shopping, so to speak."

Pausing a moment to stab at her salad and stuff some in her mouth, Rachel continued, "What do you think, Kim and Amy? What better way to forget a jerk than to meet a new one!"

So it was agreed that they would all go to Club X in Greenwich Village around eleven that evening, although Nikki didn't think she would have a very good time. After Ben, her boyfriend of a little over a year, cheated on her, and they subsequently broke up, Nikki had felt down all week, but today she had begun to think maybe it was time to make some changes. She knew it was well past time for her to become a modern woman and take charge of her life. She just wasn't entirely sure how to go about it.

All four of the friends were longtime college buddies and had grown into adulthood together as roomies in the dorms, although timid Amy was the last to join their tight group. Rachel had always been the extrovert, and her outgoing manner, while sometimes a little grating, had certainly paid off at work. She had already received a small promotion and was eagerly taking on more responsibility. Nikki's closest friend, Kim, was also an outgoing person—someone who knew what she wanted and, while less mouthy than Rachel, had a definite plan for how to get there.

Nikki, however, was more reserved, not quite as shy and conventional as Amy but not one to put herself out there in the limelight either. After a week of soul searching, she had come to the conclusion that it was time for a Nikki makeover. It wasn't that she was totally heartbroken over Ben. She realized now what a jerk he really was, just as Rachel said, but Nikki also acknowledged that her quiet personality and muted fashion style made sure that she was the last one to get noticed in a group—and at her job too!

Nikki knew she was smart, a hard worker, and if not stunningly beautiful, she was at least good-looking, with a fit body and shapely legs. For too long she had been comfortable, not pushing herself to stand out and certainly not showing her assets to their best advantage. That was the reason Nikki had settled for a boyfriend who put his needs above hers and urged her to do things she didn't want to in bed, while taking her for granted until something better came along. Changing herself might take some effort and perhaps push her out of her comfort zone, but if nothing else, she would know that she had given her best shot—at work, at play, and at love.

Nikki and Rachel were coworkers in a small publishing house in Lower Manhattan, and as they walked back to work together after lunch, Rachel apologized for being pushy. "I know I come on a little strong sometimes, but if there is anything I can do to help, you know you can count on me."

"I know," Nikki responded. "You're a good friend. I'm just not as outgoing as you, and certainly not as sophisticated either, but that's something I want to change." Pausing, she thought about it and decided to take a chance and confide in her friend. "Do you know the reason why we broke up, Ben and I?"

"No, I don't. Kim wouldn't spill it, although…nosy me…I did ask her."

"It's stupid, really. Ben and I were together for over a year, and you know we had sex—lots, actually. I thought it was good, but, well, he didn't like that he always had to use a condom."

"Really," interjected Rachel, clearly fascinated by this dirt.

"Sometimes I wonder why I didn't just give in and get birth control pills. At first I was being careful, you know, safe sex and all. But then after six months or so, Ben wanted me to get the pill so he could stop using a condom. He just started hounding me about it, getting demanding and calling me 'old-fashioned.' So, I got stubborn and said no, that I wasn't ready. Then, as you know, I discovered he was cheating on me and that was the end of us."

Nikki stopped walking and looked at Rachel to try to gauge her reaction. "I know you must think I'm really lame and backward."

Rachel gave Nikki's hand a squeeze and said, "I don't think that at all. It's your choice what you use or don't use. Ben seemed like a nice enough guy when you first started dating him, but lately he started treating you badly, standing you up and stuff like that. I'd even seen him scoping out other women when he was with you... I just didn't know how to tell you about that. And, now that I know everything, I think he's a real douche bag! You're better off without him."

"I suppose so," Nikki responded. She was glad to be through with him, but it still hurt.

"Hey, I know I'm right," Rachel said as they started walking again. "Tonight let's just have some fun—keep it light. Flirt with some hot guys and get a little drunk."

Feeling better having dished it through, Nikki said, "That sounds like a plan!"

2

IN WITH THE NEW

THAT NIGHT THE GIRLS gathered at the tiny two-bedroom apartment Nikki and Kim shared in the Village. They put some finishing touches on their makeup and admired each other's outfits before heading out. Pickup joint or not, Club X was the girls' favorite club, in part because Rachel knew one of the bouncers who always let them jump the line. If they were very lucky, they didn't even have to pay the cover. They enjoyed parading past all the people waiting patiently in line and then walking directly into the club as the velvet rope was lifted just for them.

Earlier that evening, Nikki had made a decision. Since it was out with the old boyfriend, it would also be out with the old, shy Nikki and in with a hot new look. To accomplish this, she had put on brighter makeup than usual and had done her long hair in a sexy, fun style. Nikki had also borrowed one of Kim's thigh-high miniskirts and a tight blouse and had put on her highest platform pumps.

Someday she would have to replace her white modest underwear—her "mommy-boughts," as Nikki called them—with something more risqué. However, for now at least the rest of her look was *flossy*, as Rachel would say. Nikki wondered why she hadn't dressed a bit flashier before to show off her long, lean legs and other assets.

As they did their usual parade past the waiting line of clubbers, Nikki felt a little giddy with excitement over her new style and added a little more swing to her hips as she walked. Glancing at the line, she could see some of the guys eyeing her up and down as she strutted by them. She did not plan to "go to the boneyard," as Rachel so crudely put it, with anyone tonight, but Nikki hoped to have a little fun flirting with a hot guy or two.

The club was just starting to fill as they entered, so they were able to grab a table fairly close to the small dance floor. The DJ was playing loud, thumping music, even though no one was dancing yet. They ordered some drinks from the bar and settled in to lie in wait for hot guys—or any guys that might want to dance or flirt.

Kim watched Nikki sipping her usual martini and asked how she was feeling.

"I'm fine—actually I feel good. I'm thinking it's out with the old boyfriend and in with the new one, although I don't really expect to meet anyone special here tonight. I mean, really, does anyone ever meet Mr. Right at a pickup bar?" Nikki asked her friends.

"Yeah, I think we'd have better luck on one of those online dating sites," Amy agreed.

Rachel shot Amy a look. "You know what? You need a spark in your ass." She looked around the table for support, but the other two girls just stared at her blankly. Rachel continued, "You've got to put yourself out there. And, anyway, who said we're looking for Mr. Right? We are all way too young to get stuck fucking one guy for the *rest of our lives*!" she finished, as if it were a death sentence.

Kim joined in, saying, "Aren't we here to just have some fun tonight? Let's get out there and dance."

"That's the spirit," said Rachel. "I'll buy the next round for anyone who asks a guy to dance."

"Deal," said Kim and Amy at the same time. Amy immediately looked around for a likely target. Amy might be a little shy, but she was also broke and would happily ask someone to dance if that would get her a free drink—maybe two if the guy also bought her one.

With almost no effort, the two girls found two guys willing to hit the dance floor, although some might say Amy cheated a little because she asked someone she knew from college who just happened to be there, decidedly just friend material but still fine to hang with for a while.

The girlfriends had been there for a couple hours, had a few drinks, and danced a little when they saw three gorgeous guys grab an open table across the room.

"Now that's hunkalicious," said Rachel, looking at them with interest. "Dibs on the tall one!"

"Wow, they are all so good-looking," sighed Amy.

"You go, girl," Kim urged Amy with an encouraging smile. "If you walk over, I'll go with you."

Nikki sipped her drink and said, "I'll hold the table, and I'm thinking I'll just enjoy watching tonight. You all go though, since there are only three of them anyway."

Glancing over again, Rachel announced with exasperation, "Look at them…how quickly they operate. They've already moved on those slutty girls over there, and we're too late!"

With that Rachel, Kim, and Amy turned their attention elsewhere, and pretty soon they were all dancing again with various guys, both old acquaintances and new prospects. Nikki was still holding the table and had turned down a couple offers to dance. *What is with me?* Nikki wondered. She needed to get out of the funk she had slipped into this evening.

Looking around, she saw that two of the gorgeous hunks were at the bar talking to different girls than before, but the third guy, the one that appealed the most to her, was still sitting there. He noticed her looking at him and smiled from across the room. Nikki tentatively returned the smile before looking away. She looked down at her drink and realized she wanted a refill, so she got up and headed to the bar, waving at Amy to get her to come back and hold the table. By this time the club was packed, and Nikki had to push her way into the crowd at the bar, but with so many bartenders, she wouldn't wait long to get another cosmo, her martini of choice.

While waiting, Nikki thought again about how cute the guy who had smiled at her was—just her type—and then she chortled slightly. *Well, of course he is. Men that handsome are everyone's type.* She couldn't guess his height because he was sitting, but he was clearly well built, muscular but not over the top. With his movie-star blond hair and finely chiseled face, he reminded her of the Greek god Adonis, remembered from her college lit class.

Hmmm. She wondered what his voice sounded like and what color his eyes were, maybe blue. *Well, she would play Aphrodite to his Adonis anytime…or was it Daphne*, she mused, still laughing at herself as she pictured the two of them rolling around, fucking in the clouds like Greek gods would do. College seemed like a long time ago, but it was all coming back to her now.

As she turned away from the bar with her martini, Nikki almost bumped into her Adonis fantasy, who was standing right behind her.

"Oh hi," Nikki muttered, acutely embarrassed that she had been lusting after him. She tried to sidle by, but the bar area was very crowded. She wondered if her face was blushing bright red.

Her fantasy turned out to have a very deep, sensual voice. "Hi. Ah, actually I was coming over to say hello to you," he responded. "I saw you across the room and…" He trailed off as if unsure what to say next.

"Hey, do you want to dance?" he asked abruptly.

"Well, ah, maybe, but I just got a fresh drink," Nikki said as she continued to ponder his deep, masculine voice—just the kind that made her insides tingle with excitement. The crush around the bar forced them to stand very close to each other, and she could almost feel his warmth as she looked up into his *blue* eyes—yes, they were Greek-god blue, she realized. Some might call the color sky-blue or cerulean, but for her it would be named after the gods from now on.

"Oh, of course, how stupid of me," he said, interrupting her musings.

"But I'd be happy to sit and talk with you," Nikki quickly interjected.

"Great. Follow me," he said before leading her back to his table, which was now crowded with guys and girls. He grabbed two chairs and pulled them slightly away, seeming to want a chance to talk with her alone. With the thumping music and everyone talking loudly, they only needed to be a few feet away to converse out of the entire table's earshot.

"I'm Hunter," he said, sticking his hand out to shake hers.

"Nice to meet you. I'm Nikki, and I'm here with my friends over there," she said, gesturing across the room.

"Yes, I know. I've been waiting for a chance to talk with you," he said. "You're…ah…pretty."

His deep voice and his sweet compliment did wonders for her

mood—and for other parts of her too. "Thanks. I could say the same about you," she said, smiling at him. "Ummm, not that you're pretty, of course... Just...ah...good-looking," she added, embarrassed for having called a grown man pretty.

Eventually the others went out to the dance floor, and Nikki was alone with him. They talked and flirted for more than an hour, mostly about clubs and bands they liked, and the whole time Nikki felt a growing attraction to him. He was so very hot! When their knees accidentally bumped under the table, the sexual electricity was enough to make both of them fall silent and just stare at each other.

Nikki made a mental note not to get carried away, but it was clear Hunter seemed interested in her. She kept reminding herself that while he may look like Adonis, that didn't mean he was a nice guy and, anyway, thinking again of her lit class, Nikki remembered that the Greek gods often were not very nice, especially to such plain-Jane, mere mortals like her.

Nikki was giggling about something Hunter had whispered in her ear when Rachel caught them by surprise, interrupting them loudly.

"Hi! I'm Rachel, Nikki's friend," she announced. Then she grabbed an empty chair and sat down right next to Nikki. Amy and Kim had finished dancing, and Rachel waved them over to their new table. When they arrived, Nikki introduced Hunter to the girls, and they sat down too.

Then the other two guys, whose names turned out to be Rob and Dave, returned without their dance partners. Rachel seemed engrossed in watching one of them stuff a piece of paper into his pocket, and then she turned and looked toward Nikki. Scowling, Rachel made a slight, secretive nod of her head toward the guys, but Nikki couldn't guess the message her friend was trying to convey.

The one Rachel had called dibs on earlier, Rob, said, "Hey, I'm going to the bar. Anyone want anything?"

Nikki hadn't finished her drink, but the other girls all ordered something. After he left, Amy and Kim started talking to Hunter and Dave, but Rachel kept glancing back at the bar with a disgusted look on her face. Nikki wondered what was going on. Was Rachel so thirsty that she couldn't wait another minute for her drink? Nikki was just about to offer Rachel a sip of her cosmo when Rob returned.

"That will be thirteen dollars each with tip," he announced, and the surprised girls looked at each other.

They all dug into their purses and gave Rob the money as Kim whispered to Amy, "What a cheapskate."

The girls could tell that Nikki really liked Hunter, so they continued to hang out with the other two guys. The DJ had increased the house music to an ear-splitting level, forcing them to nearly yell back and forth as they got to know each other, while Nikki and Hunter continued to whisper quietly to each other, their heads practically touching. The club was completely packed now with people crowded all around them.

Kim leaned over and whispered into Amy's ear, "Something seems to be bugging Rachel, but I can't figure it out."

"I know. I've seen her giving Rob dirty looks," Amy responded quietly.

"He does seem to be working the room. Look! He's getting the phone number of the girl who just bumped into him," Kim noted with some annoyance. "I know Rachel thought he was cute earlier, but he's hitting on everything in a skirt."

"And I've also seen Dave getting phone numbers from multiple women. What's their deal?" commented Amy.

At that point, they saw Hunter pulling out a pen and a piece of paper identical to the one that Rob had just used.

"Stop right there!" Rachel yelled loudly at Hunter from across the table. "You're all just a bunch of cheapskate playas, and you"— she pointed at Hunter—"are not going to get Nikki's phone number. I've been watching you guys all evening busily collecting girls' phone numbers like it's some kind of game. Are you keeping score, or is each one a score?" she demanded, standing up as Amy and Kim rose with her.

"What?" said Nikki. "That's not true, is it?" She looked at Hunter with indecision.

"Come on, Nikki. Stand up," urged Kim. "Rachel's right. You shouldn't give this jerk your phone number. You don't need another dirtbag in your life right now."

"Hey, wait a minute! Where do you get off calling Hunter a dirtbag?" Rob yelled, also standing up.

Reaching for Nikki's hand, Rachel told her emphatically, "They are all jerks who'll say anything to get a girl's number. And if you look at the type of slutty girls they're after, I'm sure they only want one thing. Isn't that *right*, Rob?" Turning to look at him, Rachel added, "I even heard you now lying to that girl over there, telling her you're a doctor! *Really?* A cheapskate doctor that asks for money after offering to buy you a drink."

Dave jumped into the fray, adding in a placating tone, "Yes, we *really* are doctors! We just finished our residencies today, so we're kinda broke, but we are all officially doctors now. We're celebrating, that's all."

"Celebrating!" Rachel squawked. "You're celebrating by trying to bone as many women as possible!" Looking back over her shoulder as she tugged Nikki away, Rachel yelled, "Creeps!"

Calling after them into the noisy club, Rob angrily yelled, "What of it? It's our business what we do! I've scored a long list of numbers, and I didn't ask for yours, did I?" As he sat back down, he muttered, "Wouldn't want to bang her anyway!"

Then Nikki broke free of Rachel's hold and went back to Hunter. "Is any of this true?" she asked him.

Hunter paused, too long in Nikki's opinion, and finally said, "Well, yes. It's just a stupid game, that's all." Reaching out a hand, he pleaded, "Let me explain. It's…"

But he was too late. This time it was Nikki who stomped away, and she didn't look back again.

Trying to lighten Nikki's mood, Rachel said, "It's okay… There are other fish in the sea, as the saying goes."

All the girls nodded, except Nikki, who said, "It sucks! He really is so cute."

"Yeah, they're all hotties," Kim agreed. "But they are also jerks. Imagine passing themselves off as doctors. Really…that's so lame!"

And this time even Nikki agreed. Turning to Rachel, she said, "Thank you so much for watching my back."

"That's what friends are for." Hugging Nikki, Rachel added,

"Actually it was kind of fun...outing them. Just wish I could tell all the unsuspecting girls on those lists what jerks those guys really are."

As they gathered their stuff, Nikki took one last look back at Hunter and cried, "Look at them! They're already hitting on another group of girls!"

It was true. As they turned to look, they could see Rob inviting another group of three pretty young women over to their table—and he already had his pen and paper in hand!

In disgust, Amy said, "Let's get out of here. Didn't I tell you that this place is just a pickup joint? You can't meet nice guys here."

The girls nodded in agreement as Rachel said, "You were right. This club is a regular petri douche!"

The girls laughed uproariously as they left the club together to head home.

However, Nikki continued to think about Hunter—he was just so gorgeous—but she was also aware of how close she had come to getting involved with another loser. *Wow, my jerk-dar really isn't good. Thank heavens for friends who watch out for me.* Even though the night hadn't turned out well, Nikki didn't regret deciding to give herself a makeover. In the future, she would just have to be more discerning about who she enticed with her "in with the new" look, that was all.

3

IN WITH THE NEW...LINGERIE

WHILE NIKKI WAS GLAD that Rachel had saved her from a guy on the make, she moped around about it the rest of the weekend. So on Monday, Rachel talked Nikki into some lunchtime retail therapy, and they all met at a fancy lingerie store.

"I've never shopped here before," Nikki said. "But I'm thinking I need some new undies. I'm trying to change my style to be flashier, more noticeable. I might as well make my lingerie sexier too."

"Well, this is the place to go for glamorous, risqué stuff. We'll help you pick something out," Kim said, picking up a flaming, red-and-black lacy number that sparkled with little crystals. "This would look great on you," she added, holding it out to Nikki.

"Oh, no! Really, that's way more out there than I was thinking," Nikki responded.

"At least try it on," Rachel urged. "Doesn't cost anything to try it on."

"What about this set?" Amy offered, holding up a black bra and underwear pairing that was skimpy but not as racy.

"Sure that's nice too, but if you want something truly hot, then that's the real deal," Rachel said, pointing at what Kim held.

In the dressing room Nikki first tried on the black set. Looking in the mirror, she could see that it was certainly a step up from her old, white-cotton "mommy-boughts." Longingly she touched the striking lingerie still on the hanger. The set was so pretty. The red and black lace was gorgeous and so rocking sexy! *What the hell*, Nikki challenged herself as she hurriedly tried them on before changing her mind.

Yes, this is the real thing. Nikki turned this way and that in the mirror, fingering the sparkly little crystals that hung between her breasts. Why go half measures? Anyway, it wasn't like anyone would actually see them, she realized, but she would know that under her work clothes she looked fabulous. As she rotated before the mirror, she saw that the matching hip-hugger panties were also flattering.

As Nikki emerged from the dressing room, she saw only Kim waiting for her. "It's going to be a while," Kim said. "Rachel's got a lot of items to try on, and Amy had to rush back to work for a meeting."

Looking at what Nikki held in her hand, Kim added, "Good for you. You're going to buy them, right?"

"Yes, but that's not all… I'd like to tell you something, but keep it to yourself, okay?"

"Sure, of course. What is it?"

Nikki whispered, "You know I'm making lots of changes to my looks and to other things…like how assertive I am at work." Kim nodded. "Well, my annual girlie-parts exam is coming up, and I decided I'm going to get a birth control prescription. I don't know why, but it makes me a little anxious thinking about asking my doctor for it…but it's high time I joined the modern world."

"Nikki, you shouldn't worry about asking the doctor. That's what they're there for, but…Ben was a huge jerk and I hope that his bullying didn't influence your decision," Kim said with concern.

"No, it most definitely doesn't have anything to do with him. It's just something I want to do for me as part of my full makeover, inside and out. I've even heard that with the new pills you can eliminate having your period all together. I would love that!"

"Good! I'm glad to hear it," responded Kim, giving her friend a quick hug. "I know there is a special guy out there for you. I just know it. And for that matter, there's one for me too!"

After they exited the store with three matching lingerie bags in their hands, the girlfriends walked back to work. It was a beautiful spring day in the bustling city, and they were young, carefree women starting out in their careers with a lot to look forward to.

Inside, Nikki thought that her transformation from not-quite-a-wallflower to outgoing sophisticate was coming along nicely. She felt her confidence growing. She knew life would hold surprises for her, both good and bad, and she was eager to meet them head-on.

4

CAN IT GET ANY
MORE EMBARRASSING?

A COUPLE WEEKS LATER, Nikki scheduled an appointment with Dr. Lisa Porter, her regular gynecologist. Nikki was very comfortable with her doctor, having decided long ago that she would only see a female ob-gyn. The appointments were unpleasant enough already without having a strange man staring at her down there.

Upon her arrival, Nikki signed in and a nurse, someone new she had not met before, showed her to the standard tiny, cold exam room. The nurse left her with the usual instructions to strip down to nothing and cover herself with a sheet. After the nurse left, Nikki began undressing and then remembered she had worn her new set of sexy lingerie that day.

Earlier that morning Nikki had seen the items lying in her underwear drawer, unworn and still brand-new. In that instant, she'd decided to wear them, even though she had no boyfriend to see them. If she was truly going to be this new modern woman, she could wear whatever she wanted underneath. It was her business and no one else's. Feeling secretly pretty and sexy would surely boost her confidence too.

And it did! For most of the morning, Nikki felt edgy and slightly naughty, like she was a risk-taker. Later, as things got busy, she forgot about her underwear. The glamorous, sexy feel became just part of her transformation into a cosmopolitan, confident, and outgoing woman, and she was already getting positive feedback. Her boss had called Nikki aside after a staff meeting and told her how he had appreciated her input and that he was glad she was becoming more forthright in her position at the company.

Now, however, Nikki felt momentary embarrassment at seeing her body in the risqué lingerie, but she tried to shrug it off. *What the hell!*

I'm a twenty-six-year-old career woman. It's not like it is black leather—just a few sparkles and lace. So to prove she was comfortable with her choices, Nikki hung them on top of her outerwear in plain sight on the two wall hooks, rather than hiding them underneath as she usually would with her old white undies. Wrapping the sheet around her naked body, she giggled slightly, laughing at herself for her foolishness. Surely, Lisa had seen it all and more, Nikki realized about Dr. Porter.

After sitting down on the cold exam table with its annoying rustling paper, Nikki thought about how she hated these gynecologic appointments and how she got anxious every time while she waited alone wrapped in a thin sheet. Maybe next time she would bring her cozy blanket from home. Wouldn't that be funny? But why not? She was always cold, and the room was so barren and unpleasant with nothing on the walls except charts displaying intimate body parts or things Nikki didn't want to be reminded about, such as various infections or STDs.

Then there were the stirrups! *What evil man had invented that humiliating contraption?* she thought with a grimace. Nikki always detested that part of the exam. At least her doctor put little warm socky-things over the metal and, again, at least she was a woman. It would be doubly humiliating to glance down and see a man's face peering at her vajayjay, she mused.

Nikki really liked her kind doctor and almost thought of her as a friend. Who knows? Maybe someday this same woman would be delivering her babies—that is, if she ever met a guy nice enough to marry. She'd had a string of casual boyfriends throughout her NYU years, nothing serious. Who would have thought it would be so hard to meet nice guys after college? However, it was proving difficult for all her friends.

Sitting on the table and getting colder by the minute, Nikki continued to stew over how to go about meeting someone special. Amy had been right—a pickup bar was not the place to meet nice guys.

The wait seemed especially lengthy today, exacerbating her usual anxiety about gynecologic appointments. Adding to her unease, Nikki was uncomfortable about asking for a birth control prescription and just wanted it over with. *I'm an adult,* she reminded herself. *I shouldn't be embarrassed to ask for this or anything that I need.* Gathering her fortitude, Nikki resolved to speak confidently, without any mumbling—just as she had voiced her opinion in the staff meeting earlier this morning.

"It's really taking a long time… What's the holdup today?" she said aloud, frustrated.

Then finally the door opened and in walked a doctor, but it was not Dr. Porter—and even more startlingly, it was a young guy! A couple thoughts flashed through Nikki's mind almost simultaneously: she only saw women gynecologists, and who the heck is this guy anyway at this all-female practice?

The man was looking down at her file, she could see, and even as he continued to peruse her chart, he said, "Welcome, Ms. Woods. I'm Dr. Sterling. The nurse will be joining us in just a mo—"

"*It's you!* What are you doing here?" Nikki shrieked.

Clutching the sheet tighter to her body, she realized that this was the same guy who had hit on her at Club X. Hunter looked a little different—more professional in his white lab coat. But it was him, alright.

Dr. Sterling stuttered in response, "Ah, um, I'm filling in for…" But his words trailed to a dead stop when he recognized the young woman he had tried, but failed, to hook up with a couple weeks ago. She was sitting there looking just as pretty and all, but gift-wrapped for him in a too-thin sheet. After clearing his throat, he looked her in the eye and attempted his most professional tone, saying, "I'm filling in for Dr. Porter who is sick."

Then after another glance at his clipboard, he continued. "It says here that you came in for a birth-control prescription. We…ah, usually do a full exam before…" and again he trailed off into silence as his eyes strayed to her perky nipples, which were on display through the thin fabric.

Nikki felt such acute mortification that she assumed she was blushing beet red, probably all the way from her face to her chest, but she refused to let herself look down to check. Then she spied her racy underwear displayed on the wall, and she tried desperately to figure a way that she could surreptitiously reach over and cover it up. Almost at the same moment, she saw Hunter's face blanch when he realized that he was staring at her breasts. Suddenly, he glanced back at Nikki's face, and then his eyes started anxiously shifting around the room, looking at everything but her.

"Umm," he started again.

No, no, no, Nikki silently entreated, but she was too late.

"The standard practice is to do a full exam before…" This time he ended with a guttural choking sound as his eyes locked on the very red, very sexy, lace underthings hanging at eye level just a few feet from his face, seemingly there for his personal perusal and enjoyment. At that point, Hunter just gave up trying to talk and seemed physically unable to take his eyes off the naughty, hot things. Leaning even closer, mesmerized, he stared at the dangling bright crystals on the bra that twinkled slightly in the light.

What is he thinking? Nikki asked herself. *Why is he just standing there staring at my underwear? Why won't he look away, for heaven's sake! Could this get any more embarrassing?* she wondered frantically.

Yes, it could! Suddenly a tingling awareness swept through Nikki, making her shiver. She was still attracted to Hunter—he was too damned handsome—and even in her mortification, she felt her nipples constrict into tighter buds. She realized that she still wanted him, even as she silently entreated, *Please, please, please stop looking at my underwear.* She was in a state of disbelief—at herself. How could she be so embarrassed and so hotly aroused at the same time? Nikki panicked, frantically trying to figure out how she could make this misery end.

"This isn't going to work! I thought this was an all-female practice. Isn't there a woman I can see?" she blurted out.

It seemed like it took every ounce of his willpower to fight the allure of her sexy lingerie, but he slowly turned to face Nikki, while also quickly dropping his chart to hold it awkwardly in front of his pelvis. He stared fixedly into her eyes, although it seemed to Nikki as if the sexy display on the wall still called to him.

"I'm, ah, sorry… I was just hired. I'm the first male doctor here," Hunter muttered. "It's my first day, and I'm covering lunch and also filling in for Dr. Porter, who's sick. The nurse should have told you, but if you're willing to wait a short while longer, Dr. Jones...Dr. Brenda Jones will be back from lunch."

At Nikki's nod, the young doctor turned to leave, still holding his chart in front of him like a shield.

"Wait," Nikki said, halting his progress out the door. "What were you guys really doing the other night? Was I just one more number on your list of conquests?"

Turning back, Hunter said regretfully, "I'm sorry about that. It wasn't my idea. Actually it was my roommate Rob's plan. He's kind of a jerk. We were celebrating finishing our residencies, but I only went along with it...getting a couple numbers...'cause the guys were ribbing me. I didn't plan to call any of them, well except for you, that is. And I didn't plan to see how many I could, umm, have sex with either, no matter what Rob's plan was." He paused but she didn't say anything.

Turning to leave again, he added, "I'll get the nurse to set you up with Dr. Jones. Again, sorry about this...about all of it."

She still didn't respond, so Hunter walked out and shut the door behind him, leaving her sitting there, still shocked and mortified.

Nikki realized she had been holding her breath and let it out in a whoosh. *Should I just leave?* she wondered, feeling defeated. *No! I'm going to get what I came here for!* After a few minutes, the nurse entered and let her know that Dr. Jones had come back from lunch early so Nikki would not have to wait too long. She also apologized for not telling Nikki about Dr. Sterling. She was filling in for a nurse on maternity leave and didn't realize Nikki only saw Dr. Porter.

After the nurse left, Nikki stood up, still wrapped in the sheet, and discreetly covered her lingerie. She would stick it out and get her prescription, but she realized she would blush bright red every time she saw the risqué items hanging there, especially when she remembered Hunter's stunned but hungry expression.

Finally, much later than she had planned, Nikki finished her exam and left the office.

She was both relieved and a little disappointed that she didn't see Hunter again before leaving the clinic. After that crazy night at the bar, she hadn't expected to ever see him again, but now she realized what a missed opportunity it had been. He's a doctor! And also he seemed, nice, available, and even interested in her...or *was* anyway, she thought with a sigh.

Heading back to the office after the rather long lunch, Nikki tried to dispel her gloomy mood with the thought that her friends were going to find this whole incident highly amusing. It would be the biggest dish of the month.

HER FRIENDS DEMAND THE DISH

AND SHE WAS RIGHT. Kim didn't take long to ask her how the appointment went—did she get what she wanted? Nikki responded mysteriously that she got or didn't get *way more* than she had planned, but said that she'd wait to tell all when the girls could get together. She really didn't want to have to tell this outrageous story more than once.

Hearing that Nikki had something delectable to dish, Rachel, Amy, and Kim rearranged their plans so they could meet for lunch the next day. They went to their favorite spot and were lucky to get a table in the back corner, their favorite place to chat privately and people-watch at the same time. The girls listened avidly as Nikki told her tale. First she shared that the three handsome Club X guys really were brand-new doctors, and then she explained in great detail the humiliating encounter.

When she finished, Nikki looked down morosely at her food and stirred her salad. It was the juiciest topic they'd had in a while, so the other three women excitedly chattered on about it, but Nikki still felt down about the missed opportunity. She also remembered how hot and bothered she'd felt when Hunter stared at her so intensely.

"That's incredible! I can't believe the dumb luck of having him walk in on you sitting there naked," said Amy, cutting in on Nikki's reverie.

"I was wrapped in a sheet," Nikki countered. "But…it was so thin. It felt like I was practically naked," she admitted.

"I can't believe they really *are* all doctors. Jerks, but still real, bona fide *doctors*!" said Rachel as a calculating look crossed her face.

Defending Hunter, Nikki explained, "It was all Rob's idea, and Hunter wasn't planning on calling the girls on his list. Well, except for me."

"That's what he told you?" Kim asked. "Do you believe him?"

"Well, yes I do," Nikki responded. "Oh, I don't know."

"What I want to know is why Hunter held your file in front of him like you described," Amy said. "That sounds so strange."

"Are you fucking kidding!" exclaimed Rachel as Kim and even Nikki started laughing. "Sometimes you can be so clueless."

"What! What's so funny?" Amy looked from one friend to another in confusion.

"I guess we need to spell it out for you," Kim said as Nikki started to blush.

With a conspiratorial grin, Rachel leaned over the table and then in a loud stage whisper, she dished, "Hunter got a big, bad boner looking at naked Nikki and her naughty knickers."

Again the girls laughed, and Kim added, "He was probably imagining how sexy she would look in them."

"Oh!" said a chagrined Amy. "Of course. How silly of me, but how embarrassing for you, Nikki. I'm sure you'll be happy if you don't ever see *him* again for the rest of your life."

Nikki's laughing smile disappeared from her face. "I don't know. It seems like such a missed opportunity, and now I'll never know if Hunter and I could have hit it off."

"Look," said Rachel, feeling a little guilty about the role she'd played in stopping them from hooking up at the club. "Hunter was going along with their skanky contest, so he can say anything now, but he had a list of numbers too, didn't he?"

Reassuring her friend, Kim said, "Don't worry, Nikki. As the saying goes, there are more fish in the sea."

But Nikki wished she hadn't let this one get away.

~ 6 ~
CARPE FISH

OVER THE NEXT WEEK, Nikki stewed about her lost fish. Finally an idea began to form, and she discussed it with Rachel during a quick lunchroom chat at the office.

"I really want to give Hunter another try, but I know he'll never call me, even if he still wants to," Nikki told her friend.

"Why not? If he's really interested, let him pursue you," Rachel advised.

"Well, let's see… Let me count the reasons." Nikki held up her hand and counted on three fingers. "For one thing, he doesn't have my number. Two, he probably thinks I'm in a relationship since I was there to get the pill. And three, he would never approach me now that I'm a patient."

"Hmmm," said Rachel. "You didn't actually get examined by him, so technically you really aren't his patient. That reason doesn't count."

Continuing, Rachel added, "There are many reasons a woman might get a birth control prescription, and a doctor would know that, so don't assume he thinks you have a boyfriend. But…there is the issue of him not having your number. I suppose he could get it from patient records, but even I wouldn't do something that unethical just to get a hookup. So, yeah, you're probably right. Hunter won't call."

Both women stopped talking, contemplating what could be done about it. Then Nikki leaned in toward her friend with anxious excitement. "Ever since I broke up with Ben, I've decided to make some changes in my life—take more risks, be more outgoing, dress to shine, not hide."

"I've seen your most excellent adjustments. You look great, and remember how the boss liked your new attitude," Rachel said encouragingly. "We sisters have to use what we've got, both our brains and beauty, then add some bling-bling…and sell it! Otherwise the guys get all the promotions at work."

"And all the fun after work too," Nikki agreed. "So, maybe I should call Hunter myself and ask *him* out," she announced with growing enthusiasm. "I've decided that it's time for some carpe diem in my life."

"Carp?" Rachel exclaimed. "What have fish got to do with it?"

"Not fish, Rachel. Carpe diem…it means seize the day, take charge. I've been remembering my ancient lit classes lately," Nikki said. A self-conscious smile spread across her face as she once again imagined Hunter as a Greek god in full Adonis getup and her as his Aphrodite.

"Anyway, that's what I'm going to do—take a chance and call Hunter, rather than waiting around to see if he ever tries to contact me. That's what a twenty-first-century woman should do!" Nikki finished with growing confidence.

"You go, girl!" said Rachel. "Do it today."

"Oh, well, I don't know. It's a busy day at work, maybe tom—"

Cutting her off, Rachel urged again, "Do it today! Now, before you change your mind. You can use the boss's office for privacy since he's out sick today."

Heading out of the lunchroom, Nikki said with a little less self-assurance, "Oh, okay. Why not get it over with? I'm just going to leave a message for him anyway."

As they walked down the hall, Nikki felt Rachel give her an encouraging pat on the shoulder. She started to feel a little queasy. Maybe it was the day-old leftovers she had for lunch, Nikki thought, but who was she kidding? Being a modern take-charge woman took courage, and hers seemed to be abandoning her rather quickly. Following Rachel into the boss's office, she shut the door. Using her cell, Nikki found the doctor's office number in her contacts and hit dial. As it started to ring, she quickly hung up on the call.

"What's wrong?" asked Rachel.

Motioning her friend to leave, Nikki said, "Go on. I'm not doing this with an audience."

"Okay, but don't chicken out or I'll make the call for you." Rachel winked at her before shutting the door.

7

CASTING THE HOOK

NIKKI TAPPED ON THE number again and waited nervously as the phone rang. Expecting the receptionist to take a message, Nikki was startled when she realized that she was being put through to Hunter. Before she could hang up, Nikki heard his familiar deep voice.

"Hello. This is Doctor Sterling. How can I help you?"

"Ahh, umm. This is Nikki Woods. We met a week or so ago at Club X…and again in the exam room last week."

Sounding extremely polite, Hunter replied, "Yes, I remember you, of course. I want to apologize again for not being as professional as I would have liked. I…was just caught by surprise. Actually, to be completely honest, you were about the last person on earth I expected to see sitting there waiting…" He trailed off.

After taking a deep breath, Nikki plunged ahead. "No, I'm not calling about that mess. It was embarrassing all around. I think we can agree on that."

She paused to take another calming breath, but Hunter jumped in, "Well then, was there a problem with the prescription? I'm sure Dr. Porter will be glad to—"

"No! Not that!" Nikki emphatically interrupted him. "I mean, I am calling about something personal. I was…ah… Well, you and I seemed to hit it off at the bar, but after what happened, you never got my number. I hope you don't mind being called at work, but I was wondering if you would like to go out to dinner with me this Saturday night."

Nikki sat holding the phone to her ear during what seemed like a very long pause, although it was really only a couple seconds of silence. She felt defeated, assuming he was just trying to find a nice way to say no.

Eventually Hunter said, "I'd like that very much. I wanted to call you, but after seeing you as a patient—well, sort of a patient—I couldn't look up your number in the office records. That would probably get me fired or worse."

"Well, I decided that…you know…with women's equality and all, I could just call and invite you out myself, if you don't think I'm too forward or anything."

"No. This is terrific. Now I can stop being so angry at my room-mate Rob for that stupid game he was playing…that cost me getting your number in the first place."

Feeling for once like the outgoing, self-assured woman she wanted to be, Nikki closed the deal. "How 'bout we meet at Pizza Villa at seven thirty this Saturday night? It's in the Village just off Bleecker Street."

"Sounds good. I'll see you then. Bye," Hunter said.

As she put the phone down, Nikki felt pleased with herself and a little anxious too. She had snagged a date with a very hot guy, a doctor no less. Her mom would be thrilled. However, she would just have to put it out of her mind that Hunter had already seen her racy un-mentionables. On the other hand, that might spice up the evening, she thought with a grin.

8

THE FISH IS REELED IN

HUNTER PACED BACK AND forth in front of the pizza joint. He had already scoped out a corner spot inside the quiet, little place, but he felt way too restless to sit and wait for Nikki. He could hardly believe that she had actually called and asked him on a date, in spite of everything that had happened. After trying for days to figure out how he could ethically get Nikki's phone number, he had all but given up.

Then, after his embarrassing display in the exam room, Hunter wasn't sure there was any point in even trying. He'd never lost control like that before, but knowing she was naked underneath the sheet, combined with that suggestive display of her sexy panties, had been too much. It had done him in! Hunter had spent the rest of that day trying to get it and her out of his mind. There was no frigging way he could do his job—his particular type of work—with a hard-on!

And that didn't even take into account how much he liked her as a person. They had really hit it off at the club, and their interrupted conversation had played in his mind over and over as he had tried to figure out how to connect with her again. *Damn Rob and his stupid games!* Although he wanted to blame Rob for it all, Hunter grudgingly acknowledged that he had gone along with the contest, if somewhat halfheartedly. They had treated all those girls like nothing more than conquests, even if he hadn't planned on trying to get into their pants… well, except for maybe one of them.

Hunter nodded absentmindedly to another passerby, a lady who had smiled at him when she saw the small bouquet of flowers in his hand. A man with flowers seemed to be a spectacle, either a romantic or a pansy, depending on whether a woman or a man walked by him. He checked the time on his cell phone for the tenth time, but it was his own fault for getting there twenty minutes early.

Finally, Hunter spied her walking toward him. His eyes were immediately drawn to her gorgeous long, shapely legs and sexy, spike-heeled pumps displayed beneath her short skirt. As Nikki drew closer, Hunter noticed the seductive sway of her hips in the tight attire, and he let his eyes travel up to her chest before finally landing on her face. *Shit!* She was watching him ogle her body. Hadn't he been down that road already? She was smiling at him, so Hunter guessed she didn't mind too much.

"Hi, these are for you," he said, smiling down at her.

"Thank you so much. How thoughtful of you." He watched Nikki sink her face into the soft blooms and deeply inhale their scent. For some reason, her actions looked incredibly erotic, and he sucked in his breath.

Hunter opened the door for Nikki and followed her into the restaurant. Over a pizza and some beer, they got to know each other. Each of them could tell that they were mutually attracted, but the turmoil over their first meeting and embarrassment over the second were stifling their attempts at conversation. Hunter realized the date was going nowhere fast, but he was stuck in his own little hell.

He had been sitting there trying to think of something to say, anything at all that might get his mind off what he was picturing. Watching her across the table, Nikki looked very pretty, and her tight black top accentuated her nice chest, but Hunter was distracted by images of what Nikki might have on underneath. Was she wearing the incredibly sexy red-and-black items he had seen hanging in the exam room? Or did she have something even hotter beneath her fairly modest clothes? Hunter had spent the last fifteen minutes trying not to look down at her breasts or think about her panties, but that had made his dick hard and his mind mush.

Hunter remembered his embarrassment during the abbreviated exam with Nikki. It wasn't like that had been his first one. He had been examining women patients for much of his four-year residency, and it wasn't even his first appointment that day. So what was it about this girl that had his mind wrapped up in knots? He had thought she was cute at Club X, and when they talked, Hunter had realized he wanted to ask her out. But then all that chaos about scoring girls' numbers had ruined it. He had thought it was a lost opportunity, and here he was blowing it again. He had to stop thinking about her underwear!

"Excuse me, did you hear me?" asked Nikki, leaning toward him with a vaguely irritated look on her face.

"Oh, I'm sorry," responded Hunter, sitting up a little straighter. "I guess my mind wandered. Please say it again."

"I want to ask you a personal question. Actually, my friend Rachel is the one hounding me to find out, but I guess I'm curious too."

"What do you want to know?" he asked.

"I said, that… Well, it's really none of my business, but could you tell me why you chose to become a gynecologist? I mean, it's not really a guy thing like…oh, I don't know, sports medicine or even heart surgery. Rachel said that it's because you want to…ah…look at girls' vajayjays all day," Nikki said, repeating her friend's words and blushing bright red. "I asked it nicer the first time but you weren't listening." Then she studied her salad as if it was the most interesting thing she had ever seen.

Hunter tried to hide his discomfort with her question, knowing it wasn't for the reason she would think.

"I have been teased mercilessly by my friends about this, so I hope you won't laugh when I tell you," he said. "I don't really want to be a gynecologist. I want to deliver babies, and if you study obstetrics, you also get gynecology. Since I just joined this practice, I don't have any OB patients yet but hopefully soon."

"Oh, that's interesting. Nice, really," she said, smiling now. "What made you want to deliver babies?"

Hunter wanted her full attention so he took hold of her hand and looked her directly in the eye. He wanted to see her reaction to his explanation. Would she think it sappy too, like his buddies?

"I have already delivered one baby all by myself, and that's why I want to focus on obstetrics. It was my second year in med school, and I hadn't been able to figure out what area of medicine interested me. I was riding the bus to the hospital for my rotation, and a woman went into labor. Actually she was far along and had the baby right there on the bus. I had done an EMT rotation, and I was the closest thing she had to a doctor so I helped her deliver the baby, a little boy. It was life changing for me."

Sitting back, Hunter let go of her hands and asked, "Does that seem silly to you? I had no interest in that field and suddenly I knew it was what I wanted."

Nikki reached back and gently squeezed his hands, murmuring, "No, that sounds really very sweet." But as she thought of Rachel's distrust again and how she'd been hurt in the past, Nikki pulled her hands away and asked, "This isn't just a line, is it? It sounds so fantastic. Why wasn't an ambulance called?"

"Well, if you want the full story... I learned some of it after the fact. Here goes," Hunter said, taking a swig of his beer before continuing.

"The woman, Daniela was her name... It was her first child, and she was having a bad day. She'd lost her cell phone that morning, misplaced it really, and then she felt some labor pains when she was out shopping and went home where her water broke. She left a message for her husband but didn't reach him...told him to meet her at the hospital. The couple had, like, no money so Daniela figured she would use her bus pass to ride the bus to the hospital. It was a short ride and it was her first baby so she thought she had many hours to go. It doesn't make sense in hindsight, but then again, I suppose if you're in labor, you might not always be thinking straight."

"Go on. What happened then?" asked Nikki, realizing this couldn't be a fabrication. It was too crazy to be made-up and something she could easily verify, thanks to the Internet.

"Well, I was sitting there and she started moaning, then doubling over and almost screaming. I could see she was gripping the seat like her life depended on it. I quickly said I was a med student and asked if I could help her. 'I'm going to have a baby *right now*,' she yelled at me. I told her that I'd get an ambulance there. 'Someone call 911!' I yelled, and she moaned, 'It's too late. The baby's coming. I can feel it, NOW!' Then she let out a loud, pain-filled scream and the bus driver pulled the bus over."

Hunter took another sip of beer and watched Nikki closely. Her worshipful gaze made his heart tighten with pleasure.

"From there, things happened quickly. The driver got everyone off the bus as I laid her down on a seat and washed my hands with sanitizer someone handed me. And then like magic or more like a miracle, there was this baby's head crowning and I eased it into the world. The little baby boy started crying immediately, and the passengers outside the bus cheered. I used a tissue to clean the little face and a passenger handed in a something—a shawl, I think—and I wrapped the baby up tightly and handed him to the mother.

"I didn't try to do anything more. I could hear the ambulance siren wailing and decided to wait for professionals to do the rest. The baby and mom were safe, and I had that feeling of accomplishment, of being an important part of that phenomenal moment. From that point on, what I wanted to focus on in medicine was settled."

"That's such a sweet story, amazing really!" said Nikki, smiling brightly with the sparkle of unshed tears in her eyes. "Why would your friends tease you about it? I would think they'd be envious of you knowing so clearly what you want to do with your life. Why, I'd think the story would even come in handy to impress your dates."

"Actually, I haven't really shared it much. You're the first woman on a date with me that I have told about it."

"I'm glad you told me," Nikki said. Her smile dazzled him.

"Afterward, I became a bit of a celebrity at med school. I got to ride in the ambulance because Daniela wanted me there with her, holding her hand. And the next day there was a notice in the papers, but what meant the most to me is that they gave their child my name as his middle name. Gabriel Hunter is now almost seven, and I've even been to a couple of his birthday parties. I know I won't have that kind of connection with all the babies I'll deliver, but still each one will be a little miracle. That's why I don't tell the story much. It's too personal."

After taking another drink of his beer, he added, "That's probably also why my friends teased me. It's too much for most guys, easier to just poke fun. What do you think?"

"What do I think about what?" Nikki asked, still a little dreamy-eyed.

"Is that a dumb reason to choose a career?"

"Oh no, not at all. It sounds like you just knew then what you wanted to do. I'm twenty-six and I still don't really know what I want to do with my life. I would like a good job that pays well, but I can't say I have a calling. I wish I did," Nikki said. Realizing she was still holding his hand, she gave it a little squeeze. "Thank you for sharing your story with me."

Hunter then asked Nikki about her job and her career goals and listened attentively while she talked about her recent push for more responsibility at work. After that, they quickly developed an easy camaraderie and discovered things they had in common, such as a love of movies and going to the beach. Finally, realizing they had lingered over their pizza for three hours, Hunter offered to escort her home. It was the least he could do, he said, since Nikki refused to let him pay for dinner.

"After all," she pointed out, "I asked you out."

At the door to her apartment building, they lingered and talked more all the while holding hands and looking into each other's eyes. Hunter gently caressed her hand, making small swirling circles with his thumb on the soft pad of her palm. Nikki seemed as aroused as he was, her eyes dilated and her breath coming in short little pants. He very much wanted to kiss her and hoped she would let him. Nikki swayed toward him, and his arm came around to support the small of her back, gently pulling her against his body.

"May I kiss you good night?" he asked in a low, husky voice.

"Mmm, yes," she replied, melting into him and tilting her face upward.

His heart pounding, Hunter slowly lowered his mouth to meet hers, just the gentlest sweeping touch upon her lips. His breath caught in his throat as he stood wanting and needing more. Deepening the kiss, Hunter crushed her tightly to him and stroked her lips with his tongue. He was burning with desire and wondered for perhaps the hundredth time this evening if she was wearing those so-sexy underthings. Oh, how he would love to see them on her, to slowly peel them off her body and explore her with his tongue. Thinking that he was getting dangerously carried away, he started to pull back, but then Nikki parted her lips and welcomed his kiss into her mouth. Hunter pulled her even more tightly to him.

He could taste Nikki now, the subtle flavor of her mixed with the tangy beer they had consumed with dinner. The press of her breasts to his chest, her peaked nipples pressing into him, sent a shooting thrill throughout his body. His hand ached to reach up and caress her there. Before he got carried away, Hunter started to release her, but Nikki reached up and put her arms around his neck, pulling him back to her and deepening the kiss.

It felt so good, so hot. Hunter reveled in the sensations and the awareness that this gorgeous woman wanted him as much as he wanted her. His bulging erection pressed into her belly, and he could barely stop himself from rubbing it against her. Instead, he ended the kiss and stepped firmly away, feeling unstable, as if he might lose control and yank her back, and then nothing would be able to stop him from finishing what they were starting. He needed to get away quickly. He didn't want to ruin things now.

"This was a terrific evening. Thank you," Hunter said, turning away quickly, worried that Nikki might try to restart the kiss. Very much wanting her to do just that.

"I enjoyed it too. Bye," Nikki responded, still leaning toward him.

"Thank you again. I'll call you soon," he called as he resolutely walked away.

Hunter felt young and carefree with an exciting new career to focus on, so he was not thinking about settling down. However, he didn't want Nikki to think he was just out for a quick fuck. Better to take it slowly than risk their budding friendship, especially after such a crazy, rocky start.

9

LANDING HIM
(A.K.A. BONING THE FISH)

BACK INSIDE HER APARTMENT, Nikki felt both relief and also some regret that the kiss did not go further. She had been very close to inviting him in, before Hunter had dropped his arms and stepped back. She was extremely aroused—her body tingling all over, especially down there, and Nikki could tell she was wet. All of her past feelings of inadequacy or previous hurts were gone, she realized. She wanted to explore this man, wanted to feel his warm, naked body against hers, and she had been ready to do so right now, this evening.

She predicted that sex with Hunter would be amazing, but what if she had done that and then he never called her again? Then she would definitely regret having slept with him. With satisfaction, Nikki realized that she had accomplished what she had set out to do. She had invited a cute guy out to dinner as a modern woman should be able to do, and the evening had gone very well. She had seized the day and wouldn't regret it one bit, whether he ever called her again or not. Well, who was she kidding? Of course she would be unhappy if Hunter didn't call her, but Nikki felt fairly sure that she would hear from him again sometime soon.

The next day at lunch, the three friends wanted to hear all about the date. In her usual loudmouth style, Rachel latched on to the fact that Hunter didn't pay, even though Nikki said repeatedly that he had offered, had even pulled out money but she refused it.

However, even Rachel was left without her usual retort after hearing the story of why Hunter had chosen his career. Amy thought it was all quite dreamy. Nikki wondered again how long she would wait before she got to see Hunter again. Carpe diem or not, she wasn't going to appear so needy that she called him again. It was his turn now.

She had steeled herself to wait at least a week before hearing from him, so Nikki was thrilled when Hunter called her Monday evening to ask her out for Friday. He told her that he hoped she didn't mind, but he would like to have her over for a poor man's date—a home-cooked dinner in his apartment. He explained that his two roommates would be gone. Well, actually Dave was moving into his own place now that he was employed, and Rob would be out of town for the weekend. Hunter also told her that he had become a fairly decent cook over the years, a necessity since the others couldn't even boil water. She gladly accepted the invitation, thinking she would enjoy being alone with him rather than surrounded by strangers out in public.

The week dragged slowly by until finally Friday night arrived. Nikki took extra care with her looks. It was a casual date, but she still wanted to look her sexiest. Since it was a warm spring evening, she chose a skintight, stretchy miniskirt and a pretty top that draped loosely around her. She hesitated for a moment but then chose to wear her new lingerie set that would make her feel sexy on the inside too. Smiling to herself, she wondered if maybe tonight he would actually get to see it on her.

When Nikki arrived at Hunter's two-bedroom apartment, he gave her a quick tour of the place. It was bigger than what she and Kim shared, but it needed to be, given three guys were living there together for all four years of their residency. Now that Dave was gone, the main room was once again being used as a living room. While she pretended indifference, Nikki was most interested in seeing Hunter's bedroom. It was small but private and had a twin bed. She wondered if he made an effort to clean it up and make it look nice or if he always kept it that neat.

Interrupting her musings, Hunter told her, "I'm cooking a simple meal, just steak, salad, and baked potatoes. I can get a decent meal on the table but it's never fancy."

"That sounds terrific," Nikki responded. "I think it's great that you can cook at all." She left unsaid the fact that her last boyfriend had expected her to do all the cooking and then the cleanup too.

"Can I get you a cold beer?" he offered, and she accepted.

Taking the bottle, she joined him on the New Your City version of a balcony, the fire escape, where Hunter was cooking steaks on a small portable grill. It was a beautiful evening, and she enjoyed spending time alone with him.

"So how long have you been friends with Rob?" Nikki asked.

"I met Rob and Dave when we started our residencies. Rob already had a lease on this place, and the rent is really cheap. It's also fairly close to the hospital, so it worked well. He is not such a bad guy, really."

"I can give him the benefit of the doubt, but, honestly, Rachel really dislikes him. She's still talking about that silly contest."

"That was a stupid, stupid idea," Hunter noted aloud. "I still regret that I went along with it, but as I told you before, I didn't call any of the numbers I obtained and, of course, didn't sleep with any of them either."

Thinking about her friend, Nikki said, "You know that old saying, 'The lady doth protest too much'? I think perhaps Rachel is just annoyed that Rob didn't want her number. She noticed him the minute you all walked into the club."

"Interesting," Hunter pondered. "The way he kept looking at her, I think Rob definitely would have gotten around to asking for her number, but then things got so crazy," he finished with a grimace.

"Don't you dare tell Rob," she interrupted quickly. "Rachel is a good friend, and she'd never forgive me if he found out that she thought he was cute."

Laughing, Hunter grabbed Nikki playfully and gave her a quick kiss. "I won't say a thing. Believe me, I don't want to get in the middle of anything between those two hot-tempered people, even if Rob is a friend."

Nestling closer to him as they stood on the fire escape, she murmured agreement, "Mmmm, Yep. I only want you to get in the middle of me."

Nikki could hardly believe she had made that bold come-on, but it pleased her a great deal to hear Hunter's slight gasp in response.

Once the steaks were done, they ate dinner at the small table in the dining alcove. Again, Nikki saw touches that suggested Hunter was a romantic—candles adding a soft glow to the room and quiet classical music playing in the background. The simple meal was tasty, but even more delicious was the seductive talk they playfully engaged in with each other. After dinner, they moved with their beers to the sofa and sat down, close to each other but not quite touching. Hunter clinked his beer bottle against hers in a sort of toast.

"Here's to overcoming an unusually rough start to a friendship."

"I'll toast to that," Nikki agreed with a smile.

Their fingers bumped during the impromptu toast, and Nikki liked the physical contact with him, wanting more. Deciding to fight her natural reticence, she put her drink down and reached over to take hold of his hand. Hunter smiled at her and gently squeezed her hand in response.

"I'm still so pleased that you called me after that disaster at the doctor's office," Hunter said.

"It was one of the first actions of the new me...the new outgoing and brave me," she said with a hint of pride.

"Besides the fact that I didn't have your number...couldn't ethically get it from the office records either...there was also the little problem of my complete and utter humiliation," Hunter muttered, still holding her hand but now looking away with an embarrassed shrug.

"What do you mean *your* humiliation?" she countered. "I was the one who had her bra and panties hanging on display like that... I was so mortified! I don't know what I was thinking."

"Seeing your super-sexy underthings hanging there at eye level... Well, it was extremely arousing," he said huskily. "But that was also the cause of my problem. Didn't you notice that I had to hold your file down in front of me? I think you can guess why," he said with a crooked smile.

"Oh, yes, I do remember." She laughed. "The girls thought that was *very* funny!"

"No! You didn't tell them, did you?" he retorted.

"Mmm, sorry. I was so disappointed, thinking I'd never get to go on a date with you after that, so I guess I spilled the whole story," she said, only slightly apologetic. "But to be totally honest with you..." Nikki whispered. "Well, while it was awkward for me to sit there watching you stare at my underwear, I guess the real reason I was embarrassed was that I was, well…I was also aroused. As my…" Nikki stopped, terribly self-conscious now.

"Go on," he urged, looking a little stimulated himself.

"I was also aroused," she started again in a barely there whisper, not looking at him but down at her hand still holding his. "And I could feel my nipples tighten, and, umm, other things happening to my body, and then I was thinking that I couldn't let you examine me like *that*!"

Nikki glanced up as she heard his harshly inhaled breath. He now looked very aroused, she realized, and a part of her was pleased. That newly emerging sensual woman inside her was beginning to feel her power.

In a tight voice, Hunter said, "I hope you won't be offended, but in my wildest…or maybe weirdest…fantasies, I see the two of us fucking like crazy animals right there on that exam table. I know that it could never happen, but still the idea's a real turn-on, for me anyway."

"I can hardly believe I'm going to tell you this… I've had similar fantasies since that day in the clinic." Realizing that she wanted to tell Hunter her deepest naughty secrets, Nikki smiled deliciously. "I have pictured you ripping that thin sheet off me and climbing up to join me on that table to…"

Nikki stopped talking and Hunter squeezed her hand, looking expectantly at her. He clearly wanted her to finish the sentence.

Instead she asked, "Tell me something… Would *any* set of women's underwear do that to you?"

"I think you know the answer to that. I was attracted to you when I met you at the bar. Then seeing you gift-wrapped in a sheet sitting there waiting for me, and then those glittering panties and bra… It was incredibly sexy. You were incredibly sexy!" he said in a deep, husky voice. "I just can't stop thinking about how gorgeous you would look wearing them," Hunter declared.

Everything he told her was making Nikki feel beautiful as well as hot and bothered. On a whim, she couldn't resist pulling her top down off her shoulder just enough so that Hunter could see she wore the lingerie in question. Groaning sharply under his breath, he reached up to caress her bare shoulder.

Nikki felt relaxed, uninhibited, sexy—and she liked this newly sensual woman she was becoming. She leaned over to give him a little kiss on the lips, really just a peck, but the contact sent a sizzling electric jolt that went straight down to her core. Hunter lightly grabbed her arms as she started to pull away and brought her back for another longer, deeper kiss. Nikki tingled all over inside and pressed into him. Taking this as encouragement, Hunter gently pulled her onto his lap and encircled her with his arms.

Sitting there, she could feel his arousal as her hip pushed up against the hard bulge in his pants. In the past this might have embarrassed her a little. However, the new Nikki wasn't discomfited or shy. Instead, she wanted desperately to unzip his pants to finally see his erect penis. She wanted to touch it. Wondered what he would do or think if she were that bold.

She was secretly excited to realize she could do exactly what she wanted, but Nikki also acknowledged to herself that she had more growing to do. She was just not quite that daring…not *yet*. So, she settled for squirming a little on his lap to feel the bulge rub against her ass and was rewarded with a low guttural moan from Hunter even as he continued to kiss her. She opened her mouth at the insistence of his tongue, and they spent several hot minutes learning the taste and feel of each other while her hand caressed the back of his neck.

Nikki felt one of his hands slowly slide up her leg and then under her short skirt, pausing for a few seconds to caress the top of her thigh. His touch sent shivers skittering upward and she opened her legs a little, offering him access to her inner thighs. Hunter used his palm to touch as much skin as possible and ever so slowly inched his hand upward until it brushed the lacy fabric of her underpants. A moan erupted from the back of Nikki's throat as he swirled his tongue in her mouth to the same rhythm that he swirled his fingers on her pussy.

Nikki was consumed by the stimulating sensations. She felt liberated and wildly abandoned, which was fresh…exciting! She was not new to sex. She'd had several intimate relationships, but she had always held back a little, allowed her natural reticence to rein in her sensuality. She had always felt secure and comfortable that way, but now Nikki suddenly comprehended that this had also held her back, kept her from allowing her own sensuality to fully blossom.

She finally understood that this flowering was something she could control. No man could make it happen or take it away. She alone was responsible for deciding whether to fully explore all the pleasure that her body was capable of—and Nikki decided then and there that she wanted it, wanted all the exhilarating pleasure, every last bit of it! As these freeing ideas took shape in her mind, she felt a new eroticism erupt within her and a roiling, burning arousal like she had never felt before.

Moaning, Nikki arched back to raise her breasts until they were touching his chest through the fabric of their clothing, and she opened her legs wider, using both hands to hold his face tightly to her throughout their long, passionate kiss. Hunter's breathing became ragged, and although it seemed impossible, the bulge in his pants felt like it was growing bigger.

Nikki was now in a mindless state of sensual pleasure when Hunter suddenly broke the kiss and huskily begged, "I want to see you! I want you to take off your clothes."

"Ohh," moaned Nikki, slowly opening her erotically drugged eyes to look into his passionate gaze.

"I've just got to see you in your sexy underthings. It's driving me crazy! I know you'll look so fucking hot. Please!" he begged, staring pleadingly into her eyes.

Nikki was unsure, momentarily hesitating. This was not who she had been in the past—the wild, open lover—but it was who she wanted to be now. That's why she'd bought the sexy lingerie in the first place, although she hadn't anticipated that her lover would already know what she was wearing before she even undressed. *I hope he's not disappointed.* The thought flitted briefly through her mind, as Nikki accepted that she was now ready to become the courageously erotic woman she had always wished to be.

Looking back into his eagerly waiting eyes, Nikki nodded even as she wondered how she should undress. Should she just start wriggling out of her skirt on his lap or stand up or let him take the initiative? Nikki realized that she could do it anyway *she* wanted, be *anything* she wanted. She could even turn over all control to Hunter, if that was what she wished—and it freed her to boldly ask, "How would you like me to undress?"

Hunter pleaded, "Let me undress you. I'd like to be the one to slowly take your clothes off."

Nikki nodded her consent and waited, feeling both deliciously wicked and hotly aroused. Without speaking, Hunter slowly eased her off his lap and raised her up with him as he stood. Looking down at her, he bent his mouth to give her another searing kiss before stepping back a little. Looking at him, Nikki saw that Hunter was also filled with lust and holding tightly on to his control. Standing there waiting, she felt just a little anxiety mixed in with her excited spirits. Almost holding her breath, she awaited the big reveal. *What will he think? What will he do?* she wondered breathlessly.

Hunter reached out with both hands and grasped the bottom of her blouse to slowly pull it over her head and toss it aside. He gasped when he saw Nikki in her racy bra for the first time, and she felt naughty, displayed in front of him like a stripper. His eyes were fixated on her breasts, only barely covered in red and black lace. Reaching out a hand, he gently touched the sparkling crystal beads on the short tassel between her breasts, then dragged his finger slowly across the top edge of her bra, touching both the lace and her warm skin above.

"You look beautiful," he breathed, his eyes still on her breasts, "and so fucking hot! My own living sex toy. Please tell me that I can play with you."

Now Nikki gasped quietly as she reached out to grab his shoulder. Without support, she thought her legs might give out.

"Yes, I want you to come out to play," she whispered as her hand grazed across the hot bulge in his pants.

Sucking in his breath at her light touch, he bent down and placed a kiss on the tender skin just above her bra. Holding his shoulders tightly for support, she felt his tongue caress along the same path his finger had taken. Nikki could hear her moans becoming louder in the room as she felt his hands circle behind her body to slowly unzip her skirt. How could such a mundane task feel so erotic? Then Hunter pushed the skirt down and it slid over her hips to fall in a puddle at her feet.

Nikki froze, realizing she was now almost naked in front of him, but he reassured her, breathing out, "You're so beautiful."

Hunter dropped to his knees, startling her as she looked down to see his face just inches from her panties. He stared at her pelvis, and she saw him reach out a single finger to trace along her skin just above the waistband. Then she gasped again as she watched him lean forward and kiss her there, where his fingers had just been. His tongue licked caressingly along the same path. It felt wildly erotic, as her knees got weaker and she held on tighter to his shoulders to keep from falling down. Sitting back on his heels, Hunter fixated on her pussy.

As Nikki watched, he leaned forward and kissed her there—right there!—through her panties. With a low moan, she gave in to the weakness taking over her limbs and started to waver, crumpling just as Hunter took hold of her hips to steady her. He stood up and then, with one fluid motion, swept her up into his arms and started carrying her toward his bedroom.

Hunter was still dressed and she almost completely naked, but for the first time Nikki felt uninhibited and totally carefree. She had always been the "nice girl." Now she knew what it felt like to be the hot sexpot. She liked the sensation of power it gave her and allowed herself the freedom to just enjoy the pleasurable sensations. Abandoning herself to the moment was wildly exciting.

After Hunter lowered Nikki onto his bed, he stood there looking down at her and then asked with a hint of regret, "Are you sure you want to do this?"

Shifting on his feet, Hunter looked uncomfortable, and she saw that he was rock hard and bulging inside his tight jeans.

Before Nikki answered, he swore, "I'm so fucking turned on by you! But I know it's only our second date. I'll understand if you want to wait, but we'll need to stop this right *now!*"

Brushing his hand uneasily through his hair, he groaned, "I honestly don't know if I can make myself stop once I'm naked with you. I've never felt so out of control in my life, and I'm not sure…" He started to turn away from her.

"No, wait, don't go!" Nikki called insistently. "I want you too, right now! No stopping and no…holding back. Give it to me," she stated in an authoritative, almost demanding tone.

Turning back, Hunter nodded and then quickly shed his clothes while Nikki watched him keenly. She knew he was fit but had not realized how muscular he was, with strong biceps and a well-defined chest. Her eyes were glued hungrily to his body as she watched him pull off his jeans. He had a perfect, tight ass, and she couldn't take her eyes off him as Hunter eased his briefs down. His rock-hard penis stood thickly out from him. In the past, Nikki might have taken a peek to see what the guy looked like, but with her newfound boldness she felt at ease watching Hunter and knowing that he saw her staring.

"You are so sexy!" he said, drawing her attention to his face. "I love that you feel so comfortable looking at me. It makes me think that you want me as much as I want you."

"I do! Come here," she commanded, reveling in the novel freedom of being sexually aggressive.

"Yes, ma'am," he said. "Whatever you say."

As he sat down, Hunter opened a drawer and took out a condom. Nikki was pleased that she did not have to raise the issue of protection or insist on safe sex, as she had been forced to do with some guys in the past. Appreciating Hunter's thoughtfulness and feeling protected by him, Nikki realized it could be fun to be both cared for and the aggressor all at the same time.

"Let me put it on you," she demanded with a sensual smile.

"Yes, ma'am," he said again with a huge smile. "I'm more than happy to comply with your wishes…*any* wishes you may have."

Nikki sat up and took the condom from him. Looking up at Hunter through her lowered lashes she played the flirt, very slowly ripping the package open and removing its contents. Reaching out a hand, she used just one finger to touch the end of his jutting penis and rub a small circle around the tiny opening. Hunter sucked in his breath sharply, and his body clenched in response, making her realize again the power her budding sexuality held over him.

Returning her gaze to his face, she stared deeply into Hunter's eyes as she slid her hand down over the length of him and grasped him firmly. She had touched guys before but always a little hesitantly. Not this evening. Tonight she held him tightly, confidently, with the seductive smile of a fully grown and knowing woman as she began to slowly slide her hand up and down his hot, thick penis.

Hunter gasped and shut his eyes as her hand firmly massaged his jerking pole. Up and down her hand moved, over and over. He moaned in appreciation, his dick seeming to grow bigger and hotter in her hand. Nikki smiled, loving her effect on him. Suddenly he jerked back a little and his eyes snapped open.

"I'm going to lose it!" Hunter groaned. He stopped her hand with his and pleaded in a choked whisper, "I need you right *now!*"

Finally, fully comprehending the great power she had over him, Nikki nodded, supremely pleased. She carefully unfurled the condom, rolling it slowly down his long, hard shaft. Breathing rapidly, Hunter fought for control. Nikki finished putting it on and dropped her hand as she lay down on the bed to look up at him.

Hunter leaned down and planted a quick tender kiss on her lips. He pushed aside her bra slightly to free one breast and began swirling her nipple with his tongue. Nikki moaned in pleasure as he slipped his hand down along her stomach and then inside her panties.

He whispered hoarsely into her ear, "I want to be inside you so much. Deeply inside!"

Nikki squirmed when she felt his fingers reach her moist, ready pussy and caress her clitoris. "Yes, yes," she mouthed, unable to speak. Her newfound power had evaporated as lust consumed her, and she was desperately needy for his touch.

"You're so wet for me," he groaned with his mouth still around her nipple.

"Hunter, take off the rest of my clothes now, please." It was her turn to beg.

Without a word, he eased off her panties and then, as she arched up for him, reached behind to unclasp her bra. Hunter admired her naked body, staring for a moment at her damp mound.

"You're so beautiful," he said again.

With her finally fully naked, Hunter eased himself on top of her. Nikki loved the feel of his warm body touching her all along her own, especially his chest hair grazing her sensitive, tight nipples. His penis nestled between her legs, and she could feel its hot, throbbing hardness bumping against her clitoris. Squirming under him, she tried to increase the contact where her aching pussy met his pole.

Hunter rested himself on his elbows and slowly lowered his head to kiss her. Their mouths met, and he began a slow dance with his tongue, licking the tip of her tongue and then sliding out of her mouth. Then, as if driven by sudden increased passion, he slammed his mouth hard against her in a more demanding kiss.

Nikki was on fire, and her mindless writhing increased. Breaking contact with his mouth, she urged, "Please, Hunter! Now!"

Hunter raised himself up a little and placed his pulsing penis at the opening of her vagina. Ever so slowly he entered her, and she moaned loudly at the glorious contact. Nikki raised her hands to grasp Hunter's face and bring him down to her. She kissed him passionately as she raised and lowered her hips to encourage him to move faster.

"Nikki, you feel so good," he murmured into her mouth. He trailed kisses around her face and on her neck as the speed of their pumping bodies increased and their combined moans filled the air. He continued this driving pace while he reached a hand to play with one of her breasts, squeezing and tweaking the nipple.

Lying under him, Nikki felt pleasure coursing up from her core and building in intensity. She wanted more, needed more, and reached around with both hands to grab his ass to pull him even closer to her with each of his thrusts. She felt herself tighten and clench as the sensations built. Nikki threw back her head and cried loudly, "Hunter!" as she slid over the edge into a powerful, shuddering climax.

He arched into her and groaned in pleasure, his pelvis surging into a pumping orgasm. They stayed that way for long moments, wanting their first time to go on and on. Then slowly their breathing returned to normal. Locked together in this intimate embrace, Hunter opened his eyes and smiled down at Nikki.

Looking up at him, she returned his smile and gently pulled him down to rest his head next to hers. Nikki felt his heart beating loudly.

"That was wonderful," he whispered into her ear before he rolled onto his side and wrapped his arms around her.

"Mmmm," she murmured back.

"Stay with me tonight, will you please?" he asked her, and she happily nodded in agreement as she nestled closer to him.

"Mmmm," she repeated before she drifted off to sleep.

10

OKAY, ENOUGH OF THE FISH METAPHOR...OUR LOVERS GET TO KNOW EACH OTHER BETTER

THE NEXT MORNING, HUNTER woke Nikki by kissing her on the neck, which quickly led to another delicious round of indoor sports. Nikki was grateful once again that she had taken the initiative to ask him out. Afterward, as they lay there in each other's arms, Hunter asked her to stay the weekend with him. He suggested that they play tourists in New York City, and Nikki happily agreed. As a college student and more recently a busy career woman, she had always been too busy to fully explore the city, and now she would get to do it with a handsome new boyfriend.

"I have an idea. Let's play *poor* tourists and see how many things we can do that are cheap or free," she said, remembering Hunter's tight financial straits—and to be frank, hers weren't much better with her large student loans and low-paying entry-level job.

"That's an awesome idea," he responded, opening his laptop and doing a search on "free things to do in New York City."

By mid-morning they were off with a plan for the weekend. First, a quick stop at her apartment for a change of clothes and other essentials. Nikki also left a note telling Kim where she was. Then it was off to have the cheapest lunch in Manhattan—hot dogs at Gray's Papaya, a city landmark since 1973. For the afternoon, they took the subway to Battery Park for a free round-trip ride on the Staten Island Ferry. Even though the ferry is really just a bus on water—not a fancy boat or circle tour—standing there with Hunter's arm around her on a sunny Saturday and watching as the Manhattan skyline receded was incredibly romantic.

As they glided by the Statue of Liberty, Nikki was pleased when Hunter suggested they plan a trip there on another weekend. Neither had been there before, but more importantly, Hunter was subtly telling her that they would be more than just a weekend fling. After a dull, yearlong relationship with a guy who was more interested in drinking and sports than anything she might want to do, suddenly the city was full of endless possibilities, and the thought of sharing them with Hunter was unbelievably exciting.

Later, after the return ferry trip, they went back to his apartment where Nikki accepted Hunter's humorous invitation to "Let's make fucky." The afternoon raced by in delightful multiple orgasms, and Nikki was so relaxed that she suggested spending the evening in with him lounging on the couch. However, Hunter insisted that he had promised her a weekend on the town and that's what they would do. So they showered together—which took extra time while Nikki experienced her first shower sex—and then they got a little dressed up before riding the subway all the way uptown, some eighty-six blocks, and then walking over to Fifth Avenue and Eighty-Eighth Street. It was free night at the Guggenheim Museum.

After spending nearly eight years in Manhattan, Nikki was amazed to discover that there was so much more to the city than her small Greenwich Village world. She felt very grown-up strolling down the museum's spiral walkway. They talked about art and held hands, almost never letting go. Later in the evening they splurged, eating dinner at Lucille's Bar and Grill in Times Square where they listened to free jazz music. Afterward, the weather was so warm and the night so pleasant that they strolled down Broadway almost the entire way downtown before catching a taxi for the last mile or so to Hunter's apartment.

Sunday was a wonderful mix of sleeping in, more sex, a picnic, and strolling on the High Line, a unique elevated park on Manhattan's lower west side. In the late afternoon, Hunter walked Nikki to her apartment and gave her a long, passionate kiss before leaving. He had suggested she come over for dinner, but Nikki knew Rob would be back in town. Besides, she needed to do laundry so she would have clean clothes to wear to work on Monday. However, they made plans to get together midweek for pizza and a DVD at her place.

Nikki walked into her apartment feeling like she was floating on a cloud. Kim was there gathering her dirty laundry, so the two friends went to the building's basement facilities together to take care of the weekly chore. Kim wanted to know every detail about the weekend, and Nikki was happy to relive the fun times she had with Hunter playing tourist.

Nikki ended her story by saying, "I'm so crazy about him! I feel like I was struck by lightning. I just hope he feels the same way."

"I'm sure he feels something fabulous toward you. Guys just don't drop everything to spend forty-some hours with a woman unless they've got it bad. It even sounds like he enjoys *moreplay*."

"Huh?" asked Nikki.

"You know…cuddling and fondling after sex…but it often turns into foreplay and even more sex."

"Oh, my gosh, yeeessss!" Nikki exclaimed. "He kissed, snuggled, and *mored* with me for hours Saturday afternoon. I'm surprised we made it back out of the apartment at all."

"Guess what?" Kim told her. "I'm going to be gone for several days three weeks from now for my grandma's birthday, in case you want some privacy." She gave Nikki a knowing smile.

Shrieking with excitement, Nikki hugged her friend. "Thank you for telling me! I'll invite Hunter over, and we can plan to do a sequel of playing tourist."

"Maybe you'll just want to play *house*," Kim answered, smirking.

"Hmmm, maybe…I can think of many things Hunter and I can play," Nikki bantered back as the two friends carried their finished laundry to the elevator.

At dinner on Wednesday, Nikki was thrilled when Hunter accepted her invitation to stay with her for a repeat weekend of playing tourist. They enjoyed each other's company very much, and each time they got together, they learned a little more about the other. Sharing the pizza Hunter had brought while sitting on the couch, they put off watching a movie to talk. He elaborated about his career goals and explained how things were going at the clinic.

"I'm hopeful that I'll soon have an obstetrics patient of my own. You know…I can't tell a patient to hurry up and get pregnant, but I do know of at least two couples that are trying to conceive. With any luck I'll be delivering my first baby in less than a year."

"Wow! Does that make you excited or anxious?"

"Excited, definitely excited. I did deliver babies during my residency, but they weren't *my* patients. I want to be as ready as I can so I've been spending time studying a couple nights a week on all the latest delivery techniques. What about you?" Hunter asked. "How is your job coming along?"

"I'm really trying to be more proactive, besides speaking up more in meetings and offering to take on more responsibility, I've really tried to go beyond the call of duty on any projects that come my way...to show everyone what I'm really capable of. I think it's starting to pay off, but it's not like my boss has offered to promote me or anything, at least not yet. There is an open position for assistant editor and I think I'm going to apply for the job, but I guess I'm worried that I won't get it. Then what?"

"Then you start looking for a higher-level job somewhere else," Hunter said. "Look, nothing ventured, nothing gained. We're like poster children for that motto. What if you'd never called and asked me out, and all the time I was feeling like my hands were tied at the clinic, no matter how much I wanted to call you? Think of all we would have missed."

"I don't even want to think about it," Nikki murmured. "But you're right. It took a lot of nerve for me to call you, and look how it paid off."

Hunter leaned in close to her. In a husky voice, he said, "I think it paid off very well." He pulled her into his arms and kissed her passionately. "Extremely well!" Hunter caressed her back and deepened the kiss, and Nikki squirmed in closer to him.

Easing back, Hunter groaned, "When's Kim coming home?"

"Later. Much later." And she tugged him back to kiss her again, her hands circling around his shoulders.

They never got to see their video...didn't even make it off the couch.

11

MOREPLAY

WHEN KIM WENT HOME for her grandma's birthday, the new couple enjoyed their second tourist weekend using Nikki's apartment as their base. The weekend flew by, but this time they didn't make it out of the apartment nearly as often as the first time they played New York tourists. Their "indoor sports" were just too much fun! Hunter expressed often how Nikki's relaxed boldness was a real turn-on. Nikki told him that was the "new" her, but Hunter didn't believe she could have been so very different in the past from the outgoing lover she was now. Nikki also appreciated that Hunter was always proactive about protection and never pushed her to do something she didn't want.

"I wish we could spend every night together. I hate that tonight you won't be lying next to me," Hunter said as they lounged in bed on Sunday afternoon.

"Ha!" Reaching over, Nikki playfully swatted him on the ass. "You just want your sex toy available to you twenty-four seven, admit it!"

"Well, there is that," he responded, leering playfully at her. "But really, I enjoy just being with you, just hanging out with you. What do you say, let's move in together."

"You're serious, aren't you?"

"Yes, I am. I know we've only been going out for a short time, but why not?"

Nikki looked away from his intense gaze and considered his idea. Why not? She had never lived with a guy before, but why the hell not? Truth be told, Nikki would like having her sex god handy every night as well. However, the idea of the shared closeness of living together with Hunter was what really excited her. He had quickly become her most intimate friend in a way that even her longtime girlfriends could never be. The idea seemed more natural than the current trade-off sleepover arrangements, and it just felt right, Nikki realized.

She opened her mouth, ready to exclaim, "I would *love* that," but paused to choose her words more carefully. Instead she said, "I would *like* that very much."

Nikki was wary about letting the "L-bomb" drop too soon, knowing how most guys react to such declarations. But deep inside, she guessed that what she was feeling was probably love. She wondered if Hunter felt the same way. It certainly seemed that he did.

Hunter was clearly pleased with her affirmative answer, hugging her close and kissing her cheek tenderly. Their close proximity quickly led to less talking and more cuddling—*moreplay* as Kim called it—followed by some very energetic, loud "cuddling."

Later, Nikki said she would inform Kim that she'd be moving out. Still lying in bed, the two of them started eagerly looking online for available apartments and planning their move. Before he left Sunday night, Hunter told her that they were holding a surprise party for Dave's birthday the next Friday night and Nikki and her three friends were invited.

After hugging Hunter good-bye and closing the door to the apartment, Nikki collapsed happily onto the couch. She could hardly believe all the changes in her life—a new wardrobe, a new live-in boyfriend, the chance for a promotion—and all because she decided to stop being a doormat and take charge of her life. With that mental pat on the back, Nikki smiled and went about the mundane tasks of life, such as the enormous pile of dirty laundry waiting for her.

12

GROUP PLAY

BY ELEVEN, DAVE'S SURPRISE party was in full swing on Friday night, the two-bedroom apartment filled with people. Nikki enjoyed meeting more of Hunter's friends, and her girlfriends all came to the party. Free drinks and the promise of lots of single doctors were lure enough for them to bling up in their sexiest attire. The music was loud, and the furniture had been moved to allow dancing in one corner. Kim and Amy danced all evening with different guys and seemed to be enjoying themselves. Around midnight, when Hunter left the party briefly to buy more ice, Nikki grabbed a drink and went over to chat with Kim and Amy.

"Hi," Nikki said, joining her two friends. "Where's Rachel? I haven't seen her all night."

"Well, she was hanging with us for a while," Kim responded. "But I haven't seen her in a couple hours. I can't imagine she would leave without telling us."

"I'm off to see how long the bathroom line is," said Amy. "I'll look around for her."

Almost immediately, she returned with a surprised look on her face. "You won't believe it! I don't believe it either, and I saw them with my own eyes. Rachel and Rob are in the bedroom sucking face!"

Both girls turned to her in surprise, and Kim responded, "You're right, I don't believe it. I've got to see it for myself."

Together they walked over and peered into Rob's bedroom. The lights were low, and this seemed to be the designated make-out room because several couples were spread around on chairs, the floor, and the bed. Everyone was fully dressed, but there was a lot of deep kissing and heavy groping going on, and each couple seemed oblivious to everyone else around them.

"See," Amy whispered, pointing to a pair on the bed. "I almost didn't recognize her in the dark."

Rachel sat on Rob's lap, straddling his thighs and kissing him full on. Just then, Rob broke the kiss and buried his face in her chest, and she threw her head back, moaning in obvious pleasure. Opening her eyes, Rachel noticed the three of them staring from the doorway and gave them a saucy smile and wink before kissing the top of Rob's head. Not wanting to be voyeurs, the girls turned away to go back to the living room.

Perplexed, Kim said, "I just don't get it. I thought Rachel hated Rob. She's always complaining about him."

Looking thoughtful, Nikki said, "Well, I was beginning to think that there was something going on. Several times over the past month when Rachel and I were with Hunter, we've run into Rob. They're always a little nasty to each other, but sometimes their snippy exchanges seem more hot than angry."

"What do you mean?" Kim asked, still not getting it.

"Well, for instance, Rachel and I ran into them at The Bean this week when we were getting coffee. She immediately launched into her standard attack about that old contest... She's always asking if Rob actually succeeded in boning any of them, her words not mine. But this time Rachel taunted him, saying something about how she didn't think he'd know the first thing about getting a woman off if he did manage to get any of them naked...that Rob was just all talk."

"You're kidding." Amy clearly couldn't fathom saying anything like that to a guy.

"No, she really said it, and Rob looked extremely angry—spitting, stomping angry. For a second I thought he was going to hit her or grab her...*something*...but then he just said, 'Fuck you!' Oh, and something like, all he needed was thirty minutes with her naked and it would be the best sex she'd ever had. At that point, Hunter and I walked away. We didn't want to get in the middle of *that* conversation!"

"I can't believe you didn't tell us about this," accused Kim.

"Yeah, sorry. As you know, other events took over this week and I totally forgot about it."

"What other events?" asked Amy, who was starting to look put-out.

Turning to her, Nikki looked really excited. "Hunter asked me to move in with him. Can you believe it, after just five weeks? I just got the chance to tell Kim about it last night so she can start looking for a new roommate."

"Hey, do you want to be my roomie?" Kim asked Amy.

"Really? I'd love to! You know I can't stand my current one, but I'll need to give a month's notice or I won't get my deposit back."

Nikki jumped in. "That's okay. Hunter and I will need at least that long to find a place we can afford. We're looking for something near the hospital since he'll need to be there at all hours once he starts delivering babies."

"It's settled then," announced Kim, giving Amy a quick hug. "Nikki and Hunter will have their own little *love nest*, and you and I will be roomies."

"So back to the more important topic—what the heck is happening between those two people who hate each other?" asked Kim, gesturing toward the bedroom.

"Well, I think it's a case of two opposites attracting," suggested Nikki.

"It makes total sense to me," countered Amy. "'Cause they're not opposites at all. Both of them are inquisitive, strong-minded, and extremely extroverted people."

Kim choked on a laugh and said, "Amy, you're so diplomatic. I'm sure I will learn a lot from you when we become roommates, because I would have called them both opinionated, noisy loudmouths. I love Rachel… Don't get me wrong, but…"

"I love Rachel too," Nikki joined in. "But I don't give them more than a couple weeks before they kill each other."

"I think you're right," answered Kim. "However, I think their sex will be amazing, hot, and explosive, right up until their relationship implodes."

Looking thoughtful, Amy murmured, "Mmm, I don't know. They may surprise you both, and anyway at least she'll be getting well boned and often… That's more than Kim and me!"

"Amy! Stop that right now. You've been listening to Rachel too much, picking up her bizarre slang. I want you to stay just the way you are so I can learn to be refined and demure like you," said Kim, laughing as they started heading back toward the dance floor.

Later when Nikki slow-danced with Hunter, she happily told him the news—that Amy and Kim would be roomies, and who knows about Rob and Rachel. Hunter looked pleased that it was all working out for everyone, but he was most happy for himself. Soon he would have Nikki all to himself, and he was eager to explore her body all night long, every night.

~13~

SEVERAL MONTHS LATER

NIKKI WAS VERY HAPPY about everything in her life. Her personal goal of transforming herself in subtle ways had resulted in more responsibility at work, a terrific boyfriend who was also the best roommate *ever*, and possibly soon a promotion. If that did not happen, she would start job hunting in earnest as Hunter had suggested. In the meantime, Nikki could hardly believe they had been living together for four months already.

It had taken them a month to find a place that was not too expensive. Their new, tiny one-bedroom apartment in the East Village wasn't high luxury, but with their combined furniture and a few important acquisitions—a new queen mattress, a slightly used sofa that would double as a guest bed, and a new television—it was quite cozy. Nikki adored it. She had a little more in savings than Hunter—his massive med-school loans weighed heavily on his mind—but he had insisted on splitting the cost of everything, and again she appreciated the feeling of being cared for and protected, rather than taken advantage of, as in the past.

They both worked long hours at their jobs, and Hunter continued to spend one or sometimes two nights a week at the clinic studying by himself to enhance his knowledge of obstetrics. He would stay there after it closed and hit the books or take online seminars, often not coming home until late at night. Then he would slip quietly into bed next to Nikki, trying not to wake her up.

She once suggested that he study in their apartment after they had dinner, and she would hang out in the bedroom to give him peace and quiet, but Hunter said that he felt more motivated at the clinic surrounded by the equipment of his specialty. That, and the practice also had a small medical reference library he sometimes consulted. Nikki didn't really mind too much, and the free nights often provided the chance for a girls' night out.

So one Tuesday evening, Nikki, Rachel, Amy, and Kim got together at their favorite hangout, Pizza Villa. They shared a large pizza along with a carafe of wine and dished about boyfriends, jobs, and such.

"I'm so pleased that you two like being roommates. Then I don't have to feel guilty that I deserted Kim." Nikki smiled at her friends, then looked at Rachel and added, "And speaking of roomies, I hear from Hunter that you are moving in with Rob. Is that right?"

"Are you serious?" Kim exclaimed. "We knew you had a fling with him, but really...*Rob?*"

Rachel smiled broadly as Amy joined the fray. "I told you they were like-minded people...two birds of a feather, if you ask me."

"Okay, enough already! Rob and I get along great, and he found that he couldn't swing the rent alone after Hunter moved out, so he invited me to move in. No biggie." Looking around at the skeptical faces of her friends, she became slightly annoyed.

"He's not that bad! He's actually a nice guy when you get to know him...and the boning is the best!" Rachel could never pass up a chance to shock her friends.

Addressing Nikki, she said, "Rob and I were thinking we should go on a double date sometime. Whaddya say? Rob suggested it to Hunter when he ran into him in Midtown last Tuesday evening. We were thinking maybe—"

"No, wait," interrupted Nikki. "What did you say about running into Hunter? He was at the clinic Tuesday night all evening, studying. Where did Rob say he saw him? It must have been another day."

"Umm." Rachel paused to think a moment. "No, I'm sure it was Tuesday. Rob was in Midtown running an errand. I remember because that was the only evening we spent together all week. Rob came home around eight and had just seen Hunter with a...umm. Yeah, that's about it, I think."

"What? What were you going to say?" Nikki was sure there was an explanation for why Hunter would lie about where he was, but suddenly she wondered if he really had been at the office all those nights as he'd said.

"It's nothing, I'm sure." Rachel, whose whole personality had softened in response to her new relationship with Rob, tried ineffectually to change the subject. "Hey, does anyone want more wine? I think we should order some more, don't you?" She looked at Kim and Amy for agreement, but that only made Nikki more suspicious.

"Rachel Edelstein! You tell me right now what you know. I'm sure it's nothing too, but please don't keep secrets from me."

"It's just that Rob said he ran into Hunter walking down Restaurant Row—you know, Forty-Sixth Street—with the receptionist from his clinic. Umm. I didn't really think anything about it at the time, but I didn't know he was supposed to be at work in the Village studying by himself, either."

"Ohh! Well, I'm sure there is a very good explanation."

Nikki tried to make light of it, but she felt sick inside. While she wanted to trust Hunter, Nikki had met the new receptionist and she was a total hottie. Nikki had even seen the young woman flirt with Hunter, which at the time she had ignored because all women everywhere— waitresses, sales clerks, everyone—smiled at him and flirted.

His Greek-god good looks were always a draw, and Nikki had gotten used to it. However, this was different. Hunter had lied to her about where he was, what he was doing, and worst of all, who he was with. Nikki wondered why she always seemed to attract guys who cheated. Was it some kind of deep-seated personality flaw?

The girlfriends jumped in to reassure Nikki. "I'm sure it's nothing," said Rachel again, while Kim urged, "Just ask him about it." Amy unthinkingly added, "The receptionist had probably just worked late too." But the last pretext fell flat, and they fell silent. They all knew that receptionists only work during regular office hours, and anyway, Forty-Sixth Street was nearly five miles from the clinic so they weren't just walking home.

"Why don't you just flat-out ask him?" Kim urged again.

Nikki felt like crying. Was it really possible that Hunter was cheating? They had only been together six months! However, Nikki's past boyfriends had taught her not to expect too much from them, sometimes not even trust. Hunter was a healthy young man and, like any other horny American male, why wouldn't he jump at the chance for a quick fuck with a gorgeous, willing woman?

Nikki tried to rein in her fears and her emotions. Perhaps there was another explanation. Hunter had been wonderful so far, but then again, maybe she had been too trusting, never even calling the office to check up on him. Finally, she came to a decision.

"No, I'm not going to ask Hunter about it. I'm going to trust him. That's what you do in a loving relationship."

But she also knew that Hunter had never said he loved her.

She revised her decision. "I'll give him through the weekend to tell me what's going on. Then I'll ask him point-blank."

The girlfriends reached out and gave Nikki supportive pats and smiles. Although she had made up her mind, Nikki no longer felt like partying or even dishing the dish, so she said good-bye and went home.

Later, climbing into bed alone, it was all she could do not to call and check up on him at the clinic. Lying there unable to sleep, Nikki vacillated between feeling sure there was a logical explanation and thinking the worst—that Hunter was like every other guy she had dated, a cheater who would happily stick his dick in any willing girl. Here she was, thinking that Hunter wanted and cared for her, but maybe he just liked having a ready fuck available. Maybe he had never intended more than that.

Nikki didn't want to think such bad things about him. He really did seem nice, but maybe Hunter just thought they were friends with benefits. It was all her problem, Nikki realized, filled with self-doubt. With her history of finding loser boyfriends, why did she think it would be any different now just because of a new hairstyle and different clothes? Inside she was the same, old boring Nikki. The kind of girl who guys settled for until something better came along, and certainly not nearly hot enough to hold on to a gorgeous guy like Hunter, not for long anyway.

Rolling over and pounding on the pillow, trying to get comfortable, Nikki realized that she was being slightly melodramatic. She really didn't know what was going on and why Hunter had been on Forty-Sixth Street with the sexy receptionist when he had told her he was working. Well, there was one way to find out. Nikki reached over to the nightstand for her phone, but once she had it in her hand, she just stared at it. Earlier she had made the decision to trust him, to give Hunter time to explain, and that was the mature choice. She would stick to her plan for a few more days and see what happened. Nikki rolled over and shut her eyes, determined to stop thinking about it and get some rest.

Sleep was long in coming, but when she finally did fall asleep, it was deep and she never heard Hunter come home that evening.

⌁ 14 ⌁
KEEPING SECRETS

IT WAS THURSDAY NIGHT, and Nikki was relaxing on the sofa next to Hunter as they watched the tube. She had stuck to her decision and hadn't brought up the incident, reassuring herself that Hunter's caring behavior toward her hadn't changed at all. Maybe, just maybe, there was an innocent explanation for why he had lied to her about his whereabouts, but her patience was beginning to wear thin.

Then out of the blue, Hunter asked, "Do you realize that tomorrow is exactly six months since our first date when you took me out for pizza?"

"Really." *Where is this going?* Nikki wondered anxiously. Was he preparing to tell her that it had been nice while it lasted, but now he'd found something better?

Interrupting her private worries, Hunter queried, "Did you keep the night open like I asked?"

"Umm, yes."

"Great! Would you consider wearing your sexy red-and-black lingerie again? I think it's really hot knowing you have them on underneath your clothes…our little secret. Also maybe wear a dress. We're going somewhere fancy."

Nikki sucked in a large rush of air. She hadn't realized that she had been holding her breath. She also stopped worrying about whatever Hunter had been up to last Tuesday. Clearly he still wanted her and had even remembered their six-month anniversary! Nikki was filled with pleasure and a dose of relief, if not complete reassurance.

"Sure, I will, and you can take them off me later in the evening." She smiled deliciously at Hunter and winked.

All through the next day at work, Nikki was thrilled every time she recalled that Hunter had remembered something as romantic as a six-month milestone. She could hardly wait for the day to end. Occasionally, however, nagging doubt rose up again, but each time Nikki would tell herself she was being ridiculous. Hunter wouldn't have planned a special celebration if he were planning to dump her.

After arriving home from work, Nikki dressed for the evening in her sexiest short, little evening number—something new she had just purchased. Earlier in the afternoon, she'd played hooky for an hour and had gone for a haircut. The stylist had done a very good job of blow-drying Nikki's longish brown hair into an attractive full style. Looking in the mirror with her makeup on, Nikki felt confident that she looked both pretty and sexy.

She was surprised when Hunter took her to an elegant place on Restaurant Row. He must have told them it was a special night because he and Nikki were seated in a little alcove that felt very secluded. They sat side by side, their shoulders touching, alone in their private thoughts.

"How did we score such an exclusive table?" Nikki asked.

"I got help from the new receptionist who has a special 'in' here. Her boyfriend is a waiter, and on Tuesday she brought me over to see the place. I kept that secret from you for a few days…that I hadn't been studying. I feel relieved that I can finally tell you about it. Silly, but it felt like I was lying to you."

Instantly, Nikki felt great relief. *Thank God I kept my mouth shut.* Hunter had just been planning this big surprise. The fact that he mentioned the receptionist had a boyfriend was an added bonus. In her excitement, Nikki turned and gave Hunter a huge hug and a wet kiss. Before she pulled back, Hunter grabbed her to extend the kiss into something deep and hot that left Nikki panting and tingling.

"I love this place. It's so very romantic, and thank you for remembering our six-month anniversary," she exclaimed.

Then the waiter arrived with menus, and Nikki was shocked at the exorbitant prices. Although she didn't say anything, she was concerned, knowing that Hunter still had massive student loans, along with paying his share of the cost of the new furniture and monthly rent. Nikki decided to order the least expensive thing on the menu and skip the salad, saying she'd had a big lunch. Even so, Hunter ordered Nikki's favorite martini for her and later a bottle of sparkling wine although she tried to demur, saying they didn't need to go all out.

But he insisted, and after their waiter poured the bubbly, Hunter raised his glass and made a toast. "To my beautiful Nikki. I'm so glad you've come into my life."

"Thank you, Hunter. I'm glad you are in mine too!"

The meal was delicious, and they talked quietly about nothing… and everything…as lovers can sometimes do, while holding hands in their quiet corner. As they finished the bottle of bubbly, Nikki was becoming a little woozy from the alcohol, and Hunter's gentle caresses on her back were sending hot, tingling vibrations down her spine. Her thighs were clenched together at the wicked sensations.

"You got me drunk on purpose, didn't you? You want to take advantage of me later this evening," she teased with a glimmer in her eye.

"What can I say? Even here in the restaurant, I want to slide my hand under your dress and run my fingers over the lace covering your pussy," he whispered hotly into her ear as his hand gently squeezed her thigh. "It's pretty much all I've been thinking about for the last hour."

"So let's get out of here," Nikki said, quivering in response.

"Check, please!" Hunter called out with a laugh.

After they left the restaurant and were walking along the sidewalk trying to catch a taxi, Hunter told her, "I hope you don't mind, but I need to stop by the clinic for a few minutes. I forgot some files at the end of the day that I need to go over later tonight."

Nikki was more than a little unhappy at the idea that Hunter planned to interrupt their magical night for work. His naughty banter in the restaurant made her want to go straight home and strip his clothes off. However, she knew Hunter wouldn't ask if he didn't really need to go there. She wanted to pout but instead said, "Well, it is on the way, so okay. But I hope it won't take too long. I want to get home for some fun, if you get my drift."

"Absolutely! I'm one hundred percent with you there."

Once inside the taxicab, Hunter pulled Nikki into his arms and slowly brought his mouth down to hers. After a few minutes of hot, demanding kisses, she was giggling and ready to agree to anything he wanted. They pulled up in front of the brownstone that housed the clinic, and she hurriedly got out, wanting to get this over with as quickly as possible.

"Okay, let's get those files and get on home," she said, smiling at him.

～15～
PLAYING DOCTOR

HUNTER UNLOCKED THE DOOR to the building and turned off the security code after they entered. Gesturing to the lobby sofa, he said, "Why don't you just wait here while I get what I need? Let's keep the lights off so no one comes snooping, and I've got the front door locked again."

"Okay, but hurry, please," Nikki said, giving him a quick kiss on the cheek before sitting down.

"I'll be quick," he replied, smiling back at her.

She sat down on the sofa and relaxed backward, letting her eyes drift shut. She was beginning to realize that she was more than a little drunk, but in a good way. *I guess I had more wine than I thought.* She wanted to hold on to the sensual feelings from their brief ride in the taxi—the feel of his hands sliding around her body, his wet kisses trailing along her neckline, then his tongue playing in her mouth. Nikki groaned aloud and moved restlessly. Grabbing some files seemed to be taking a long time. *What is he doing, anyway?* she wondered as she saw him going from room to room.

"Hey, what are you doing back there?" she called playfully down the hall. "It looks like you're straightening up the place. I thought you just had to get some files."

"Oh, I just can't find what I need. It'll just be another minute, I promise," he called back from inside an exam room.

Almost immediately after that, Nikki was surprised to see Hunter walking toward her with only one small file in his hand. Strangely, he now wore his lab coat and a stethoscope around his neck.

"What's going on?" she asked, pouting. "It looks like you are getting ready to actually work."

Hunter came to a stop in front of her. Looking down, he smiled—his sexy dimples on maximum—and said huskily, "Well, I was thinking… Remember how we fantasized about getting down and dirty here a while ago? Would you like to celebrate our six months together back here at the site of our arousing fiasco? I think it's time we finish your exam *properly*."

Nikki gasped, so surprised that she jumped to her feet. "You're kidding, right?" She teased, "I was right. That *is* why you were plying me with alcohol! You want to take advantage of your patient…you *naughty* doctor, you!"

"So, how about it? Let's…*play doctor*," Hunter said, grinning mischievously.

Nikki looked him up and down and was struck by how handsome he looked in his professional attire—the white lab coat setting off his golden tan and blond, blue-eyed Adonis looks even in the darkened room. He was every woman's fantasy doctor—handsome, thoroughly masculine, and ready to give her *very* personal service.

Hunter returned her perusal, letting his eyes slide slowly, caressingly down her body. He gave her such a hot, lascivious look that it sent an electric jolt coursing straight to her sex. The combination of alcohol and the sudden rush of desire made Nikki dizzy, and she wobbled in her high heels. Hunter quickly reached out and dragged her into his arms before she could tumble back down onto the couch. He gave her a passionate kiss, his tongue pulsing in and out of her mouth seductively, before pulling back to wait for her answer.

After imagining the many possibilities of the erotic game he was proposing, Nikki leaned provocatively in toward him and demanded, "Dr. Sterling! Examine me, please! I have aches all over that need to be checked out…thoroughly."

A wide, cocky grin spread across Hunter's face as he hungrily stared at Nikki. "I want to rip your clothes off right here in the lobby, but I also want to play with you in there." He gestured back to an exam room. Affecting his most professional doctorly demeanor, Hunter looked down at his file and formally requested, "Ms. Woods, why don't you follow me to the examination room."

"Yes, Doctor," she replied, giggling as he pulled her by the hand down the hall.

"Oh, wow!" Surprised, Nikki stopped at the threshold and gazed around the small room. Replacing the stark overhead lights were many small votive candles placed everywhere, which gave the usually sterile room a romantic atmosphere. Soft music played on the sound system, and the exam table had a soft sheet on it instead of crinkly tissue paper.

"It's beautiful, really...and pretty music too!" she exclaimed.

"That's one small change I've made already here," he said, dropping character for a moment. "I thought patients would be more relaxed with some quiet music to listen to while they wait, and they already had a sound system in place so I asked the other doctors to give it a try. We've gotten good responses to it so far."

Also dropping character, Nikki voiced a small worry. "Playing naughty doctor with you sounds really hot, but what about someone coming in here, another doctor or the cleaning staff or something? I don't want you to get into trouble."

"I've been planning this for a while. Actually, that's partly why I've been studying here a couple nights a week. Now I know everyone's schedule, and the chance of anyone showing up here tonight is almost nil," he said, obviously proud of his ruse and all the effort he had put into this evening.

Clearing his throat, Hunter transformed back into sexy doctor mode and reached out one finger to let it slowly trail down Nikki's body in her tight, short dress. She tingled everywhere he touched her.

"Ms. Woods. Please take off your clothes. Here is a sheet for you to wrap your body in....and keep your bra and underwear on for now. I'll take those off myself," he said wickedly.

But rather than leave the room as was convention, Hunter closed the door behind himself and leaned lazily back against it to watch. Maybe it was the alcohol from dinner or maybe it was the craziness of the location, but Nikki was totally intoxicated with a wild desire beyond anything she had experienced before. She was both light-headedly woozy and magnificently aroused at the same time.

Nikki looked at Hunter, and a slow, seductive smile lit her face as she realized how far she had come. Not only was the "new" Nikki brave enough to perform a deliberate striptease for his viewing pleasure, but she would enjoy every minute of it too. With her gaze locked on his eyes, she slowly grasped the hem of her dress and raised it inch by inch until her panties were just starting to peek out.

Turning, Nikki looked over her shoulder at him as she raised it farther to reveal her lace-covered fanny, then she twerked for him like a star stripper. Hunter was watching her intently, a small naughty smile playing on his lips, and Nikki felt his gaze upon her body like a hot brand. It made her pussy clench and her breasts tighten.

Reveling in the feel of being a seductress, Nikki continued turning around until she again faced him. She raised her dress the rest of the way to reveal herself fully to him, then pulled it off. After throwing the dress onto a chair, Nikki strutted seductively to the exam table. She turned around and sat on it with crossed legs, swinging a sexy high-heeled pump a little to accentuate her long legs. Then, rather than wrapping herself in the sheet Hunter had given her, Nikki slowly pulled it across her body, enjoying the feel of the soft material gliding across her skin before she let it slide off to drop to the floor. By way of finale, Nikki leaned back on her hands—her legs still glamorously crossed—arched her back, and provocatively thrust her breasts upward on display.

"I'm *ready*, doctor," she singsonged as she slowly eased herself back to almost lying down, still thrusting her bosom in the air.

Dropping the file to the floor, Hunter choked. "Well, I'm ready too… That's for sure."

He stalked slowly toward her, leering at her lingerie-covered body. "Thank you for remembering to wear your hot panties and bra. I can still see them in my mind so clearly hanging there on the wall," he said, nodding his head toward the hooks. "When I saw them there six months ago, all I could think about was what they would look like on your body. It was a little distracting."

Leaning casually over her, he put his stethoscope into his ears. "This may shock you just a little," he said with an impish grin as he placed it on her breast and slid it under her bra.

"It's freezing!" Nikki shrieked. "What did you do?" She sucked in her breath sharply as she felt the ice-cold metal gliding over an already peaked, aching nipple.

Moaning, she arched upward into it.

Smiling wickedly, he said, "I had it in the freezer. Do you like it?" He moved the shocking metal slowly to her other breast. "This is only the beginning. I promise you this will be an examination unlike anything you've had before."

Really getting into the game, Nikki imagined that he was nothing more than a clinical physician—practically a stranger to her—and this formal, professional man was about to do very improper things to her body. Curling, tightening sensations skittered down from her aching nipples to her pussy, and she began to pant as she listened to the doctor's sexy voice talk about what he had in store for her.

"Hmm," he said as he pulled out the stethoscope and placed it on the counter, "everything seems in order but I'll need to examine your breasts thoroughly, just to be sure." After sliding one hand under her back, he expertly snapped open the bra, all the while staring hotly down at her.

Feeling the bra come undone, Nikki murmured, "My, my, Doctor, you do have dexterous fingers, don't you?"

"The better to examine you with, my dear."

Hunter slowly pulled the bra off, kissed it, and turned to hang it almost reverently on the wall. He arranged it a little until it looked just like it did six months ago, hanging there with the rhinestones twinkling on top. As he turned back to her, he said, "I think you'll find, Ms. Woods, that it's not just my fingers that are dexterous."

Staring down at her now-naked chest, he slowly lowered his mouth and reached out his tongue to swirl languidly around one of the nipples. His hand came up to gently fondle her other breast, meticulously caressing the entire mound as if he was doing the most erotic breast exam ever. The pressure of his hand intensified as he began to squeeze and play with her nipple while his mouth latched on to suck deeply on the other one. Moaning audibly now, Nikki reached up and clasped his head to her chest.

Rising up slightly, he said, "I'm sorry, Ms. Woods, but I must insist that you leave your hands by your sides. As a doctor, I need the freedom to *thoroughly* examine you."

There was a dangerous, authoritative glint to his eye that made her shiver. "I wouldn't want to have to use restraints, but..." Hunter let it trail off as she sucked in her breath at his shocking threat. She obediently released his head and laid her hands by her sides, even as she continued to arch her back toward him.

"Dr. Sterling!" she exclaimed. "You're very, *very* wicked!"

"My sweet Ms. Woods. I just want to give you the most personal, intimate care that I can."

Enjoying the kinky game, Nikki murmured, "I'm sorry, Doctor. Please continue. I'll comply with whatever *position* you require from me, I promise." Feeling wildly sinful herself, she swirled her shoulders around to make her breasts jiggle slightly in front of his face. Standing over her, Hunter eyed her hungrily as he reached out and tweaked both her nipples sharply with his fingers.

"Oh!" she exclaimed at the faintly painful pinch. "Oh, you are so bad!" But she didn't raise her hands to stop him. She was following doctor's orders.

Switching breasts, he continued flicking one nipple with his fingers and sucking ardently on the other. Then his hands moved to explore around her body. It felt so very good that Nikki wanted badly to grab on to him again. Having to hold herself back made it that much more enthralling. She rocked her head slightly from side to side as her moans grew louder, her legs spreading open almost of their own volition. She could tell that she was getting wet. Slowly he raised his head from her breast and then kissed her on the lips, his tongue sliding in and out of her mouth as a low groan escaped from him to meld with Nikki's panting moans.

Standing up, he taunted, "You're a very good patient, Ms. Woods, but let's see how truly obedient and responsive you can be, shall we?"

Nikki was so overwhelmed that all she could do was nod in answer. Breathless, she felt edgy, hot, and swollen.

"I want to test your somatic senses, so please, Ms. Woods, shut your eyes and keep them shut. Noncompliance will result in restraints and a blindfold. Understood?"

Nikki nodded again before shutting her eyes. She listened intently as he moved about, opening a drawer and picking something up. She felt a wafting tingle fluff down her body, across her belly, and down her thighs to her ankles. Nikki moaned at the delightful pleasure. Then the featherlight touch swirled around her breasts and she recognized it. Hunter was using a feather to stimulate her skin.

"Good responses," the doctor noted. Then sternly, "Hold still now."

Nikki mewled at the sharp pricks that trailed along her body. Everywhere the points stung her, her skin quivered until her entire body was trembling. It took all her willpower to keep her eyes shut. Even though this was just a game—she could end it at any time—she felt helpless and vulnerable. It heightened her remaining senses and made everything seem bigger, more pronounced. When she felt the points rolling up her thigh, she keened loudly, wanting him to go all the way up but at the same time not wanting it.

"You may open your eyes now, Ms. Woods." He showed her a silver metal object. "Your response to the Wartenberg neurowheel was highly satisfactory."

Then Hunter took out a latex glove and pulled it on with a snap. Nikki jumped slightly at the loud sound. He winked and wiggled his fingers in front of her face before dragging a latex-covered finger slowly down her body, making her pant. In his most professional tone he instructed, "I want your full cooperation as I continue with the internal part of the exam. Do you understand?"

He gazed down at her sexy red-and-black lace panties and slid a hand underneath the hem, making doctorly "mmm, mmm" sounds as he went. His gloved fingers felt slightly different, more palpably tactile than bare skin. Nikki felt his hand caress along her skin to her mound, searching until his finger found her clitoris. He fondled her tight bud, and she squirmed and pressed her pelvis into his hand, her eyes drifting shut and her mind centering on the delicious sensations coursing through her body. The good doctor brought her right to the edge of ecstasy before moving away from her clit.

Nikki almost whimpered as she bucked once uselessly into the air, her hands clenching the sides of the table to keep from grabbing his hand to put it back where she wanted it. Then his finger slid into her vagina, questing and teasing everywhere inside her. Finding her G-spot, Hunter tickled this ultimate erogenous zone until Nikki was whimpering and writhing mindlessly on the exam table. She was so close, panting and on the verge, and then he eased his finger out of her. *No!* she wanted to scream.

She watched as he dragged his gloved hand out from inside her panties. He raised his hand and held up one finger for her to see. Then he pulled the glove off with another startling snap.

"You're exceedingly wet, Ms. Woods. I think I should examine your condition further."

As Hunter walked slowly to the end of the table to stand facing her, he trailed his hand down her body, leaving tingles along the way. Hunter reached both hands to the outsides of her hips and, in one swift motion, pulled her panties down and off. He kissed the little scrap of cloth and then hung it on a hook just as it was before, murmuring, "Perfect!"

Nikki watched him reach under the table and flip up the exam-table stirrups. Startled, she cried out, "You can't be serious! What are you doing? I hate those!"

Taking on a faux stern tone, Hunter answered, "I believe, Ms. Woods, that you promised full cooperation. Did you not understand?"

"Well…mmm, ah," Nikki responded, not sure where this was going or if she would like it.

Still wearing his white lab coat and with an air of authority, he stared into her eyes as if to dare her to object further. Not saying anything, he reached up and grasped both her ankles in a strong grip. With one fluid movement, he yanked on her legs and pulled her along the exam table toward him. Nikki gasped as she watched his eyes move from her face down to the vee between her spread legs. She was spellbound, watching his tongue slip out of his mouth to lick his lips and wondering what he was going to do next.

After removing Nikki's shoes, Hunter placed both of her heels into the stirrups. Then he reached up and tugged her hips down until her thighs were wide open and her buttocks on the edge of the table.

Lowering himself down onto a stool between her legs, he never took his eyes off her wet pussy.

Nikki felt so exposed and open to him—both at his mercy and titillated at the same time. Hunter's hands came up to fondle the insides of her thighs. Then, even though she was watching him through half-closed eyes, she jumped in shock when she felt his tongue on her clitoris.

"Oh my," Nikki gasped and writhed on the table. "Oooohhh, ahh."

Hunter knew unerringly just what to do with his mouth to tease her, to stimulate and arouse her until she was on the edge of aching pleasure.

"Yes, oh, more please," Nikki begged as she moved and tilted her pelvis in rhythm with his mouth. As the feelings grew more and more intense, she realized that she was about to go over the top. Hunter flicked his tongue, striking her clit—once, twice—and Nikki exploded into a huge climax that had her whole body quaking and shuddering. She almost lost consciousness for a moment, consumed by the whirling sensations.

As she came down from the high, she saw that Hunter has risen to his feet. He was breathing hard.

"All right," he choked out, "enough playing doctor. I'm so hard that it hurts. I want you now…right now!"

"Yes, I want you too. Come here," she urged him.

Hunter pushed her, almost roughly, back up the cushioned table, not even taking the time to remove his clothes as he climbed up after her. Crawling up along her body, he then knelt with his legs on either side of her. Hurriedly, almost frantically, he unzipped his pants with one hand and shoved his clothes down while Nikki pulled his erection free. With a grunt, Hunter plunged his hot, hard rod inside her and let his whole weight down on her for a moment.

"Oh, that feels so good," he groaned out.

Quickly rising back up on his arms, he pumped in and out of her wildly. She planted her feet down on either side of him and used the table to push up to meet each of his pumping thrusts. Both of them were moaning even as they passionately kissed each other, her arms wrapped around his head. Their most sensitive and intimate body parts slammed into each other faster and faster until they both cried out in simultaneous orgasms. Hunter thrust a few more times as he moaned in pleasure before coming to rest. Nikki dragged him down on top of her. Both were panting and breathless.

After a while, Nikki murmured, "I can hear your heart beating so loudly." She planted a quick kiss on his cheek. "That was wild and hot and ohhhh so good!"

Hunter raised himself back up on his elbows and looked down at her, saying earnestly the words she longed to hear.

"I love you, Ms. Nikki Woods."

Looking into his beautiful blue eyes, she joyfully answered him. "I love you too, Hunter. So very much!"

Rolling to her side with his backside against the wall, Hunter pulled her back to cradle within his arms. Reaching down, he fumbled in the pocket of the lab coat he still wore as she watched his face, smiling with pleasure in his embrace. Slowly, Hunter drew his hand out and raised it so she could see that he held a ring—a diamond ring!

"Nikki, I love you. I know we've only been together for six months, but I also know, really truly know, that I want to spend the rest of my life with you. Will you marry me?" he asked as he offered the ring to her.

Nikki was almost speechless with amazement and surprise. She took it from him and looked down at the pretty little ring. "I, ah, Hunter that's…wow, that's unexpect—"

"I know it seems sudden and maybe too soon, and, well, if you want, we can have a long engagement for our families' sake, if nothing else. But I know I will always want you in my life."

Taking a quick breath, he continued rapidly, "The diamond is small, I realize that, but I promise you something bigger later when I can afford it…when *we* can afford it. Then we'll get whatever you want. I'm still a new doctor in huge debt, so things might be a little tight at first, but I promise you a long life with me loving you and caring for you and…"

"*It's perfect!*" she cried, cutting him off this time. "The ring is perfect. You picked it out and I love it!"

"Well?" he asked, looking into her eyes.

"Yes, I'll marry you…now or later. It doesn't matter. I'm happy just knowing I get to spend the rest of my life with you," Nikki exclaimed ecstatically before kissing him passionately on the mouth.

Then Hunter carefully took the ring from her hands and slowly, lovingly slid it onto her finger. "It's official now. We're engaged and you're going to be my wife," he pronounced in a voice that seemed to indicate he was as amazed by this as she.

"Thank you," Nikki murmured. "But I have one little request in order to marry you—something that I think will be nonnegotiable." Nikki sounded stern but she was also smiling.

"What? What is it?" Hunter asked, holding his breath. He would make it work, no matter what it was.

"Well…" Nikki said, smiling broadly at him. "My one nonnegotiable requirement is that we make *playing doctor* right here in your office an annual event, celebrating our anniversary each year. What do you say?"

"Hell, yes! That's what I say! We're going to have one wild, hot life together if this is any indication."

With that pronouncement Hunter ended further discussion, lowering his mouth to hers for a long erotic kiss.

One could say he had started another conversation, but of a different sort.

READ ON FOR A SNEAK PEEK AT
ONE OF THE THREE NOVELLAS IN THE
NEXT EROTIC ROMANCE ANTHOLOGY
FROM KATE ALLURE

Lawyering Up

COMING SOON FROM
SOURCEBOOKS CASABLANCA

Of Unsound Mind and Body

AN OLD-TIME LAWYER'S OFFICE

I OPENED THE ANTIQUE, beautifully crafted, heavy oak doors and squinted into the dim interior. The part-time secretary, Mrs. Meyer, welcomed me and surprisingly gave me a motherly hug, offering her condolences. She introduced me to the other couple there—an elderly gentleman and his wife—who had been providing daily care and cooking for Auntie for the last five years. This had been a perfect part-time job for them and an act of love too, I suspected, seeing their sadness.

"Mr. Ross will be right out in a minute," Mrs. Meyer said. As she returned to her old-fashioned desk, I settled onto a worn but comfortable leather chair.

Looking around, I saw that nothing had changed. It looked exactly the same as the last time I was here, a few years ago when I was helping Auntie with her will and selling off some farmland. Probably nothing had changed in fifty years—the ancient brown leather sofa and two matching chairs near the front with a low railing separating this sitting area from a massive lawyer's desk and smaller secretarial one were all exactly as they had always been. There was a solitary Tiffany floor lamp and two green-glass banker's desk lamps. They were probably valuable antiques now, but they gave off little light, leaving the entire high-ceilinged room perpetually dim even on this bright afternoon. The only nod to modernity was a corner workstation that held a desktop computer and a small printer. The setting reminded me of those old-time black-and-white TV shows—all that was missing was Perry Mason walking out from the back room.

Just then the door to the back opened, and I stood to greet Franklin Ross. My mouth dropped open and I stared in surprise as the mysterious stranger from the funeral emerged through the door instead. Without his shades, his gaze was even more penetrating, his dark, almost-black eyes drawing me into their secretive depths. Never breaking eye contact, he swung open the low gate and stalked straight toward me. I startled and froze—a deer in the headlights response. Then the tingling was back in a cascading rush that left me slightly dizzy.

"Hello, Ms. Jensen. I'm Franklin Ross...Junior." His hand was outstretched, and I reached out to place my hand in his. His fingers were long and lean—his grip strong as he easily encircled my smaller hand. The minute our fingers touched, I experienced an electric jolt that sizzled up my arm and straight down my body. Deep inside, my pelvis tightened in acknowledgment of the irresistible sexual attraction I felt toward this stranger. I wondered if that gasp I had heard was mine.

When I didn't immediately speak, he continued, "My dad is sorry he could not be here to see you today. He's retired and living in Arizona now. I work for a large practice in Omaha but have kept this office open to handle a few remaining cases and long-standing clients. It's a pleasure to finally meet you, Ms. Jensen. My father spoke often about your kindness toward your aunt Elizabeth."

I was in shock. Never in my life had I experienced such an immediate, overpowering lust and absolutely never ever for a complete stranger, but I managed to mutter the expected response.

"Ummm...It's nice to meet you too."

I realized something then. *Young* Mr. Ross had stepped closer and was still holding on to my hand, his other hand having settled on top to capture mine between his two large, warm ones. His dark eyes pulled me in—like the hypnotic gaze of a snake—and I was caught. Breathless, I wondered if he was feeling this extraordinary attraction too.

He cleared his throat then, a deep rumbling sound, as he seemed to realize what he was doing. Abruptly he dropped my hand and stepped backward, but our eyes were still locked together, both of us breathing hard. It was as if we were alone in a strange, intimate cocoon. Slowly we became aware that the other occupants of the room had risen and were staring at us. The mood broken, I felt suddenly bereft, adrift on a sensual haze.

Mr. Ross Jr., repeated the introductions and invited us to sit again. I listened with only half an ear to the reading of the will, catching a phrase here and there…"of sound mind and body"…"hereby bequeath"…and so on. I mostly knew its contents already but was gratified to see how thrilled the elderly couple was to receive a small bequest—pretty much the remainder of Auntie's bank account. Their gratitude was sincere, and I realized how much Auntie valued their help over the years. I knew her personal effects would be mine, but I dreaded the sad work of going through her things. She had also left me the homestead and the remaining three acres, the rest of the land having been sold off years before. Then we were standing again, shaking hands and saying our good-byes.

"Ms. Jensen, would you mind staying a few minutes so we can go over some details?" asked the lawyer. "Also, I need to report that there have been two offers for the property, in case you don't want to retain it."

"Really? Yes, I believe I'll need to sell it, since I live in Philadelphia."

I waved to the departing caretakers. The secretary was still at her computer station, but with the other couple gone, the intimacy returned immediately. I wondered again if he felt the same sizzling connection.

"Why don't you follow me to my desk, Miss Jensen."

"Please, call me Liza," I responded breathlessly.

He smiled. "That's a beautiful name…for a beautiful woman." Suddenly he seemed to realize what he had said, and he jumped in before I could respond. "I'm sorry! That must have seemed forward."

I was momentarily speechless. I wanted to tell him he could say anything he wanted in that deep sensual voice. Ask anything!

"I…ahh…thank you, Franklin," I managed, wondering where my sanity had gone.

He indicated a guest chair and I sat. "I go by Lucky Hawk or just Hawk, my middle name. My dad has always been Franklin, and… well…I like the identification with my mother's Omaha tribe."

I was struck dumb, again.

Hawk! He was called Hawk!

Shivers ran down my spine. How strange that I had already known. Not *really* known, of course, but still—his predatory boldness, his sense of being above us all—I had felt it so strongly at the cemetery. It was almost as if he was a living embodiment of the Native American belief that humans could take on the animal characteristics of their namesakes.

I very much wanted to tell Hawk about my eerie preconception, but he would have thought me crazy. It was easier to just sit there quietly as he explained the particulars of my inheritance. My palms were sweaty and the quivering arousal continued unabated as I listened to Hawk, his deep soothing voice like a warm fog slowly wrapping around me.

Did he feel anything at all? Maybe this was all in my addled, sex-deprived mind. I wanted to slyly glance at his crotch—the sure sign of a man's desire—but the large desk was a wall between us. I was beginning to find it hard to sit still—my lust making me twitchy. Still he talked on quietly with his eyes locked on mine, almost never breaking contact. It seemed as though there was a question in them—or was it just my imagination?

Perhaps an hour later we finished up. I had signed lots of documents, and the homestead was now officially mine. There were two markedly different bids for the property. A developer offered a lot of cash but would tear the structure down to build several homes. The second, for substantially less, was a consortium of public and private interests that wanted to turn the homestead into a museum. I wasn't sure what to do. I could sell it today if I wanted, but I decided instead to give myself a few days to consider both offers. Then we were standing by the door, ready to depart. Mrs. Meyer had already left after hugging me good-bye. Now it was just us two—just the need to say good-bye. It was almost painful, a sense of pulling apart something that wanted to stay connected, but that was meaningless. We weren't anything to each other, virtually strangers, really.

Hawk too seemed to be stalling before the inevitable parting.

"Where are you staying?" he asked suddenly. "At the homestead?"

"Oh no. I found a little hotel in Hastings."

Gesturing to the couch, Hawk said, "Since there isn't a decent hotel within forty miles, I just sleep right there on the rare times that I need to come down from Omaha. It's actually pretty comfortable to stretch out…"

He trailed off then, seeing the oddly strained look on my face. Staring at the large sofa, I could almost see Hawk lying there on his back, if not completely naked, then perhaps with his chest bare. In my mind, I was there with him, both of us naked, and we weren't sleeping. I guessed his thoughts were similar, because simultaneously, we turned back to each other, bright, proper smiles on our faces. I thanked Hawk again for his help, then after a quick, succinct shaking of hands, I went out the door. There it was again, that bereft emptiness that made me want to turn back. I started briskly walking toward the car and heard the door reopen.

"Hey," he called. "Would you like to grab some dinner before you head out of town? The local diner actually makes a pretty good burger."

Turning back to Hawk, I felt absolutely giddy. I realized my happiness was over the top—it was just a quick dinner after all—but there was no stopping the surging excitement.

"Sure. That sounds good!"

～ Scene 3 ～
A RUN-DOWN HONKY-TONK BAR AND GRILL

I WAITED WHILE HAWK shut off the lights and locked the door. No fancy alarm system needed in this small town. I noticed he had taken off his suit jacket and tie and left them in the office. He looked less formidable with his shirt unbuttoned and his sleeves rolled up, but still totally gorgeous, the white cotton contrasting with his dark, reddish-brown skin. I now knew this was not a tan but his natural Native American coloring, and I wanted to see more of his bare skin.

We strolled diagonally across Main Street to the only establishment in Willow Pond that served food. We didn't say much as we walked, and I wondered what the night would bring. This man was unlike any I had met before, an intensely masculine combination of virile and suave. The trepidation was back—like prey, I felt skittish and hyperaware of the man next to me.

Inside, the place was surprisingly packed, which was unexpected in this sleepy little town, but it was Friday night, after all. Loud country music was playing, and through the haze of smoke and dim lighting, I could see some guys gathered around a pool table in the back. We managed to find two spots squeezed together at the crowded bar, and I felt the now-familiar electricity zing up my leg when our thighs bumped together as we sat down. By the way he hesitated when we touched, I guessed he felt it too.

"Don't expect any fancy martinis or fine wine, but you can get your basic well drinks…and about every beer known to man." Hawk laughed.

The din was so loud that we needed to lean close to talk—our heads almost touching—and I shivered at the feel of his breath on my ear. We ordered burgers, and he urged me to try an unusual cocktail, the only drink they excelled in, but he wouldn't tell me what it was. When the drinks arrived we clinked glasses.

"To new friends," I said and took a big gulp. "Wow! This is sweet… really, *really* sweet."

"It's called a Kool-Aid Caddy in honor of Hastings, where Kool-Aid was invented."

"Okay then, in honor of Hastings…bottoms up." I tilted the glass and started gulping it down. I was thirstier than I realized after the afternoon in the sun. Drinking too fast, I choked.

"Careful," he admonished. As I coughed and spluttered, Hawk patted my lower back with his warm hand. "Only small sips, and let them trickle slowly down your throat. Then you can truly appreciate the nectar of the gods…of Nebraska." He laughed.

"Ah, you're no fun," I flirted boldly. "How are you going to take advantage of me if you don't get me drunk? And, anyway, I don't even taste any alcohol in this."

"All that sugar masks the vodka. If you drink it too fast on an empty stomach, you'll be drunk as a skunk."

Then he paused and tilted his head to stare at me, seeming to reconsider my words. Slowly, Hawk broke into a wicked grin and stopped patting me. Instead, he started making slow, swirling caresses on my lower back that were more drugging than the alcohol.

Leaning in, he whispered, "Would you like me to take advantage of you?" His husky voice was another caress. "We've only just met, but I'm finding it hard to keep my hands off you."

I laughed—well pleased to know Hawk was as interested in me as I was in him. I leaned into his shoulder, preparing what I hoped would be a smart, seductive comeback.

Just then, some locals interrupted us, breaking the mood. From the smiles and backslaps, it was clear they were old high-school buddies and had been good friends before Hawk left for college and a law career in the big city. They talked for a few minutes and wished each other well before the guys departed. I appreciated this brief chance to see another side of Hawk—a hometown boy who would always be welcomed back.

It made him seem less of a stranger to me. He was someone's friend and hopefully would be mine too.

With the arrival of the meal, we ordered a second round of drinks, then began devouring our food. As we ate, we learned about each other: both single, both devoted to our careers, both living in big cities. One difference became obvious too, although it wasn't expressly stated—he made a lot of money and I didn't. It occurred to me that if I sold to the developer, I would have a wad of cash, but I pushed the thought aside. I was having a wonderful time with Hawk and grateful to let the ennui flow out of me as the alcohol flowed in. But where was this going? Was this just a casual dinner, or what?

Hawk's earlier comment seemed accurate—he couldn't seem to keep his hands off me, touching me on the shoulder, caressing my lower back, even trailing his finger along the line of my jaw. I found myself leaning into his touch and "accidentally" pressing my thigh against his. It would have been perfect except that I knew we lived too far apart for this to turn into a real relationship—but it was still great fun flirting with such a gorgeous guy.

As our plates were cleared, I asked the bartender for a glass of water, wondering what would happen next. Would Hawk make a play for me—try to seduce me? I wasn't ready to say good-bye to him, but I wasn't sure I was ready for sex with a stranger, either. Then, from behind me, I heard a woman's happy screech.

"*Oh my God!* Lucky Hawk! How are you? It's so good to see you!"

I looked over my shoulder to find a pretty woman gleefully grabbing on to Hawk. She was dressed to attract, sky-high heels, skintight jeans, lots of cleavage—the woman was stacked!—and too much makeup and gaudy jewelry. Hawk was smiling, hugging her back, muttering about old times.

I turned my back to her, ostensibly to thank the bartender for the water but really to decide how to extricate myself from the evening without losing face. I had thought Hawk was interested in me, but would this virile man want to take a chance on me, when a sure bet was now available?

"Lucky, Sweetie. *Pleeeeease* come dance with me!" the interloper purred, pulling on his arm. "It'll be just like old times."

Some part of me rebelled at giving up that easily, so I turned around fully to face the woman defiantly and let her know there was competition. But I didn't expect to win.

Hawk said, "Wynona, I'd like you to meet Liza Jensen. We were just finishing up dinner."

"Oh!" She giggled, eyeing me with scorn. "I didn't see you there… such dark clothes and all." Wynona laughed again—at me—before turning her sole attention to Lucky Hawk.

I felt ugly and plain! My clothes were the antithesis of feminine, the exact opposite of sexy. Underneath I knew my figure couldn't compete with hers.

Before I could respond, Wynona stepped closer and slid her hand playfully up Hawk's arm. "I'm sure your business client won't mind you having a *little* fun," she whined. "She looks ready to leave anyway."

"The thing is, Wynona. I was already having fun with Miss Jensen. And she's not my client. Our business is now finished…at least our *work* business," Hawk said, throwing me a blistering look.

He wanted me!

The simmering desire I had felt all evening thrummed larger, making me feel more attractive and sexy. *He wanted me!* But was I really the kind of woman that could satisfy a man who literally dripped sex appeal? Not previously, surely. Would I even have the courage to put it all out there, to dive headlong into the pursuit of pure pleasure with this man?

"Humph!" Wynona sniffed. "I remember what you like, Lucky. Big-city girls don't know the first thing about pleasing a guy. Once you figure that out, you know where to find me—if I'm still available, that is." She gave him a quick kiss on the cheek and then gave me another derisive glance before walking off.

"Old girlfriend?" I asked, trying to sound sardonic rather than jealous.

"Yeah, uhhh…we go way back, but that was a long time ago. Sorry about that."

I told Hawk it was nothing, but in truth, I needed a moment to sort out the roiling mixture of desire, jealousy, and trepidation coursing through me—all this about a man I had just met. Excusing myself to the ladies' room, I left him sitting there…after double-checking that Wynona was otherwise occupied.

Once there, I looked myself over in the bathroom mirror. *Yuck!* My look was more undertaker than hot babe. Not a problem if all I wanted was to go to my hotel alone. Staring at my reflection, I tried to decide what I really wanted. There was definitely something sizzling between us. I could feel it with certainty, as if it were spelled out in one of Hawk's legal documents. Even so, sex with a stranger? Was I *really* thinking of doing that? It gave me pause—words from the reading of the will came to mind. Was I of "sound mind and body" in actually contemplating a one-night stand, something I'd never done before, not even in college?

But I couldn't just walk away—I hadn't felt this alive, this vibrant, in a very long time. Still looking at myself in the mirror, I realized that I did know what I wanted, and he was sitting out there waiting for me. Squaring my shoulders, I made the bold—for me, anyway—decision to pursue a one-night stand with a man I hardly knew.

I took several calming breaths.

Now, how to change from funeral director to femme fatale? I wondered. I took off the shapeless jacket, rolled up my sleeves, and unbuttoned my cream-colored silk blouse till just a hint of my bra showed, thankful that I wore pretty pale-pink lingerie adorned with lace. There was nothing I could do about the ugly skirt and flats, but I fluffed my hair and rummaged in my purse. Ahhh, there it was—my favorite lipstick. It would be obvious to Hawk that I had performed an impromptu makeover, but I didn't mind him knowing I had done this for him. Adding a bright layer of scarlet, I pouted in the mirror. My lush lips now looked delectably kissable.

When I returned to Lucky Hawk, he smiled appreciatively at me and stood up. I could see that there were two filled shot glasses on the bar, and he said, "I would like to dance with you, but first let's celebrate our new friendship with a toast."

I nodded agreement, and he handed me one. Raising the other, Hawk said, "In the words of my Omaha ancestors, 'Ask questions from your heart and you will be answered from the heart.'" He tilted his glass and drank it all in one gulp.

I wondered at the proverb's meaning but liked the sense of loving honesty. Following his example, I put the glass to my lips and downed it all, feeling the burning tequila trail hotly down my throat.

After giving me a naughty grin, he said, "If that isn't enough to allow me to…as you said…*take advantage of you*, I've got some wine back at the office."

Then he led me to the small dance floor. He pulled me close, and we swayed to the romantic beat of the music. His hand once again made slow circles on my lower back, and the delicate sensation flooded me with warmth. Our bodies were pressed together, and I could feel he was hard against my belly. I wanted it pressed lower, ached to feel his bulge where it belonged. I raised my eyes to his and saw that he was staring at my mouth.

"You have the most deliciously luscious lips I've ever seen," he said. "I've wanted to kiss them since the moment I saw you this afternoon."

Then he bent his head to me and kissed me while we continued to move slowly in place. His tongue danced in and out of my open mouth, and he tasted of tequila. It felt perfect, but then he pulled back. I couldn't help leaning into him, following his mouth with mine. I needed more!

"Look," he groaned. "I could beat around the bush. I could invite you to the office for a glass of wine or I could make some other excuse to get you alone, but we're both adults…that's not how I operate. I want to be direct and to the point with you. Is that okay?"

"Yes," I breathed, in a sensual haze that made talking increasingly difficult.

"I want to take you back to my office, strip you naked, and make love to you."

He waited patiently and assuredly for my reply, staring into my eyes and seeming to will me to say what he wanted to hear. I already knew that Hawk was a good lawyer; his stories this evening told me he was used to getting his way through carefully elucidated language. I learned now that he was also a consummate closer. Whispering huskily, he added, "The couch will do for starters. There, I will kiss you senseless. The chairs might be fun too. But bending you over the top of the desk, that is where I want to fuck you."

The haze burst into a blaze of heat, and I sensed his words right down to my tingling cunt. Nothing else mattered now—I needed to screw this man, feel him banging me over and over. I managed a single nod of acquiescence.

Without another word, Hawk took my hand, turned, and led me out of the bar. It was all I could do not to run across the street. It was wickedly exciting, the idea of having sex with him right there in his law office. Suddenly that old practice with its large, ancient furnishings was the sexiest place on earth. We both walked briskly, not saying a word as he fished the keys out of his pocket. Once there, he quickly unlocked the door. I was finally about to be fucked, and I laughed in delighted anticipation.

ACKNOWLEDGMENTS

It gives me great pleasure to extend my heartfelt thanks to a few who have helped make this debut novel possible. First, this book would not have gotten off the ground without my sweet, sexy, and oh-so-supportive husband and my dear friend and personal editor, Anna. Then I owe tremendous gratitude to Deb Werksman at Sourcebooks, Inc., for taking a chance on me and to my wonderful agent, Louise Fury of The Bent Agency, for her invaluable assistance. Finally—before the hook pulls me off the stage—I offer a shout-out to my family and friends who have all encouraged and supported me.

About the Author

Kate Allure has been a storyteller her entire life, writing plays, short
stories, and dance librettos throughout her childhood and later for
semiprof   g
included   y
Ballet ar   d
writing,   ;s
sensual y
    Foll